MW01249012

Dancing Across the Keys

By

Curie Nova

ISBN: 0-7596-7391-8

This book is printed on acid free paper.

1stBooks - rev. 12/11/01

This book is dedicated to all the beautiful people out there who are forever young.

I wish to thank Attorney Joseph J. Bileti, whose assistance with the legal scenes was invaluable.   Without Joe's help the courtroom scenes, and conversations between the attorneys, would have sounded phony and trite. Thank you so much Joe, for your expert advice.

I also thank my fiancé Robert, and my son Nicholas, for reading, and rereading this book until I got it "just right."

Foreword

Every Sunday @ 3:00 P.M., twelve incredible people, all over the age of fifty-five, meet me at a magnificent mansion in La Jolla, California. There we discuss their once most privately held thoughts and religiously guarded secrets.

This group, which started out as my research subjects, quickly became my most treasured friends. They have no reservations about allowing me into every intimate crevice of their lives. I've heard it said that most senior citizens, as a rule, don't trust younger people too much, but my group trusts me. You see—my group is being interviewed for a thought-provoking book that I'm writing about aging, and how older people truly feel about themselves. For some, the mental and physical havoc set in motion by simply reaching a certain age is devastating, especially if the person was once physically attractive and full of vigor. Personally, I think most people, if they develop and maintain a certain sense of eloquence, get sexier as they age.

It was my curiosity about how seniors get along in today's racy, impersonal, digital world that prompted me to form the group. One member, who is 63, still can't get the hang of computers and won't even attempt to send an email. And the mystery of how fax machines work just boggles the mind of another, who is only 65.

I'm not implying that seniors are stupid—far from it. But let's face it, a lot of the technical things that are important for us to know today weren't as relevant, say as little as twenty years ago. Another thing I'm *not* saying is that the people in my group are old. I've seen 30 year olds who act more ancient than others do at 80. But since the fear of aging can sneak in on some as early as age 35, being over 50 can take some people right over the edge.

And it's not just the technical aspect of senior living that I wanted to write about. My first pre-requisite was honesty, no matter how raw or embarrassing the questions.

When I first set out to write this book, I had intended to interview each member privately—one-on-one. But that plan changed when I met Rachel Maxwell, an eccentric, energetic, 63-year-old socialite and the owner of August House, a prestigious art gallery in Downtown La Jolla, California.

Soon after Rachel and I met, she became impassioned and fascinated by my seniors project. With little effort, she convinced me to allow her to co-author the book and suggested that we conduct the interviews in a group setting at her sprawling, 12 bedroom estate.

I was immediately taken with the beautiful, glamorous and wealthy woman, and readily accepted her generous offer.

The interviewees included people from vastly different walks of life. This was essential to me so that the book's focus wouldn't be on a certain ethnic or economic group, which might leave the reader with one-dimensional views and opinions.

At first, I was apprehensive about mixing the diverse backgrounds, as the subjects ranged from the extremely wealthy to the incredibly poor. But Rachel alleviated my concerns about that, and explained how mixing the group might stimulate more colorful responses.

Thus, we began our journey, facing tough questions head-on, some as sensitive and private as their sex lives to the more emotional ones, like how they feel about life-long dreams that were abandoned or shattered, and the dreams that came true.

I dug deep to uncover the naked truth to these, and other delicate questions, and I listened as the group bared their souls to me.

Things were progressing extremely well, and we looked forward to seeing each other on Sundays. Then, one quiet Monday morning, our cozy world was violently shattered when one of the members of our little group was gruesomely bludgeoned to death. Because our group included some of San Diego's most wealthy and powerful people, the grizzly act made headlines all across the nation.

Like poison arrows, sharp tongues began to whiz by from every direction. A steady onslaught of news reporters, some of which implied that I had formed some sort of cult, stirred the emotions of bewildered, saddened family members, and feverish senior citizens' groups, both of which demanded from me immediate answers. Many began to question my motives and made my life miserable. Without warning, I found myself smack in the middle of an intense ethical and emotional battle, and each session had been neatly tape-recorded by me for the entire world to hear.

I felt enormous guilt, and sometimes regret, for having formed the group. What had started out as a tell-all of what it's like to be over fifty-five had turned into a hellish nightmare.

But through these experiences, we all learned the real meaning of friendship, forgiveness, and unconditional love. We also saw hatred and stupidity in all its glory. We journeyed down a long and perilous road together, and in the end, discovered a lot about ourselves, and about each other. For some, it was the first time that they had ever ventured beyond their own world, and tasted what it's like to be wealthy and glamorous. Conversely, others learned that being wealthy was not a guarantee of happiness. As for me, I accomplished my goal of learning the joys of youth at whatever age by peeking into the secret lives of some mighty beautiful people. I also learned how to trust, and to have faith in the tremendous power of love.

Chapter One

"Introducing Rachel"

It was a rainy day in November 2000 when I met Rachel Maxell, one of San Diego's most influential socialites. It had been raining all morning, and in San Diego, the slightest drizzle can result in an unyielding traffic jam, so I decided to leave early for my 1:00 o'clock appointment in downtown La Jolla.

The instant I stepped out of my front door, I twisted my ankle and stumbled clumsily into the wet grass just beyond my driveway. I sure felt like a fool, looking around to see if anyone saw me sprawled onto the wet pavement. Hurriedly, I sprang up, retrieved my briefcase and purse from the yard, and ran to my car. By the time I reached it, I was soaked, and felt downright hideous. Trying to force my hair not to frizz, I took my hands and pressed it hard against my head. But within minutes I saw my once cute, stylish hairdo turn into a misshapen Afro.

"What the hell," I thought to myself and headed to August House, the most prestigious art gallery in San Diego. Since I didn't have time to change my clothes or fix my hair, I figured I'd just blame my frumpy appearance on the rain.

As my car pulled onto the freeway, thoughts of selling some of my art swirled around in my mind. I had hoped to get a good price so that I could fund research for a book on aging I had hoped to write. I had already began working on my aging project, and had even assembled a small group of people, all over fifty-five, to participate in intensive interviews. I could hardly wait to get started on what I considered to be the first book to honestly capture the significant, uncensored thoughts of older people.

What do more mature people dream about? What do they think, feel, and hope for? Do they still have fantasies and motives like younger people have? And don't forget the sex. I wanted to write about everything from what goes on in their heads during the arousal stages, down to the actual act itself. Surely, I figured, the chemicals in the brain that activate the libido must change at a certain age, and I wanted to find out how.

In my opinion, fifty-five is certainly not considered old, but seemed like a good starting point to me. I wanted to know how they feel about their bodies, and if they still hold the romantic ideals of their more youthful years?

Other than the usual guesses I could make about how they feel about death, or fears about getting or being old, I wanted to truly know if they hadn't achieved their dreams, what specific fears or events prevented them from doing so. Were they terrified of dying, and failing to achieve what they dreamed their lives would be?

1

I decided to write this book because I believe that young people want to know these things. And I was planning to capture the truth by conducting a series of interviews with people from different walks of life, from the independently wealthy to some living in poverty.

The difference between how the wealthy and the poor feel about getting old was intriguing to me. I assumed the rich feel that they have more material possessions to leave behind, but what about the things that money can't buy? Things like peace of mind, happiness, feeling wanted, loving and being loved? Those with wealth, who were also thoughtful with the ability to receive and give love, to me, were like jewels. Those without riches, but who embraced life with joy, self-love and grace, were in my mind, wealthy beyond measure.

I was certain a project so detailed would consume considerable time, so my next step was to raise the money needed to fund the research. After a few feeble failed attempts to secure a sponsor, I decided to fund the project myself, and that's why I was selling some of my paintings.

Over the years, I had collected several valuable pieces of fine art, and felt my project justified the liquidation of at least some of them.

As I plodded along on the freeway, the traffic stopped and started, and the noon crowd helped to transform the interstate into a parking lot.

My rearview mirror kept reminding me of just how awful I looked. I so wanted to make a good impression on who I thought to be the owner of August House, Suzanne Sullivan. She had agreed to meet with me at the recommendation of my best friend, Diana, a cute dark haired girl I met years ago while attending a public speaking seminar.

"I hope Suzanne's more interested in my art than in the way I look," I mumbled to myself. I checked my briefcase for the papers on my paintings to make sure they survived the tumble in the wet grass.

The clock in my car played cruel tricks on me, as the digital numbers clicked ahead in seemingly fast motion, but I was determined that nothing would delay me from getting to my appointment on time. The constant rain was unusual for that time of year in San Diego. Drivers customarily reduce their speed to a snail's pace during a light mist, so today's rainstorm had them totally mystified about how to maneuver their automobiles through the downpour.

I finally reached the gallery, just in time for my appointment. I swung into a parking space and dashed from the car.

August House occupies one of the most impressive buildings in downtown La Jolla, and what makes it even more spectacular is its breathtaking view of the Pacific Ocean. If you've ever been to Downtown La Jolla you'll know what I mean. The impressive architecture is very upscale, but not at all pretentious. Every detail of the shops, from the little bakery on the corner to the elegant restaurants, exudes charm and good taste. August House is situated in the center of town.

With briefcase in hand, I pulled open one of the heavy double glass doors and stepped into a large, marbled-floored foyer. The door closed and shut off all the sounds of the outside traffic.

A well-dressed, 50ish looking, blond haired man, who was scanning a computer screen and looking into a large, gold-edged appointment book, glanced at me, but didn't speak. I walked up to him.

"Excuse me. Sorry to drip all over your floor, but I can't help it. I'm here to see Suzanne Sullivan. I have a 1:00 o'clock appointment."

"Your name?" asked the rigid man, who had a foreign accent, perhaps Scandinavian, and stood so straight it appeared that he'd snap if he tried to bend at the waist.

"Curie Nova."

"Miss Nova. Yes. Well, Miss Sullivan has been detained. I'll let Mrs. Maxwell know that you're here. Perhaps she can help you."

"Thank you," I said, as I wiped raindrops from my briefcase with my shirtsleeve.

I had no idea who Mrs. Maxwell was, but I lived in Scripps Ranch, which was more than an hour drive away, which turned into two hours in the rain, just to see Suzanne, and I wasn't leaving August House until I saw her. I figured Mrs. Maxwell must be Suzanne's secretary.

The stone-faced man picked up the telephone and punched in two numbers. "Mrs. Maxwell, there's a Curie Nova here to see Miss Sullivan. Would you care to speak with her?" He nodded a couple of times. "Yes, ma'am," he said, and then hung up the phone.

"I'm sorry, Miss Nova. I'll have Miss Sullivan call you when she returns. Does she have your telephone number?"

"Look," I said defensively and leaning forward to read his gold-plated name badge. "Look, Stephen. I've driven through two hours of stop and slow traffic to make it to this appointment with Suzanne. When will she be back? I'd hate to drive all the way back to Scripps Ranch, just to turn around and come back. I don't mind waiting. Is that OK—for me to wait here?"

"Yes. You may wait."

"Stiff old robot," I thought to myself as I took a seat on a sofa that faced the ocean. The rain had started to let up a little, but the sky was still filled with patches of dark clouds.

I looked around the lavishly decorated foyer, recognizing world-famous and incredibly expensive works of art that I had only before seen in fine art books and magazines. Precision, gallery lighting illuminated smooth, elegant sculptures. Suspended from the high ceiling was a massive, sparkling, smoke-blue, teardrop crystal chandelier. Atop an antique mahogany table in front of the sofa was a collection of strategically placed books and periodicals.

I reached over and grabbed the San Diego Magazine, which had a cover picture of a woman with striking, waist-length red hair. The caption read, "Clarise Jorgensen, a designer for the soul."

I immediately recognized her name, as her company had also been featured on issues of Fortune, Time and Forbes Magazines.

The woman looked like a forty-year-old gypsy with dangling gold earrings and several bracelets around each arm. Her makeup was flawless, and her penetrating green eyes seemed to stare right through me. Just as I was about to open the magazine to read the story of the mysterious-looking red head, Mr. Roboto, Stephen, approached.

"Excuse me, Miss Nova. Miss Sullivan called and said that it will be at least a half-hour more before she returns. Mrs. Maxwell will see you." I returned the magazine to the precise spot on the table from which I took it.

"Thank you," I said, and picked up my brief case. "Who is Mrs. Maxwell?"

"Follow me," instructed Stephen, without acknowledging my question.

"Follow me," I silently mimicked when he turned his back to lead the way.

Stephen led me to another set of double doors that opened into the gigantic main gallery. "Wait here," he said, and disappeared into one of the offices along the wall.

I looked around the intimidating room. It was filled with exquisite works of art, and lots of beautiful crystal. Sculptures in every medium occupied prominent places throughout the room. Paintings and drawings of every kind, from the Old Masters to modern day masterpieces, were displayed on easels, the walls, and atop tables.

A thin, stylishly dressed woman walked up. The polished and elegant lady appeared to be in her fifties.

"Hello Miss Nova. I'm Rachel Maxwell. Suzanne is my daughter. Is there anything I can do for you?"

I was caught off guard when I heard that Suzanne was her daughter. I was mentally prepared to address Rachel Maxwell as the secretary. Diana had neglected to mention Rachel to me.

"I'm not sure. I spoke with Suzanne a couple of days ago about some art I'm interested in selling. She asked me to come in today at 1:00, so here I am."

"I see. Suzanne didn't tell me about your appointment, or your art. She should be here in less than half an hour, so since you've waited this long, if you'd like to continue to wait, you may do so."

"Thank you. I'd like to do that."

"You may wait in here if you like, take a look around."

"Sure, thank you."

Mrs. Maxwell walked to a tea set atop a cherry wooden table. She turned and peered at me through expensive, designer eyeglasses.

I felt embarrassed with her blatant stare. I had wiped the rain from my face with my palm, and my makeup was smeared. I was certain I looked like a vagabond, and definitely felt like a ragbag standing next to Rachel. The well-dressed and perfectly made-up woman smiled a faint smile, but didn't say a word.

"Suzanne is your daughter?" I asked, trying to make conversation with the distant woman.

"Yes. She runs August House for me."

"Oh," was all I could think to say. After a few uncomfortable seconds, I blurted out, "where's your ladies' room? I'd like to dry off and freshen up a bit."

"Go through the door over there," she pointed, "and make a right."

"Thank you," I said, and hurried out of the room.

I wanted to kick myself for being tongue tied in front of Mrs. Maxwell. I looked in the mirror and realized that I did look like a ragbag. I fixed my makeup and ran my fingers through my hair. When I returned from the restroom, Mrs. Maxwell was pouring a cup of tea from a delicate-looking porcelain teapot.

"Would you care to join me for tea?"

"Oh, no thank you. It's such a pleasure to meet you, Mrs. Maxwell. You have a most wondrous art gallery."

"Thank you dear. You said you spoke with Suzanne regarding some paintings you're trying to sell?"

"Yes. She said she might be able to help me."

"Why are you selling your art, dear? What type of art is it? What did you say your name was?"

"It's Curie Nova." I spoke loud and clear in case she had a problem with her hearing. "I acquired this art from one of my trips to Switzerland. To be honest, Mrs. Maxwell, I'm not thoroughly familiar with this artist, and that's why I'm bringing it to Suzanne to take a look at. It's a series of drawings by a German painter named Willi Geiger. I understand he painted only a few pieces, and that some of his paintings are worth more than others. I'm looking for some guidance on the series I have."

After I stopped talking, I realized that I sounded like a crazed lunatic, yelling, and trying to answer all her questions in one fell swoop.

"I see. But Curie, I'm not hard of hearing. There's no need to yell."

"Yes, I'm sorry."

"Well Curie, you still haven't told me why you are selling your art."

"Oh, of course. Well, Mrs. Maxwell," I stammered. "I'm a writer, and to help fund the research on my next book, I'm afraid I'm going to have to sell some of my precious art."

"How did you come about talking with Suzanne about it?"

"Actually, my best friend, Diana, told me about August House and how splendid it is. She suggested I call, and I did. Suzanne was very kind, and knowledgeable, and asked me to meet her here today."

"If you're a good writer, why hasn't your writing helped you to fund your research? Are you published?"

"Yes, as a matter of fact, I am. But my novel hasn't been released yet. In the meantime, I'm starting on another book, but unlike the first, which was more a retrospective, the content of this one will be compiled almost entirely from interviews."

"Interviews? Who will you interview? What type of interviews?"

I was delighted that Mrs. Maxwell asked those questions. I had a sudden desire to ask her if she knew anyone who would be interested in being interviewed for my book. Her curiosity caused me to sense that she, too, would make a perfect interviewee. But she seemed so aloof. Not only was I uncertain about how I should approach asking her, but also I was apprehensive about whether she would take my book or me seriously. A woman of her obvious wealth would probably not concern herself with sharing the most intimate details of her life with a stranger, I thought.

Rachel took a seat near the cherry table, and awaited my response.

"I'm interviewing men and women fifty-five and over about their lives. I plan to take the most intriguing interviews and publish them. It's actually a book about aging. The reason I'm interviewing people over fifty-five is that I want to discover all about the aging process—well, not exactly the process, but about the thoughts of older people. I'm not saying that fifty-five is old, or anything, but I had to start somewhere, and I decided that fifty-five was a good age to start. And I don't want to write from a clinical point of view, you know, like many books I've read authored by physicians, psychiatrists or research scientists, but from life experiences of real, candid people, not laboratory subjects."

Rachel's eyes lit up and she flashed a smile of perfect dentures. Suddenly, there was an air of softness about the elegant and refined woman as she stood up, and smoothed back her blonde hair, which was pulled back tightly in a neatly pinned braid. She reminded me of the older version of Grace Kelley, and her voice was deep and rich, like Greta Garbo's.

As Rachel stood, my eyes followed her perfectly manicured red fingernails. I watched her palms as they slid, almost in slow motion, across the front of her skirt, smoothing it before she took a step. It was like her every move was choreographed.

"Tell me more about this book, Curie," she said as she glided smoothly to the table to pour another cup of tea.

I felt like a little girl being asked about a school project. Mrs. Maxwell refilled her teacup and walked towards a beautiful mocha-colored velvet divan.

"Come, sit with me."

"I hope I'm dry enough. I'd hate to ruin your beautiful sofa."

"You're just fine dear. Come, sit."

I obeyed the graceful, venerable woman like an obedient puppy. Although her face showed signs of aging, it was apparent to me that she had once been a great beauty. Perfectly arched eyebrows framed her clear, blue eyes. Even her aristocratic air added to her charm.

"I think I will have a cup of tea, Mrs. Maxwell. I'll pour," I said. As soon as those words escaped my lips I thought to myself, "as regal as she's acting, I'm surprised there's not a servant in here to pour for us."

I poured my tea, and returned to the sofa to join "Lady Maxwell," as I had instantly dubbed her.

"You see, Mrs. Maxwell..."

"Please dear, call me Rachel."

"Yes. You see Rachel—I have questions about aging that simply haven't been answered. The answers I get from books are too clinical, and the words are disguised by all types of boring, textbook terms. And writers who do approach the subject in down-to-earth terms end up adding cute words, to address this most important subject. I'm looking to capture the naked, unadulterated truth about what it's like to be, say 55, 60, 70, even 80, years old. And humdrum things like, oh, I can't drive any more because my sight is failing, is definitely not the sort of thing I'm looking for."

"What sort of things are you looking for?"

"I have prepared several questions that I'll be asking everyone that I interview. Some people will be asked more questions than others will, depending upon how they respond. If someone is open and elaborates on any given question, I'll carry that topic further, with a series of sub-questions. Interviews of the people who are not willing to bare their hearts and souls to me will probably not be published. I'm only interesting in capturing the candid views.

"How will you know whether your subjects are telling you the truth?"

"Oh, I'll know, Rachel. They'll know, too. Because everyone interviewed will be anonymously published. And when there's a veil to separate people from their truth, it's easier for one to say what's really on one's mind, don't you agree?"

"I find it easy to say what's on my mind all the time, Curie. But yes, I do see what you mean. I must say, your book sounds like it will be rather interesting."

"I'm certain it will be." Just then, a sudden rush of bravado overcame me. "Rachel, I know you've just met me, and I know you're probably extremely busy with August House, but would you do me the honor of allowing me to interview you for my book? If you can't, I'll understand. I'm enjoying talking with you Mrs. Maxwell, I mean Rachel, and I think you would contribute greatly to my work. I won't publish your name, I promise. Although I'll use a fictitious name for you, everything else in your chapter will be the real you, of course."

7

"Curie, I must admit, I am rather curious about your little project. I have some time tomorrow morning. Why don't you tell me more about it then and I'll see if I want to go further."

Just then Suzanne walked in.

"You must be Curie," she said while wiping water from her face. "I'm sorry to drip all over you, but I seem to have misplaced my umbrella. I'm Suzanne Sullivan. Stephen said you were here."

Suzanne extended her wet hand.

"Yes. I'm Curie Nova. It's a pleasure to meet you Miss Sullivan." We shook hands then I turned to face Rachel.

"I'm looking forward to coming back tomorrow for our meeting. What would be a good time, Rachel?"

"Why don't you come to my home instead? There we both will be more comfortable. I'll have Suzanne give you directions. I'll see you tomorrow at 10:00 sharp."

Suzanne looked puzzled at the casual manner in which I spoke to her mother, but she didn't question me about the meeting Rachel had arranged.

"You're here about the Geiger's, right?" asked Suzanne.

"Yes."

Rachel interrupted us.

"Give Curie my address, won't you Suzanne?" She left the room before Suzanne could respond.

"Thank you, Rachel," I said, presuming that Rachel was still within hearing distance. I followed Suzanne into her office, where we talked for more than an hour about my paintings. She promised to get back with me, and I felt hopeful that I would soon be launching my project.

"Thank you Suzanne. It was well worth the wait."

She handed me her card, on the back of which she had written Rachel's address and phone number.

Chapter Two

"You Oh, So Fabulous Woman"

It was 9:50 A.M. when I pulled into a long drive and up to an ornate, iron gate. Rachel's house was grander than I could ever have imagined. Plush landscaping made it barely visible. Just ahead was another stretch of driveway. I took a deep breath before pressing the gate buzzer. My eyes were transfixed on the small portion of the incredible Maxwell Estate that I could see from the gate. I took another deep breath. I was apprehensive about questioning the woman I had nicknamed "Lady Maxwell."

As soon as I pressed the buzzer, the gate swung open. It was obvious that someone could see my car on a monitor from inside the house. It was now 9:53. Although I was nervous, I felt extremely grateful to be visiting such an elegant lady who, with her obvious wealth, could have published her own book, but had consented to the possibility of being a part of mine.

I walked up to the front door of the fortress and rang the doorbell. Within seconds, the door opened and Rachel stepped out wearing a beautiful nautical pants suit. I had expected to see a uniformed maid.

"Come in Curie. You're ahead of schedule. I like that."

"Being prompt is most important to me, Rachel. I don't like wasting mine, or anyone else's time."

"Then we're going to get along just fine," she said, and guided me through a foyer and into the living room, which was decorated so magnificently that it almost overwhelmed me.

Works of original art tastefully filled the vast room. Expensive, decorative vases of various sizes were filled with fresh, exotic flowers, which were reflected by large mirrors in ornate frames. Original oil paintings and watercolors hung on every wall like they had been placed there with geometrical precision. Most of the furniture in the room looked like antiques, but there were lavish modern pieces among the arrangement, which made the homes I'd seen on "Lifestyles of the Rich and Famous" look like slums."

"We'll talk in here," Rachel said, as she motioned for me to follow her.

We entered another magnificent room with clear glass walls. The view was a most spectacular one of the grand Pacific Ocean.

I had never before seen such an incredible room—not even in magazines. A desk made entirely of glass occupied the center of the big room. In one of the rear corners was a stately, white Grand piano.

"You have such a beautiful home, Rachel," I said as I tried to take in everything at once.

"Thank you Curie. You should see this room at night. This house was my late husband, Philip's, pride and joy. He supervised every part of its construction, down to the tiniest detail. I'll show you around later. But first, let's get you set up. You can place your things over there," she said, pointing to the desk in the center of the room.

I removed my laptop, notebook, pencils, and tape recorder from my overstuffed case and placed everything atop a pad on the big glass desk. I had brought along the laptop and recorder so that I could type Rachel's responses, thereby staring at the computer monitor instead of at her.

Although Rachel hadn't yet consented to my interview, I came prepared to convince her to do so. If she consented, I planned to tape our conversation, but I figured steady eye contact might make her leave out some important details, so I had brought along a host of props to occupy my eyes while she talked. When the moments seemed right, I would give her undivided eye-to-eye contact and encourage her candor. I had worked out my strategy well in advance the night before. I didn't want to miss a word or a sigh of the discussion I believed to be arranged by fate.

Rachel guided me on an extended tour of her beautiful estate. She excitedly moved about the massive house, like she was the one seeing it for the first time. I figured she was probably thirty years older than I was, but it was apparent that Rachel had taken good care of herself. I knew people a lot younger than her who would have tired moving about her huge mansion. I wasn't sure how old Rachel was. And I didn't care. For the sake of my book, her age was important, but personally I just saw her as a fascinating woman.

After the tour ended, we returned to the glass room to begin our discussion.

"I must admit, Curie, the nature of your book intrigues me. You know, once you reach a certain age most people don't give a damn about what you think anymore. Oh, there are some who pretend to be interested, like relatives, you know, those who expect to inherit something once you die, or people who want you to donate money to every charitable organization in the world, but very few who really care what you think."

"I disagree, Rachel, and that's why I'm writing this book. I believe that there are a lot of people who care about what older people think, it's just that, like I said yesterday, the thoughts are usually communicated to us by some psychologist, or researcher, who uses words other than those used by the people they've spoken with. I want to use your words, Rachel, and the words of others like you, who've experienced so many things. I sense there's a lot to be discovered and shared, not just in your past, but what you think now. How you think today, you see. But let me warn you Rachel, my questions are blunt. In order to get real answers I have to ask real questions. And I don't mean questions that have been selected to show that I respect you as a more mature person. I'm talking about words that I would use if I were interviewing my best friend. So, if at any time you feel uncomfortable, that's the time that I'll really want you to dig deep to pull your honest, deep down inside answers. I don't think that you're the sort of woman who would be shy in showing real passion, but there are some people that I plan to interview who haven't stoked the fires of their hearts in a long time."

"What kind of people are you interviewing, Curie?"

"Some have given up on their dreams, thinking they're too old to care about what lies ahead, and others are lonely, and haven't been kissed, or held, in a long time. Others are just happy, satisfied, and gifted people. I want to hear straightforward answers, because you see, many older people are still achieving great things, running major corporations, are active in politics, well most politicians are older, but you know what I mean. Many of the things I just said apply to people of all ages, but society doesn't see it that way. The increased health concerns are there, I'm sure, but there's a lot more to older people than just conversations about Medicare. If you're embarrassed by anything I say, just say so, then proceed to answer the question anyway, OK? Those are the only rules. Are you game, Rachel?"

"Let's get started, Curie."

"You mean right now?" I said, pretending to be surprised. "First of all, thank you Rachel. Now, with that out of the way, in order to better understand your responses, I'll need to know more about you. So let's start at the beginning."

Rachel's housekeeper entered the room carrying a tray of drinks, fruits and cheeses.

"Thank you Gertie," said Rachel. "Curie, this is my friend and housekeeper Gertie Ortiz. Gertie, this is Curie Nova. You'll be seeing a lot of her around here, if I like what goes on today," she added.

"It's nice to meet you, Miss Nova," said Gertie in a heavy Spanish accent.

"It's a pleasure to meet you, too, Gertie," I responded, and helped myself to the snack tray. After I made myself comfortable again, I sat down to begin my interview with Rachel.

"Rachel, when and where were you born?" I turned on my laptop, and then the tape recorder. I nodded, and Rachel started her response.

"I was born in Chicago, Illinois in December 1935. My father was a successful businessman and, despite the devastation he suffered during the depression, he rose to great heights. He owned a lot of land. And he was a genius at buying real estate. He also inherited a great deal of money and other property from his father, who had made a fortune from factories that were spread all over the United States."

I hadn't asked Rachel about how she came to be wealthy, but I was thankful that she volunteered to tell me. I was surprised to hear that she was born in 1935. Rachel didn't look like a spring chicken, but she certainly didn't look sixty-five.

11

"You made reference to your late husband earlier. Tell me Rachel, are you married now?"

"I've been married three times, Curie. My first husband, John, passed away more than thirty years ago. I was only twenty-three when we married. We were married for over eight years, then he passed away...heart attack. We had some precious years together. He was quite a man, Curie. Handsome, successful, fun."

"How did you feel when he died?"

"Naturally, I was devastated. We didn't have any children, so I was all alone. There I was only thirty-one and a widow. But I survived, as you can see."

"You said your first husband was named John. You remarried, when?"

"Four years after John passed away. I met a handsome doctor named Philip Davenport. He was thirty-three and I was thirty-five. Oh, people talked because I was a patient of the hospital where I met him, but what did I care? We married six months later. Then we immediately adopted Suzanne. She was only two months old. John and I couldn't have children of our own. To tell you the truth I wasn't ready for children when I married Philip. But he told me the sad story of a beautiful little girl who was up for adoption. He said the mother was an unwed, very young, scared teenager who wasn't prepared to take care of the baby. So Philip asked me, no, begged me, to consider adopting her. He said the mother was a pitiful, young thing, and that he had fallen in love with the little girl the minute she was born. I had more money than I knew what to do with, so I figured adopting a child who could really use a good home would be the right thing to do."

"Was having a young baby like that, with no experience with children, difficult for you?"

"Not at all. The minute I saw Suzanne I felt the same way as Philip did. There we were, newlyweds, with a baby," she said and laughed. Then her voice changed to a somber tone.

"I think of Philip every day. He passed away five years after we were married. There I was, twice widowed already, but now with a child. Oh God," she sighed.

"How did you and Dr. Davenport meet?"

"I was having some surgery done. He wasn't my doctor—my gynecologist. At the time I met Philip I hadn't been interested in anyone since my John passed away. But the minute I laid eyes on Philip I knew I had to have him. The sparks just flew all over the place. So I did what came naturally. I asked him out. I didn't know or care whether he was married at the time. Fortunately for me he wasn't. Within a few months' time, after my recovery, I had Dr. Davenport eating out of the palm of my hand. It was a whirlwind romance."

"Are you involved with a man now?"

"Oh, I have friends that take me out to dinner, concerts, that sort of thing."

"Do you have sex with any of these friends—in other words, are any of these men more special to you than another?"

"My goodness, Curie. You didn't waste any time getting to that question, did you?"

I didn't respond.

"Yes, I do still have sex if that's what you're getting at."

"How often and do you reach orgasm most times, some times, hardly ever, or never?" I had begun to sound like the clinicians I had criticized. Rachel looked at me, not with a look of embarrassment or shock, but one of curiosity.

"I've never been asked that question before, not even when I was a young girl. I must say, Curie, when you say blunt, you really mean it. You did warn me, however. And this is one of those moments you were talking about when I get uncomfortable I should especially answer, is that right?" she asked while laughing and nodding her head.

"That's right," I said and smiled a look of comfort her way. I looked at her pensively and asked if it was OK to turn on some music. I had brought along some compact disks and a portable player. I switched off the recorder and selected the soundtrack from the movie Runaway Bride, starring Julia Roberts and Richard Gere. I selected Eric Clapton's song, "It Was You," and turned up the volume.

We sat there sipping coffee while listening to the emotional song of a woman who dallied with the affections of a man who had fallen hopelessly in love with her. Eric Clapton expressively wove the story of a woman who created a grand vision of splendor for her enamored worshiper, then withdrew her love and disappeared from his life. The sad song played out the drama of a heart-wrenching breach of trust and the devastation it brought to a man desperately in love.

When the emotional song ended, I turned down the volume to continue our interview. The song had worked its magic and changed Rachel's mood. Her beautiful blue eyes softened, and she appeared more relaxed. My mood had changed also, and I stopped being the official interviewer and shut off my laptop. I turned to Rachel and smiled. Rachel broke the silence.

"Curie, I've only had sex with two of the men I'm now seeing on a regular basis. All of these men are just my friends. I guess you could call them fucking friends. But I have never had an orgasm with either of them."

I was surprised by the very candor for which I had asked. I hid my surprise, and looked her straight in the eyes, nodding for her to continue.

"Curie, I orgasm any time I feel like it. I have one of the best vibrators money can buy. It is truly a 'magic wand'. And I use it quite often. I may be old, but I'm not dead," she firmly stated and laughed. "I love sex, always have. I'm going to tell you some things I've never told anyone," she whispered and leaned forward.

"When I use my vibrator I fantasize about that actor, Tim Robbins. I'll tell you more details about that fantasy later, and I'll also let you know if I want you to use my real name. Who knows, maybe I'll want the world to know who I really am. After all, what do I have to lose? I have more money than I'll ever spend in these few years I probably have left, and I am way past caring what others think about me."

"What about sex, Rachel? I'd like to hear more about your fantasies, but first I'd like to clarify something you said earlier. You said that you are sleeping with two of your friends. Tell me more about that—your sexual urges."

"Why of course, Curie. It's not sick or anything. I'm not sick. I still have energy, I'm still a woman, and I still have sex."

"Elaborate, Rachel."

"I still have a pretty decent body, thanks to exercise and taking special care of myself. I haven't had any plastic surgery, well not yet, anyway. So when I'm with a friend, I put on my sexiest outfit and tease the hell out of him. I usually date younger men because it just works out that way. Anyway, I like to play the sexy game, you know the flirting, creating it in my head first. Then, I act out what I've created in my mind with the man I'm with. They seem to love it, and I feel vitalized by it, being desired that way," Rachel said with a gleam in her eyes.

"Now what about your fantasies?"

"One of my favorites is, while I'm at dinner with one of my male friends, I go to the ladies room. After I walk out of the restroom, I see a tall, dark, good looking young man who catches my attention. We flirt with each other for a few minutes, then he hurriedly takes me to an unoccupied room in the restaurant, like an office, leans me against the desk, runs his hands up my thighs, lifts my skirt, pulls down my panties, and we just go to town. We have some of the best fucking sex I've ever had. Just as quietly as he approached me, he leaves the room. Then I compose myself, go to the ladies room to freshen up, and then walk back to the table to re-join my dinner date. I'm sitting there, Curie," she said as she laughed, "feeling like I'm floating, and reliving visions of me and the young stranger all throughout dinner. That's my favorite fantasy."

"May I borrow that fantasy, Rachel?" I asked playfully while fanning my face with my open palm. "I'm going out to dinner tonight, and it will come in real handy. Tell me Rachel, why did you refer to the man in your fantasy as young? How old do you imagine him to be, and what type of man is he? Rich, poor, black, white?"

"That's more than one question, Curie," she said then laughed again. "Well, my fantasy man's age changes depending upon the mood I'm in. One day he might be 25, then another he could be 50, 60. He's not a poor man. I don't see him as some worker in the restaurant. He's a sexy, young Mel Gibson type. A very horny Mel Gibson type."

I laughed very loud.

"Would you like to take a break, Rachel? I'd like to use your ladies room, I said while shutting off the recorder.

"Do you remember where it is?"

"No, I'm afraid I'd get lost."

"I'll show you," she said and escorted me down the hall.

"I'll be right back, Curie. I have to make a phone call."

"OK," I said through the bathroom door.

I felt totally at ease with Rachel. I hadn't expected her to be so easy to talk to, or that she would share her thoughts so freely. She seemed happy that I was giving her my total attention, and our interview was going exactly as I had hoped. Her honesty was drawing me closer to her, and I began to see her as someone I'd like to remain friends with after the interviews had concluded. After meeting me only yesterday, this extremely wealthy and glamorous woman was sharing her home and heart with me. I was definitely convinced that we were destined to meet.

Rachel had told me that she doesn't waste time beating around the bush, and that she could size up a person in seconds. I didn't know if Rachel was this comfortable with everyone she met, and I hoped she wasn't. Although I had anticipated that our meeting would turn into an interview, I felt that everything was happening too fast. I splashed water on my face.

I returned to the glass room and moved closer to the wall of glass and stared out at the ocean. The view was breathtaking, and I felt that Rachel was most fortunate to have such a magnificent presentation of nature every day. I heard her approaching footsteps.

"It is so beautiful here, Rachel," I turned to greet her.

"Yes. It is beautiful, Curie. I feel like praying every time I enter this particular room. It is so open, and I feel so close to everything outside that window—the ocean, the trees, and every drop of sand, everything."

And I believed her. She looked like a little girl staring out of the window experiencing her world, the one she had seen many times before, like she was seeing it for the first time. I was very pleased that she was sharing it with me. Although I knew that she dyed her golden blonde hair, on her it looked natural.

I glanced at my watch. "OK, are you ready to resume our interview?"

"You know, Curie, I had a brain flash while you were in the restroom. You know how you told me you plan to conduct several interviews?"

"Yes," I said, anxious to hear what she was getting at.

"Well, rather than spreading yourself all over town, conducting one interview at a time, why don't you just gather your group and do a collective series of interviews? Just think, not only will it save you time, but energy as well. With everyone together, I think it would also stimulate some pretty interesting discussions. You can even hold the interviews here, at my house, if you'd like. God knows I have the room."

"That's sounds like a pretty good proposition, Rachel, but are you sure you want to do this? Remember that you'll be inviting strangers into your home. Including you, there are eleven people on my list to interview. And they come from every walk of life, from some who live here in La Jolla to others who live in National City. And I'm not going to get tacky, Rachel, but National City has its share of slums. As a matter of fact, one of the ladies I'm interviewing lives in an apartment there that you could probably not even imagine, living the way you do."

"Curie, I'm very much aware that there are people of varying backgrounds and stations in life living on earth. And I know that you're not implying that I'm a snob, so I won't insult you that way. Believe me, Curie, it won't matter to me. Who knows, maybe I'll make some new friends."

"You are really brave, Rachel, thank you."

"No need to thank me. You were a stranger when I met you just a day ago when you walked into my gallery shivering and dripping wet. And here you are, already, right here in my home, and we're getting along just fine. Now, I don't expect it will be that way with everyone. I may never see any of these people again after the interviews are over. But, let's not try to speculate too much about that. Don't worry."

"Consider me worry free."

"By the way, Curie. Will it be OK with you if I invite one of my good friends to join the group? Her name is Clarise Jorgensen. She started out as a client of the gallery. Over the years, we have become very close friends. Her views are a bit outlandish, but I think you'll find her quite interesting."

"Of course, invite her," I said, as the face of the mysterious-looking redhead flashed across my mind. "She's the kind of person I want to interview—she sounds like she'll make a good addition to the group. I saw her picture on the cover of a magazine in your gallery. Now we have a dozen members in the group."

"When would you like to have our first group meeting?"

"Let me contact the others first and make sure that they won't mind being interviewed in a group setting. Some of the questions are pretty personal, remember? When I first set up these interviews, it was with the understanding that they were to be one-on-one."

"Just so you'll know, any day of the week except Saturdays and Mondays are good for me. On Mondays I have a series of things to which I'm already committed. And Saturdays belong strictly to me."

"I'll check with the others this afternoon and give you a call this evening. Oh, by the way, Rachel. Just so you'll know, I told the others that for participating, I'd be giving each a $1000 stipend to donate to their favorite charity. There are a couple of members who will probably need to keep it for them because they need the money. I have no problem with that."

"Well, why don't you let me help you with that, Curie. I'll cover the charity donations. You just concentrate on writing the best book you'll ever write."

"Rachel, I can't let you do that?" I protested.

"Oh yes you can, and you will. I think it's wonderful that you are perceptive enough to make your donation available to some of the lesser fortunate members to use for their own personal expenses. Now, I don't want to hear any more about it."

"OK Rachel, I accept, and am looking forward to proceeding as soon as possible."

I was happy that Rachel had opted to pay the stipend. Although Suzanne said the estimated value of my art to be around $10,000, we were nowhere near a sale.

"Sounds like a plan," said Rachel as I started gathering my things. "I'm sure you'll see just how practical getting everyone together will be. You can finish your book way ahead of schedule. I'm just happy to be involved. Oh by the way, I'll probably do this project under my real name. I'm not shy. By the way, Curie, we never talked about my third husband, Gary Maxwell. I think it was when we started talking about sex, and we never came back to the subject of my marriages."

"You're right, Rachel. Remind to me to ask you about Mr. Maxwell at a later date."

"I'll remind you," she said, then gently squeezed my arm.

I was taken with her expression of kindness and generosity.

"Rachel, you are an incredible woman. I'm very happy that you have consented to help me with the book, and thank you so much for inviting the group into your lovely home for this project."

"Well, Curie, now that you're being grateful, it's time for me to tell you that I do have an ulterior motive behind my generosity. What would you say if I told you that I'd like to help you write the book? I'm always volunteering for this board, or that charity, or to host this dinner…you get the picture. For a change I'd like to work on something that I can really sink my teeth into. Suzanne practically runs the gallery, so I'm not needed there on a daily basis anymore. Your project enthralled me from the very beginning. I'd hate to just be one of the people in the group being interviewed. I want to play an active part from start to finish."

I suppressed my initial impulse to say no. I knew that Rachel would make a very important ally and a formidable enemy. Besides, I was extremely fond of Rachel.

"Rachel, I'd be honored to have your help. We'll make one hell of a writing team."

"I'm glad you think so. Now, let's roll up our sleeves and write a book. Don't forget to call me this evening. I'm sure Suzanne already gave you my

17

telephone number. Here's my cell number, too. I'll probably be at dinner when you call. Feel free to reach me at the restaurant."

"If you see any Mel Gibson types, send them my way," I said in jest.

Rachel hadn't wasted any time in becoming an active project participant. Although I though that she was somewhat pushy, I admired her commanding and positive attitude.

"Goodbye, Rachel. I'll talk with you this evening. I best get to Mr. Bradley's. He's one of my interviews. Instead of interviewing him, I'll just cover our new arrangement."

I left Rachel's with a new sense of purpose and direction. What had started out as a chance meeting during an unusual Southern California rainstorm had turned into collaboration with one of San Diego's most influential women. I appreciated the way Rachel didn't flaunt her wealth. Her cultured manner and incredible estate was evidence enough of her considerable fortune.

Chapter Three

"Take Two"

I raced to get to my next appointment with Mr. Johnson, a 63-year-old machinist.

Bradley, a very dark-skinned, slightly overweight African American, had thick gray hair encircling his balding head. He had agreed to a one-on-one, private interview, so I felt anxious about telling him of the change in plans.

When I first approached Bradley, he said that he would be uncomfortable giving personal information about himself. But after assuring him that his name would never be made public, and that he would be helping a lot of other people by sharing his thoughts and experiences, he consented.

His wife, Rhonda, a kind and lively woman, was excited about her husband being a part of the book. She was standing on her front porch when I pulled in front of their home.

The Johnson's lived in Imperial Beach in a small, but neatly kept house. I could see Mr. Johnson peering out of his living room curtains as I headed up the walkway to greet Rhonda.

"Hello Curie," cheerfully greeted Mrs. Johnson. She stepped off her little concrete porch and walked out to meet me.

"Come on in, Bradley's waiting for you inside."

"Thank you Mrs. Johnson. How have you been?"

"Oh fine. Come right on in."

Bradley moved away from the window and stood in the doorway. He grabbed my hand and gave it a vigorous handshake.

"Hi, Curie. Good to see you. Ready to grill me?"

"Oh, I won't grill you Bradley. You'll see. It will be harmless. But I have to tell you that there's been a change in plans."

"What kind of change?"

Rhonda had stepped out of the room and returned carrying three tall glasses of tea.

"I made this sun tea myself this morning. I put it out on the back porch early this morning. It's really good."

"Thank you very much. I've been out and about all day, so this tea is just what I need."

I had spoken to Rhonda on many occasions since meeting her and Bradley a couple of years ago. I had volunteered to help make identification pictures of the neighborhood children. The Johnson's were there with their four grandchildren, and made it a point of thanking each volunteer personally that day. I was touched at their sincere show of appreciation, and later that day spent almost an hour talking with them.

When I decided to write my book, Bradley immediately came to mind as someone that would make a good interviewee. He was so talkative, and funny. I didn't want to interview a man and his wife, because I was afraid that it would make answering the touchy questions awkward. So between the two of them, I decided that Bradley would make the more interesting candidate.

"Like I was saying earlier, there's a change in plans, and I'd like to explain it to you both. Rather than interview you here, Mr. Johnson, Bradley, I've decided to hold group interviews at the home of a woman who lives in La Jolla. Her name is Rachel Maxwell, and..."

"Hold on. Did you say La Jolla?"

"Yes. She's really a very friendly and kind woman. She looks like those rich types, you know what I mean, all stuffy and such. But when you meet Rachel, you'll see, just like I did, that she's just like you and me, except she's filthy rich."

Bradley and Rhonda stared at one another.

"I don't know about this, Curie," said Bradley, who was still looking at Rhonda. "Those folks in La Jolla might not appreciate having a black man walk up in some rich white woman's house," he said with raised eyebrows.

"Bradley, come on, don't give me that look. I don't give a hoot about what the people in La Jolla will appreciate, neither does Rachel, and neither should you. Anyway, if it'll make you feel better, her house is gated. By the time you get out of your car you'll be well within the gates. So you don't have to worry about any nosy neighbors, because there are none that can see beyond the gate. The atmosphere there is free and easy, not at all like you're probably imagining. I know, because I thought that her house would be stuffy and too upscale, if you know what I mean. I'm not going to lie to you; her house is a magnificent mansion. But Rachel's no snob. Her house is elegant, but it's her that makes it inviting."

Bradley had a great deal of pride and made it clear that he didn't want others looking down on him. He also had a lot of pride about his work, and had explained the intricacies of his profession in detail to me that day I met him.

He earned a modest income, and had raised five girls and three boys. He beamed with satisfaction the day I met his grandchildren. Two of his sons still lived in the San Diego area, another had moved to Atlanta. His daughters were all married, and he said that made him happy. He told me that he was proud of all of his children, but was glad they were all grown up and on their own.

I sat in silence, sipping my sun team, while Rhonda and Bradley discussed Bradley going to Rachel's to interview.

"OK, Curie. I'll do it for you, although I have to tell you I'm not too happy about going to La Jolla."

"I assure you that Rachel will welcome you, and the rest of the group, with open arms. Rachel will also be helping me write the book."

That put him somewhat more at ease. In Bradley's mind, Rachel as the co-author made her seem more official and not just some rich woman volunteering to run the show.

After about thirty more minutes of talking about Rachel, Bradley was eager to get started.

After drinking two glasses of sun tea, I stood up to use the restroom.

"Rhonda, may I please use your bathroom?"

"Of course you can use the bathroom. You remember where it is, don't you?"

"Yes, I do. I'll be right back."

I had visited the Johnson's on several occasions since meeting them and knew every inch of their little, neatly kept house.

The tiny bathroom just off the living room was overcrowded with bottles, boxes, and towels, but it looked very organized in a disorganized sort of way. Through the door of the bathroom I could hear Rhonda and Bradley talking.

"You sure you want to go out to that woman's house in La Jolla, Bradley? I didn't mind at first when Curie was gonna be coming over here to do the interviewing, but I don't know about this now," I heard Rhonda say.

"It'll be all right, Rhonda. You heard what Curie said about this woman. She sounds like a pretty nice lady, and Curie will be there. Now that I've told her I would go, I don't see any harm in doing it just once. If it ain't right over there, I just won't go back a second time."

At that moment I flushed the toilet to signal to the Johnson's that I would soon be returning to the living room. They shifted topics as I washed my hands and emerged from the bathroom.

"Now, tell me Mr. Johnson. Since you're the first person I've spoken with about the change, you get to be the one to select what day of the week we hold the interviews. It will take about four or five sessions, just one day a week. And, oh, by the way, Saturdays and Mondays are out."

"Well, you know I don't get home from work until about 6:30, so Tuesday through Friday it would have to be after 7:30 before I could get over to La Jolla."

"What about Sundays, perhaps after Church, say around 3:00?"

"That would work out OK with me."

"Great. If the others agree to everything, then how about we begin our first interview this Sunday?"

"Fine with me."

"I want you both to know how much I appreciate this."

"Glad to help you out, Curie. Nobody's ever asked me to do nothing like this before, you know, to be a part of a book."

"With your insight, Bradley, I'm sure it will be a best seller."

Bradley flashed a big grin.

"Thank you both. Bradley, I'll call you later after I've spoken with the others and give you directions to Rachel's."

I left the Johnson's and returned home to call the rest of the group.

Chapter Four

"Presenting...The Cast"

Convincing everyone to meet at Rachel's on Sundays was easier than I had anticipated. But I knew the real work was yet to begin. It was already Thursday, and I had to prepare to interview twelve people. Now I wasn't sure if I wanted to thank Rachel for her idea or bop myself over the head for listening to her. But all in all I knew that her proposal was a good one.

I turned on my laptop to construct the players. That's how I looked at them, as players in a big production—so I dubbed the project "The Curie Affair".

I rummaged through my notes to find my list of interviewees. Skipping Rachel, whose name I had penciled in at the top of my list, I moved on to the second name.

"Jonathan Severied, age 59. White male. Married. President of the San Diego division of World Bank. Handsome, wealthy, aging lines on forehead and around mouth, but has sex appeal. Father of my best friend, Diana. Influential, friendly. Consented to being interviewed as a favor to Diana."

I added the last statement to remind myself that Mr. Severied wasn't enthusiastic about sharing his deepest secrets with me, but Diana had coaxed her father into agreeing. Jonathan, a silver-haired, always busy man, said that he couldn't promise that he'd be at every session, but would try his best to attend as many as time permitted. He found it hard to deny Diana anything.

I took my pen and wrote in the name of the woman who graced the cover of The San Diego Magazine.

"Clarise Jorgensen. 61 year old, self-professed psychic. Single white female of Danish descent. Reads Tarot cards. Very thin and shapely. New-age gypsy look in her style of dress. Striking, waist-length, probably dyed, red hair, with fair, freckled skin. Facial features remind me of the redheaded version of Shirley Maclaine. Made a fortune as the owner of a production and design company that produces commercials and artwork for television and print. Lives in Sunset Cliffs. Friend of Rachel's."

Her company, CC West Coast, Inc. Her award-winning designs adorned the covers of countless magazines and books, and television commercials her company produced had earned countless awards.

The San Diego Magazine article described Clarise as "the mystical designer who creates from her soul." In the article, Clarise said her success came from the fact that she is in touch with her spiritual self, and that she didn't begin any creative work without first consulting her higher intelligence. Her fascinating approach to life captivated me, and I was anxious to hear her new-age responses to my questions.

I moved to the next person on the list.

"Judith Levine. 63-year-old Jewish female. Single. Lives in Old Town with her older sister, Moira. Agreed to be interviewed after coercion by Moira when she overhead me talking to family physician, Dr. Samuelson. The Levine's and I see the same doctor."

Moira describes her sister as an "old maid" who is afraid to get married. She overheard Dr. Samuelson and me discussing the project one morning and asked if she could volunteer her sister.

"Why aren't you volunteering yourself?" I asked the intrusive woman.

"Because my sister, Judith, has lived a much more confined life."

I surmised if her sister was a prude, what excitement could she possibly bring to the group? What experiences could she share? But I decided to withhold judgment, and told Moira to let me know if Judith was interested.

Moira convinced Judith that being interviewed could be fun, and a way to get out of the house and make some new friends.

She invited me to lunch to introduce me to Judith. I liked Judith well enough, but wondered why her jaws seemed to be clenched, like she couldn't relax, and her brown eyes looked spiritless, like she was hiding a lot of secrets behind her fixed stare. Her short brown haircut was awfully unbecoming. I wondered what Judith looked like when she smiled and considered her a real challenge. I could hardly wait to hear how she would respond to some of the more racy and intimate questions concerning her sex life, if she had one. I guessed that she didn't.

I felt like a voyeur, getting all worked up about peering into the private lives of my subjects. Reminding myself that this was being done in the name of research, and to truly create an interesting book on aging, I readily dismissed my own insecurities about the sensitive questions I would be asking and my motives for asking them.

Judith was at first dead set against being interviewed, but after constant appeals by Moira, she finally agreed.

When I called Judith to tell her that we would be meeting as a group she adamantly refused. She said that she just couldn't talk in front of others. I later persuaded Moira to convince Judith that she didn't have to answer any questions she was uncomfortable with. But since I hadn't given Rachel or any of the others that luxury, I hoped that I could change her mind later.

Moira successfully influenced her sister to go along with the new arrangement. Because Moira was outspoken and persuasive, I initially felt that she would contribute more to the book. But, then, after seeing how Moira was able to influence her sister's actions, I decided that getting to the heart of Judith's insecurities might, in fact, provide a much more interesting insight for the readers, thus adding more value to the book.

Moving down the list, was my next subject, Andy.

"Andrew McEwen. 69 years old. White male of Irish descent. Married. Recently retired president of an investment firm in Scripps Ranch where I once worked. Very caring, smiles a lot. Lives in Torrey Pines. Ex-football player for the Chicago Bears. Retired early from football due to knee injury. Once very handsome man, still in good shape, but looks are fading, has full head of shiny, white hair. To stay in shape, walks three miles a day. Avid golfer."

Before Andy retired, he was a fast moving, high-spirited, wealth building, take no prisoners, company president. I remember the many memos we used to get from him. Most contained quotes from great philosophers and famous football coaches, especially his favorite, Vince Lombardi. Most of the memos were geared towards winning in the midst of brutal competition. They also contained pearls of wisdom from the great political and military leader, Dwight D. Eisenhower. Then there were his own quotes on how to save time, money, energy, and working smart…that sort of thing.

The inspiring memos instilled a regimented work ethic and desire to surpass goals in most of us. He had a saying that he placed in the footer of every memo. "When the winners get hungry they eat the losers."

Those who took offense at Andy's candid quips, or who didn't realize the power of the words he shared, didn't last too long at the firm. I looked forward to Andy's memos. They didn't inspire me to become the best investment banker in town, but I took many of his philosophies to heart and set out to become the writer I had so long dreamed of becoming.

When I asked Andy to participate in my project, he laughed at first, and said I couldn't be serious. He said that he had given all the advice he cared to give, and that he wasn't interested in spending time away from his golf game. After several attempts, he finally gave in, saying that he admired my tenacity. When I called him to tell him there was a change in venue, that we would be meeting at Rachel's, he readily accepted the idea.

Andy had met Rachel, but admitted that he didn't know her well, except for what he had read about her in the many magazine and newspaper stories that had been published about her, and August House. Andy thought that Rachel's idea was a brilliant one, which he agreed would save time. He even said that he was surprised that he didn't think of the idea himself.

Next on the list was gentle Sarah.

"Sarah Jenkins. Single. Youngest member of the group. 56 years old white woman. Lives in National City. Kind, seemingly unhappy. Lives in one bedroom apartment in dangerous, trash-littered neighborhood. Former critical care nurse. Quit nursing after spending time as a patient in psychiatric hospital over thirty years ago due to severe emotional problems. Now lives quiet existence alone in sparsely furnished apartment."

I met Sarah in Downtown San Diego. I gave her a ride home when her car stalled in the middle of Broad Street, which runs through the center of downtown San Diego. My car was behind hers, and when the traffic signal turned green, her beat up old brown Chevy Nova didn't move.

Cars behind mine started honking their horns. I tried to drive around her, but was blocked in by a steady stream of non-stop traffic. I was about to honk my horn, too, but noticed that the woman ahead of me was hysterical, obviously upset that her car wouldn't start.

I jumped from my car and ran up to her window. That made the drivers behind me even madder.

"Hey. What do you think you're doing?" yelled one angry driver.

"To hell with them," I told the distressed, mousy looking woman. "Just calm down. I'll get you some help."

Her stringy long brown hair looked clean, but in bad need of a trim.

"Excuse me, gentlemen," I shouted to two men standing on a nearby corner. "Can you help me push this car out of traffic?"

They immediately came over and helped get the car out of the street. After repeated failed attempts to start the engine, the men gave up and walked away.

"I feel so sorry for you," I told the frightened woman. "Unfortunately, you'll have to get your car towed."

She looked to me that she didn't have any money, so out of pity I volunteered to drive her home.

"Where do you live? What's your name?"

"I live in National City. My name is Sarah. Sarah Jenkins."

"Well, Sarah Jenkins, I know you probably didn't want to leave your car like that, but what else could you do?"

She didn't respond, and appeared ill at ease about accepting a ride from a stranger.

I talked non-stop, trying to get her to feel more comfortable with me. By the time we got near her apartment building, she seemed more at ease, and even began to talk a little.

She smiled faintly as we pulled into her apartment complex.

"Relax. A tow company is on the way to get your car to you. I hope the cops don't get to it first."

"I am so grateful to you. Thank you so much for helping me. Would you like to come inside and have a glass of water?"

I wanted to refuse. Her apartment building gave me the woolies. The parking lot was littered with paper and beer cans, and people milling about made me uneasy.

Totally abandoning conventional wisdom, I accepted Sarah's invitation. She handed me a plastic cup. I thanked her, but I didn't drink the water. I placed it on a little table that was almost bare, except for a pretty, little porcelain statue of a robin. Beside the table was a green, badly worn recliner. I looked around the tiny, skimpily furnished apartment and then at Sarah. Seeing her live this way evoked even more pity from me, so I decided to stay and talk with her for a few minutes. She was a kind lady who I assumed had experienced some problems in the past and ended up in a bad situation.

After writing down her address and phone number, I again reassured her that her car would be brought to her, and left. From time to time I called her, but she didn't have much to say. But one day, out of the blue, Sarah told me that she had been institutionalized in a mental hospital. She caught me totally off-guard, and I told her that it didn't matter to me, and that I enjoyed talking with her. Her gesture of trust that day endeared me even more to her, so when I decided to write my book I immediately thought about Sarah.

"I don't think anything I'd have to say would interest anyone," she told me the day I asked her.

"Oh, I disagree."

"I don't spend too much time away from my apartment, and I probably wouldn't fit into the group, but I'll try."

"That's all I can ask, Sarah."

I truly wanted to hear what Sarah had to say, and I had faith that over time she would see my project as a way to open up and share her life, and not as guilt to repay me for helping her with her stalled car.

Moving on down the list, I came to my next character, and I do mean character, Joe.

"Joseph Addington. 68-year-old white male. Lives in El Cajon. Bags groceries at Von's Grocery Store. Retired mailroom clerk. Oldest daughter, 50, still lives at home to help take care of Joe's ailing wife. Joe works to supplement his Social Security income."

I met Joe while he was working for the insurance company where Diana is a senior vice president. Joe was the mailroom clerk who delivered mail to the top floor executives. He was a hard working man who felt the company forced him to retire from a job he loved.

I once heard Joe say that if he ever stopped working he believed he'd die. I didn't know if that meant he couldn't afford to stop working, or if he just liked working. When I heard he was bagging groceries at Von's, Diana said that he needed the money.

One day I drove to Von's to ask Joe, a skinny, chain smoker with a very thin layer of gray hair, to be a part of my book.

"I'm not sure if I can get away from work to do it."

"Joe, I promise that I won't interrupt you while you're at work."

27

"My wife needs me on my days off."

"Joe, I'm serving refreshments, even beer, after each interview."

"Since you put it that way, OK, I accept.

Joe liked to drink beer, and his meager income didn't allow him to buy it very often. His Social Security checks went to pay his rent.

When I called Joe to inform him about conducting the interviews at Rachel's house instead, he balked.

But I told him that Rachel was very wealthy and generous, and that he'd be meeting all types of people that could possibly open the door to a job that was less hard on his feet. I reminded Joe about the $1000 stipend that we were donating to each interviewee for their favorite charity.

"You know, Joe, if your own circumstances warrant it, there is no shame in accepting the money for your own use."

"I could sure use that money to help out at home. And by the way, I'm also gonna need some help getting back and forth to La Jolla. I don't own no car, have to catch a bus everywhere I go, or ride my bike."

"I'll pay your transportation expenses, and even send a taxi for you, if necessary. Now you have no more problems, or excuses."

I scanned my list again.

"Miss Phyllis Sanders. 57-year-old real estate agent. African American. Widowed. Has worked as an independent real estate broker for over 30 years. Smart, sophisticated woman. Lives in Del Mar. Doesn't take everything in life so seriously."

Phyllis helped me to locate my house when I moved to San Diego from Memphis, Tennessee. Diana said that Phyllis was the sharpest agent in the San Diego area. Although Del Mar was almost an hour's drive from San Diego, Phyllis helped her clients find the perfect house wherever they wanted to live.

When I asked Phyllis if I could interview her, she was excited until I told her everyone in my book would be over fifty-five years old.

"Who do you think I am, some old, washed up woman?" she quipped.

"Washed up? Hell, you're more vibrant than most people I know. Old...please. You don't know the meaning of the word, and neither do I. Besides, I need a sister's point of view in the book. You're witty, and full of controversy. I like that."

Although Phyllis was one of two African American women interviewees, their ideas and views were considerably different. Phyllis had an opposite personality and more worldly background than the other woman, Beatrice.

Phyllis readily accepted the change of plans to conduct the interviews at Rachel's. She said she looked forward to seeing the inside of the La Jolla mansion and that it might lead to more real estate business.

Carmen was next on my list.

"Carmen Santiago. Married. 61-year-old Puerto Rican. Lives in Mission Beach. Professional singer and piano player. Works steadily at nightclub in Downtown San Diego. Full of energy. Customers love her. Packs the house on weekends."

Carmen, an attractive animated woman with precision-cut, light-brown dyed hair, jumped at the chance to be interviewed. One night, after one of her sets, I asked her to be a part of my project. I almost had to yell the invitation to her through the noise being made by the capacity crowd. As soon as she returned to the stage, she proudly announced that she was going to be featured in an upcoming book and pointed her finger my way, motioning for me to come on stage.

"Damn," I exclaimed out aloud. I didn't go to the stage, but smiled and waved as people turned to look my way. When I told Carmen about Rachel's, she liked the idea.

"It will be a wonderful change of scenery," she declared.

The next name on my list was Bradley's.

"Bradley Johnson. 63-year-old African American machinist. Married. Lives in Imperial Beach. Proud, religious man."

I couldn't imagine Bradley answering questions about his sex life. I hoped that he wouldn't be offended and open up once the group started sharing their own lives.

"Bradley will probably think I'm perverted," I thought aloud.

Next to last was Frank.

"Frank Johansen. 72-year-old ex-military man. White male. Married for the fourth time. Lives in Ocean Beach. Former army pilot. Served in World War II. Feisty, but serious. Almost too serious. Likes to debate. Weathered look. Looks every bit of 72."

Frank, a dead ringer for Lloyd Bridges, is my fiancé, Robert's, uncle. I met Frank about six months after Robert and I started dating. Robert wasn't sure at first if he wanted his uncle Frank sharing his secrets with me, but after I presented him with my list of others, he figured that if they were willing, that the process was probably harmless.

Frank liked it when others took an interest in him. Most of our conversations ended up with him telling stories of his military life. He had lived such a controlled life—one I wanted to include as a contrast to today's more freethinking society.

Last but not least, I finished my list with Miss Beatrice.

"Beatrice Davis. 65 years old, divorced. African American female. Lives in Pacific Beach. On fixed income, but would never admit it. Has in-home baby-sitting service that has dwindled to tending two children. Kind woman who has lots of friends."

29

Beatrice and I met on the beach while she had the two kids in tow. One of them broke took off running and bumped into me.

"Well, where are you going?" I asked the little curly-headed boy. I heard Beatrice calling out the child's name.

"Travis, you know better than that," she shouted as she approached us.

"He almost out-ran you," I said, laughing.

"He knows better than to run off like that," she said in a huff. "These children will drive you crazy if you let 'em, but I won't let 'em."

After chastising the little boy, Beatrice and I sat on the beach and talked more about her and her in-home business. She described it in glowing terms, akin to a Fortune 500 corporation.

Whenever I went to the ocean in Pacific Beach, I looked for Beatrice. I often saw her there with the two children, lecturing one or the other about the dangers of running off towards the water. When I decided to write my book, I asked her if she would consent to being interviewed. She readily accepted, but changed her mind when I told her there would be group interviews. After repeated telephone calls, I was finally able to convince her to change her mind.

The cast was ready, and I geared up to manifest my vision of ageless wisdom and beauty.

Chapter Five

"It's Show Time!!"

Rachel took her role as my co-writer very seriously. On Saturday, she called to go over the arrangements for the upcoming Sunday afternoon. Everyone in the group had agreed to a 3:00 P.M. start time.

"Everything's perfect for our charter group," Rachel's voice enthusiastically rang out through the telephone.

"Charter group? You sound like we'll be doing this again with a different group of people."

"You never know. Once we get started, we just might want to continue this project with a new group, with a whole new set of questions."

"I don't think so Rachel. This group seems more than I can handle. Now that tomorrow's our first interview, I must admit I'm getting just a little bit anxious."

"Don't worry. You'll see that everyone will get along splendidly."

"Some of these people have never even been to La Jolla, Rachel, let alone inside a palace like you have."

"Don't be ridiculous, Curie. It's just a house, and all will be made to feel welcome in my home. You're worrying too much. Don't underestimate them."

"Rachel, you haven't even met them, except for Clarise. And I haven't met her. I've just read about her firm. And Rachel, your home is not just a house. It's a mansion."

"I think I've met Andy McEwen before. I believe he golfed at a charity tournament I once sponsored," she said, ignoring my last comment. "I'll make everyone feel right at home, you'll see."

"You're right. I'm worrying too much."

"I know I'm right."

"Everyone has directions to your house. Go over your list and make sure you remember all the names. Beatrice and Joe will be the one's arriving by taxi. Have a good night.

I'll see you tomorrow."

"Good night, Curie. Till tomorrow."

Robert went out with friends, but I decided to stay in and go to bed early. The next morning I rose early in anticipation of seeing the group. After running errands all over town, by 1:30, I was headed to Rachel's. I arrived to set up.

Rachel's house looked even more beautiful the second time. By 3:00, everyone, except Joe, had arrived.

Gertie escorted the group to a sitting room, where she had set up hor'duerves. Rachel and I were waiting in the glass room, where twelve chairs were arranged in an arc, facing the ocean. I set up my tape recorder and stood before the empty chairs. Moments later the group entered the room and took a seat.

"Now that most of you have had a chance to freshen up a bit, let's get started. First of all, I'd like to thank all you very much for taking the time from your busy lives to participate in this project. As you know, I will be conducting interviews. I recommend you relax and get comfortable, because before this project is over, we're going to spend a lot of time together and know a lot about one another. If at any time you need to excuse yourselves, please feel free. If you're like me, you'll get lost in this massive house just trying to find the restroom. Don't worry. You'll end up back here sooner or later."

Just then Beatrice blurted out a loud laugh. "I know what you mean. This is some house. Rachel, if you ever decide to sell, I think that lady over there is a real estate agent," said Beatrice while pointing to Phyllis. "Give her your card, girl."

Phyllis, who looked so sophisticated in wearing a tailored black pants suit, didn't respond to Beatrice's chiding. Her short, silver-frosted Afro was very becoming and framed her beautiful brown face perfectly. Although Phyllis had laugh lines that folded every time she smiled, she was still an attractive woman, tall with graceful long arms and legs.

Gertie entered the room escorting Joe.

"Welcome Joe," I greeted him. "I was afraid that you wouldn't make it. Let me introduce you to everyone. On second thought, why don't we go around the room and formally introduce ourselves? I'll start."

"Gertie, show Joe to the refreshments," said Rachel. "And Joe, I'll show you where everything is later. For now, just help yourself and then join us for a very exciting first meeting."

"Sure thing," he said, and followed Gertie over to the table, where he overfilled his plate with small sandwiches.

He looked uncomfortable and I sensed that he felt out of place in Rachel's palace. He kept turning around to look at me, as if he wasn't sure if he should be taking food from the refreshment table while the group waited. His old, worn, blue jeans hung loosely from his skinny frame, and stringy tufts of gray hair jutted from underneath a dirty red cap. Against the backdrop of beautiful crystal glasses and bowls, Joe looked like a bum who had wandered in off the street. I wanted to walk over and snatch the cap from his head.

While Joe munched on his plate of finger sandwiches and slurped iced tea, I began. I clicked on the tape recorder.

"Now. Let's get started," I announced. "I'm Curie Nova. I was born and raised in Memphis, Tennessee. I've lived in Scripps Ranch in San Diego for over five years. I'm a writer, and when this book, of which all of you will be a part, is completed, it will be my fifth publication. OK, enough about me. Why don't we start with you Phyllis, and work our way around. And oh, yes, I'd like to thank Rachel for allowing us to gather at her lovely home."

Everyone looked at Rachel and smiled. Jonathan led with applause, and the group followed, with a round of staggered thank you's. Rachel smiled and took a quick bow, then sat at one end of the arc."

"Phyllis, why don't you begin," I announced.

"OK, sure. My name is Phyllis Sanders and I live In Del Mar. I grew up in Atlanta, and moved to San Diego when I was about twenty-nine. I've lived all over the San Diego area at one time or another. I own a real estate firm, and can assist you and your friends to find the perfect house," she added.

Everyone smiled, and Phyllis continued.

"I'm a widow. I like young, good-looking men, so nobody in this room will have to worry about me hitting on them, except maybe old Jonathan over there, with his rich self."

The group broke out in laugher, and applause.

"Thank you Phyllis. Clarise, why don't you go ahead."

"Yes, thank you. I'm Clarise Jorgensen. I was born in Copenhagen, Denmark. I moved to America, New York, when I was seventeen, where I attended the Julliard School of Dance. I was a ballet dancer for many years, performing all over the world. After retiring from dancing, I desired to stay connected to the arts, in one form or another, so I founded CC's West Coast, a production and design company. We do a lot of creative things there, but I won't get into all that just now. I also read tarot cards, so if anyone would like a reading some time, please let me know. As a member of this group, your readings will be complimentary."

"Thank you Clarise. That's very generous of you," I said. The group applauded Clarise's introduction, and then Carmen stood.

Carmen's shapely legs defied her age. Although she was showing signs of aging around her eyes, she looked athletic and full of energy. I attributed it to the fact that she danced feverishly almost nightly during her club act.

"Buenos Dios, Senors, Senoritas, and Senoras. I, like you, Clarise, am also an artist," she said, smiling at Clarise. "I am also a singer. My name is Carmen Santiago. I come from Puerto Rico. I have not performed all over the world, but I do a fantastic show Wednesday through Sunday at Santistiban's in Downtown San Diego. You all must come to see my show. I sing, dance, play the piano, and I even tell jokes, whenever the spirit moves me. I've been married to the same sexy man, David, for over 40 years. I flirt with a lot of men, but David knows that I love him and only him. Gracias."

Carmen, who loves an audience, did a little dance, then returned to her seat. The group applauded.

"One night I hope the group can come and see your show, Carmen. Santistiban's is a very lively place. And everyone, you have got to see Carmen dance. She's electrifying."

"That's great, Carmen," added Rachel. "You know, I think we're all going to become very good friends. Everyone seems to be so relaxed with each other. Why don't you go ahead, Jonathan?"

I started feeling more at ease standing before the group, with Rachel to my right in the Arc near the door.

"I'm Jonathan Severied," said Jonathan who possessed a commanding and distinctive voice. "I'm President of the San Diego division of World Bank. And I'm sorry, Phyllis, but my wife, Elizabeth, and I have been happily married for a long, long time."

Jonathan took his seat, and the group applauded his short introduction.

Jonathan was a handsome man. He looked immaculate dressed in a white polo shirt and white slacks. His demeanor was sophisticated, and his arrogant air gave me the impression that, although he was married, he was still quite a lady's man. His expensive haircut and manicured nails were in deep contrast to Joe, who looked like he hadn't had a professional haircut in ages, and whose fingernails were brittle and uneven.

"It's all right that you're married, Jonathan," said Phyllis. "We'll just have to confine our dates to every Sunday at 3:00."

"It's a deal," said Jonathan.

Andy was next. He looked comfortable in his golf shirt and khaki pants. It had been almost a month since I had seen Andy. I hadn't noticed before, but his face was showing signs of advanced aging. He took his eyeglasses from his front pocket and placed them on. He stood and faced the arc.

"I'm Andy McEwen. I'm retired from an investment firm in Scripps Ranch. My wife's name is Virginia. The game of football is my passion, but I am also a pretty good golfer. Thank you."

The group applauded, but I hesitated before moving on. I had hoped that Andy would elaborate, but he sat down. He had omitted, seemingly on purpose, that he used to be president of one of the most prestigious and successful investment firms in San Diego.

"I used to work at Andy's investment firm," I volunteered. "He was the shrewdest businessman I've ever had the privilege of being associated with. Thank you Andy," I said, and looked over at Joe.

Joe had finished eating his sandwiches and placed his plate underneath his chair. It created an eyesore in the exquisitely decorated room, and I was tempted to walk over and remove it. I pulled my attention back to Joe.

"My name's Joseph, but everybody just calls me Joe. After hearing all this fancy talk about golfing, and banking, and dancing, I don't know if I should tell you what I do for a living. I don't even know what I'm doing here. I been working all my life. Was working at an insurance company, but they said it was time for Old Joe to go, so I started working at Von's grocery store over near where I live in El Cajon."

I felt embarrassed that Joe was introducing himself in such a negative way. I hoped he wouldn't ramble on.

"I like fishing, if anyone ever wants to go with me, I'd be more than happy to show you some of my secret spots where the fish almost jump into the boat." Everyone gave Joe a hand.

"Thanks, Joe. I might just take you up on that fishing trip," I said to help Joe feel comfortable.

Jonathan looked at Joe as if silently questioning why I had invited him to be a part of the group. I hoped that Joe, or anyone else, didn't noticed Jonathan's glaring, obvious look of disdain.

"Judith, why don't you go next," I said to shift the focus off Joe.

Judith's frizzy brown hair looked more like an Afro than Phyllis' did. Despite her wealth, which according to Moira, was from a considerable inheritance from their father, Judith dressed like an old woman of meager means. Her plain blue polyester slacks and flower print shirt made her look even older than she was. Her eyeglasses dangled from a gold chain around her neck. She groped for her glasses as she spoke, then placed the out-of-date lenses on her face.

"Hello everyone. My name is Judith Levine. And I don't know what I'm doing here either, to tell you the truth. I don't know what I could possibly say that anyone would want to write in a book, but my sister Moira talked me into being here, so here I am."

She nervously sat down and looked towards Beatrice. Phyllis alone clapped, and the others joined her in staggered applause.

"Oh, my turn?" asked Beatrice. "O.K. My name is Beatrice Davis. I own a baby-sitting service. I live in Pacific Beach, not too far from the ocean. I walk there with the children I keep most days. I've been divorced so long I don't even remember when. Did you hear that, Jonathan, I'm single if you're interested."

Beatrice received a hearty applause.

Jonathan was obviously the hit with the ladies. I looked over at Sarah, who was sitting at the end of the arc on the left.

"Sarah, would you like to introduce yourself to the group?"

She hesitated, afraid to speak.

"It's O.K. Sarah," I coaxed. "We're all friends here. Before we get through, there won't be a thing about you that we won't know, so you may as well get started now."

Sarah stood, but did not make eye contact with anyone.

"My name is Sarah Jenkins. I live in National City. I don't know what else to tell you."

"That's just fine, Sarah," I said, as I led the applause for Sarah's introduction.

The room grew uncomfortably quiet after the faint applause ended. Rachel, who looked like royalty wearing a flowing, lavender chiffon dress, came to my rescue.

"And I know you have all been talking about me for the past few days. I'm the mean old lady who asked you all to come over to my house for these interviews. Curie and I have only known each other for a few days, but I know that, like me, you were all fascinated by the book she's writing. I'm Rachel Maxwell. I own August House Art Gallery. I'm originally from Chicago, but I've lived in California for quite a number of years. I'm very excited about the project...by the way Curie," she said, and turned to look at me. "I don't like calling our gathering a project. Why don't we name ourselves?"

"The other night, I was thinking about that, too," I said. "What shall we call the group?"

"How about the Dirty Dozen?" suggested Andy.

The group roared with laughter.

"Oh, God!" said Rachel. "We may end up talking dirty before the evening is over, but I don't know if I actually want to be called dirty."

"How about 'The Gabbies,' you know, because we'll be coming here to gab," yelled out Beatrice.

"Gabbies, huh. I like that," I said. Anyone else have a suggestion?"

"I know," said Clarise. "How about Nova's Arc?"

"Clarise, that's perfect," Andy zealously shouted.

Others in the group voiced comments of agreement.

I put Clarise's suggestion to a vote.

"All in favor of Nova's Arc raise their hand."

All hands were raised.

"Nova's Arc it is. Rachel, would you like to continue with your introduction?" I asked.

"I'm quite done. Thank you everyone."

"Thank you Rachel, said Clarise, who led the applause this time.

The group cheerfully joined in.

"Frank," I said to signal that it was his turn.

Frank stood tall, and I felt like I should salute him.

"I'm Captain Frank Johansen, retired Army. I spend most of my time now raising money for various veterans' organizations. I read everything I can get my hands on, and I'm married too, Phyllis and Beatrice. But I've been married four times already. If I decide to marry for a fifth time, I'll give you both a call."

The group broke out in lighthearted laughter and applauded Frank's introduction.

After the laughter died down, I turned to Bradley.

"And now, last but certainly not least, is Mr. Bradley Johnson. Bradley, why don't you stand and tell the group a little about yourself?"

Bradley stood and walked up front near me to make his introduction.

"I'm Bradley Johnson and I'm a machinist. Been one all my life, it seems like, and I'm married, too."

He turned around and looked at me.

"Curie, you'll have to find some single men for these beautiful women in the room," said Bradley, interrupting his introduction.

"You're right Bradley," was all I said, and waited for him to continue.

"My wife Rhonda and I live over in Imperial Beach. We like it there."

Bradley didn't know what else to say so I began to applaud. The others joined me, and he returned to his seat.

"OK," I said, to signal that the introductions had ended.

"Now that we all know each other a little better, let's get started with the meaty part—the interviews. But first, why don't we take a fifteen minute break?" I announced.

Everyone left the room except Rachel and me. I clicked off my recorder.

"Thank you so very much for suggesting these group interviews, Rachel. I think everything is going quite well, don't you think?"

"Excellent, Curie. You're doing a fine job. Do you need any help?"

"Oh no. I just want to check my recorder."

"Then I'll go freshen up."

Everyone had gathered in the sitting room where Gertie had placed more refreshments. The beautiful room was filled with the aroma of fresh, baked goods.

"Isn't this house magnificent?" Phyllis commented to Beatrice, who was admiring a crystal glass she had taken from the refreshment table.

"I feel like I've died and gone to heaven. This woman must have more money than Bill Gates."

"She's loaded, that's for sure," said Phyllis. "And she's so nice. I'm going to enjoy coming out here every Sunday. Everybody else is nice, too."

"Old Joe over there is kinda weird, and that Sarah. Now that's one strange woman."

"Beatrice, cut that out. You just met them. I'm sure they're nice, too. Not everyone is as open as you are. Besides, Curie wants to have all types of people in her book. It would be pretty boring if we were all alike."

"Oh, I didn't mean no harm, Phyllis. I'll see you later. I'm gonna find a map and make my way to the rest room," she joked.

Clarise walked up to Phyllis.

"I have a referral I'd like to give you, Phyllis. A friend's daughter is moving here from Tucson. She just got married, so she and her husband will want to find a house. Get with me after the meeting."

"Thank you Clarise. I didn't mean to turn this into a sales meeting, though."

"Don't be silly, Phyllis. It's good to know that you have a real estate firm. I'll send more business your way. I have lots of friends."

Phyllis smiled, and the two women shook hands.

"I'll take good care of them. Thanks again, Clarise."

Everyone returned to the glass room to begin the interviews. When the group quieted, I began.

"Are we ready? There are only a few ground rules, and I'd like to get them out of the way," I said while rubbing my palms together.

"First, put all pre-conceived notions of what you think we'll be talking about out of your mind. Although I have some prepared questions, there's no telling where our discussions will lead us. We are on a journey together, you see. What I am trying to accomplish is to enlighten people about certain aspects of aging. There are people all over the world just like you, and one purpose of this project is to validate their feelings and thoughts. Another is to expose your peers, who may think differently than you, to diverse opinions, your opinions, so that they can see their lives from different perspectives. Everyone is multi-faceted, and I'd like to shake up some of the pre-conceived notions of what life is like as you mature. Then there are the younger generations I'd like to reach. Let them know what they can expect from an uncensored, down-to-earth point of view."

The group carefully listened as I laid out the plan for our project. I went on to explain the importance of being completely open, so that we would capture meaningful stories to both enlighten and entertain our readers.

"Contrary to what some of you may believe, the younger generation is very much interested in what you have to say. I've talked to many young people who are curious about what it's like, and I mean what it's really like, to get older. Most form their opinions based on what they see on television, what they hear from their own parents, and other relatives and friends. But when it comes to some of the things that they really want to know, many tell me that they don't feel they get a straight answer. They don't know how you feel about sex, mortality, and your quality of life. I can see that you are all vital, interesting people, and I sense that you all have very fulfilling lives. Let's share them with others."

Rachel stood and addressed the group.

"Everyone, we are on a quest together. We'll keep moving until we reach our destination—and that is one of enlightenment for everyone who will be reading this book. And we'll probably discover a lot about ourselves in the process. Next, be totally honest in your responses. The purpose of this book is to help others understand that people over a certain age have hopes, dreams, fantasies, feelings, and interesting thoughts, just like everyone else. Several of you are in professionally powerful positions. Don't worry—what you say will be published anonymously."

"That's right," I interjected. "I have signed a document for each of you explaining this," I said as I held up a copy of the document. I expect that every one of you will sign it, too, as it releases your taped answers for my publication. Please take the one with your name on it before you leave, and if you have any questions, please ask Rachel or me. Lastly, let's have fun. We are gathered here today for the first of several special meetings. I feel extremely privileged that you have consented to join me here at Rachel's to help bring this project, 'Nova's Arc' to what I know will be an overwhelming success. With that said, let's get started."

"Oh, by the way," I added, "After I ask a question, anyone that wants to respond, please raise your hand. I'll call your name, so that we can keep things organized for the recording, then you may proceed with your response. Ready? Let's go!"

I cleared my throat, clicked on my recorder, and officially began the interviews.

"Question one. Is there anyone in the room who is no longer sexually active?"

Everyone except Rachel looked shocked. They weren't prepared for my first question to be about their sex lives. Joe, who was laughing, quieted, then raised his hand.

"Yes, Joe," I said.

"Hate to admit it, but me."

"Thank you Joe. Could you elaborate please?"

"Just what I said. Me. I haven't had any in so long I believe I've forgotten what it feels like."

"Why are you no longer sexually active, Joe? Is it because of your age?"

"My wife's been sick a long time. Even if she wasn't I don't know if I'd even be interested in having sex. I work, go home, have a cold beer when I can afford it, sleep, and then I get up and start all over again. Since my wife got sick, I ain't cared too much about having no sex."

"Have you thought about the sex act itself?"

"I used to a lot, but now I don't."

"Why not now? Do you masturbate?"

"Heavens woman. No!"

"Thank you, Joe. Is there anyone else in the room who is no longer sexually active?"

Judith's hand made it halfway up, and then she quickly lowered it.

"Judith," I asked, "did I see you raise your hand?"

Everyone turned to look at Judith.

"What are you all looking at?" she snapped.

"We're waiting for you to be honest and tell us if you're getting any. Come on now, don't be shy," teased Beatrice. There were spurts of laughter from the group. Although I tried to contain my laughter, I found myself laughing, too.

The look on Judith's face indicated that she didn't find Beatrice's outburst, or our laughter, amusing.

"Well," she stammered. "My not having relations has nothing to do with my age. I haven't had sex since I was a young girl, and I didn't see what all the hullabaloo was about then, so now that I'm old, I'm sure not gonna humiliate myself by doing it now."

"Why would having sex be humiliating to you?" I couldn't resist asking her.

"Curie, this is embarrassing. I really don't want to talk about this with all these men in the room," she protested.

"Judith, I'd like for you to see these men just as friends taking part in a group discussion, just as yourself, while we're here together. After all, they too will answer questions that they may find a bit embarrassing to discuss in front of ladies. But you've got to keep the goal of the book in mind. We want to educate others. Somewhere out there is another woman just like you who has never received pleasure from having sexual relations with a man. They, too, may think that it's too late to ever know what it's like to be in ecstasy, to be intimate, to make passionate love to a man. If you're just not interested in sex, that's one thing, and that's OK. But if there's a woman out there who thinks that sex is humiliating, at whatever age, if we explore that issue a bit, maybe we can help. Do you understand, Judith?"

"Yes, Curie. I understand quite well. Go on to someone else right now. I'll answer your questions later, perhaps."

Just then Sarah, who had been silent almost the entire afternoon, stood up.

"I used to love sex," said Sarah in a flat, monotone voice. "I stopped having sex after I lost my fiancé. He was so handsome, so kind, and so in love with me. We never got married though. I never found anyone quite like him, and I knew that I never would, so I didn't try to find a replacement. I live a pretty sheltered life now, so I don't meet very many men. Besides, the ones in my neighborhood hardly speak to me. Most of them look pretty dangerous anyway. But there are some nice ones, I'm sure. I do fantasize. I fantasize about me and my fiancé— the man I am still in love with, although he's dead now. But most of my longings have nothing to do with…"

Sarah's words trailed off. Her confession unnerved me. Her eyes had a far-away look, and she never looked me or anyone else, in the eyes while she spoke. I withheld judgment about Sarah, and continued the interviews, although I was curious as to what she didn't say.

"You say you fantasize, Sarah. About what specifically do you fantasize?

"I fantasize about when I was a young girl and I was the happiest woman in the world. I was engaged to a wonderful man who took me to beautiful places all over the country. I didn't live in National City at the time—and my fiancé lived right here in La Jolla. We were going to live in a house with a pretty view, like this one. That never happened. So now, I just imagine us together, making love the way we used to, so tender, so sweet."

Sarah was making the others and me uncomfortable. I began to wonder if this group interview was a good idea. But I had asked for honesty, and that's exactly what Sarah was giving, even if her unhappy tale of love lost did make the rest of us feel ill at ease.

"OK," I said in as upbeat a tone as I could to try and break the spiritless mood Sarah had set.

"So, the three of you seem to be saying that you haven't stopped having sex because of your age. It appears that the reasons are physically impaired partner and disinterest, no pleasure in the past, and trauma from an experience involving a former lover. At least no one said they stopped because of physical pain, or because they couldn't get aroused. For those of you who are still enjoying the garden of earthly delights, it's time for you."

Just then, Bradley raised his hand.

"Yes, Bradley," I acknowledged.

"I fall in the category that is not having sex."

"Oh really," I asked with surprise, wondering why he waited so long to respond.

"Yes," he said. "Me and Rhonda, that's my wife," he continued and stood to face the group, "haven't done that in a lot of years now. We used to sleep in the same bed, but now we have two little twin beds. She stays on her side of the room at night, and I stay on mine. At our age, we're as innocent as little children when it comes to sex."

"Is that the way you both want it, or does Rhonda want it and you don't, or vice versa?

"Oh, that's the way we both want it. We've raised eight children, so we've had plenty of sex. Don't need to do that sort or stuff now, as old as we are."

"Thank you Bradley."

I could almost hear the thoughts of some of the others as Bradley explained that he doesn't desire sex anymore. I wanted to find out more why he seemed to associate sex with having children only. I suspected his religious beliefs had something to do with it.

"Bradley," I called out after a few silent moments. "Why, besides the reasons you've already given, do you say you've had enough sex? Is there a cut-off age?"

"In a way there is a cut-off period. Look at me. I'm not exactly the sexiest man alive, anymore, like I used to be. And, Rhonda, although I love my wife, ain't no spring chicken either. I don't look at her like that anymore."

My suspicion was wrong. It was obvious that religion had nothing to do with his reasons.

"Do you miss having sex with your wife?"

"No. We'll sometimes I do. Depends on what I'm doing. If I'm watching some television show, and all the girls are almost buck-naked, then I might think about it."

"What do you think about when you're watching the, as you called it, buck-naked girls?"

"Curie, you know what I think about, don't you? I think about their young bodies. And I'll betcha their breasts are fake, but they still look good, and I think about touching them."

"Do you touch yourself when you're looking at these girls?"

"No, I don't do no freaky stuff like that!" Bradley yelled.

"Freaky stuff like what, Bradley?"

"Don't play dumb, Curie. Freaky stuff like playing with myself."

"Then call me a freak, Bradley. Do you still get an erection?"

"Good God, girl! You ain't got no shame. I'm a religious man you know."

Bradley's candid answers didn't sound like he was thinking about religion when staring at scantily dressed women on television.

"Yes, I know Bradley, and I respect that. God knows that we are sexual beings. He made us that way, remember. I don't remember ever reading in the Bible that you must stop having sex with your wife after a certain age. And I don't remember seeing the exact words, 'thou shall not talk about sex'.

"Have you asked Rhonda if she would like to have sex?"

"No, but she's the kind of woman that if she wanted it, believe me, she'd tell me."

"What if she didn't? What if you're assuming that she no longer wants to have sex? If you came home tonight, with fresh flowers, poured a glass of wine, or fruit juice, into two beautiful glasses, put on some jazz or other sexy music, dimmed the lights and lit a candle, how do you think she'd respond?"

"She might like it. Then again, she might say I've lot my mind."

"Bradley, would you help out the group by doing just that tonight? I'm sure Rachel will part with a few of her lovely flowers. And if you don't have any long-stemmed glasses, I'm sure Rachel will part with two of those too. When you go home, try what I just described. Fool around with Rhonda, you know, flirt and smooch with her. Even if she doesn't get in the mood to have sex, it might make her feel sexy? You know what I mean, Bradley? Next Sunday, tell the group what happened, whether she liked it. Could you do that for us Bradley? You see I'd like to know if you've assumed that Rhonda is no longer interested in romance. Romance and sex are two different things. If she looks at you like you're crazy and tells you to stop smooching, then we'll know you're right, and that she's not interested. But, if she smooches back, or returns your affections, then maybe you've assumed wrong. Could you help us out?"

"Sure. Sounds like fun."

"Great. Get with Rachel, or me, before you leave. We'll make sure you have flowers, glasses, and even candles if you need those. Is that OK with you Rachel?"

"Absolutely! I can't wait until next Sunday to hear the results."

"Thank you Rachel. Oh by the way, everyone, I don't remember if I told you that Rachel will be assisting me in writing the book, of which I've yet to title. I'm telling you this so that if she asks you some questions too, you'll know that she's not just being nosy, but is helping to clarify points for the purpose of the book."

"Why don't we take a fifteen minute break, then we'll move on to those of you who still have intimate relations with your mate."

Frank walked up to me after everyone left the room.

"Curie, I must tell you that you're asking some pretty personal and downright lewd questions."

"Well I told you that I would do that way ahead of time, Frank. After all, how in the world am I going to publish an interesting and meaningful book about people of a certain age group, specifically older people, if I don't ask challenging, thought-provoking questions? Most people already know that when you reach a certain age your bones ache, or you run out of breath faster, or your hearing or vision diminishes. The readers won't be interested in that sort of stuff. Don't you think that if your wife had assumed that you didn't want sex, but she did, and neither of you were open enough to bring up the subject, reading it here might get a discussion going, and just might get some sex going too?"

"You may have a point, Curie. But sex isn't everything. I don't believe that sex is as important to some people as it sounds like it is to you."

"That's where I think you're wrong, Frank. There is no shame in discussing one of the most intimate things that two people can do together. If they don't want to, so be it. For people approaching the age of some of you in the group, it might just reassure them that it's OK to still want your husband or lover sexually. Or for those who are years younger, believe me when I say we're downright curious about your sexual lives. I stare at my fiancé's parents and wonder if they still have sex, or whether his father still gets a hard-on for his mother. And there is Viagra® to help kick start the old lighting rod," I said, while laughing.

"Never tried it," admitted Frank.

"Don't you think it would be sexy—imagine—even at your age—having your pants unzipped while you and your wife are having afternoon tea. Think about it—while sipping afternoon tea, your wife is putting honey in her tea and on your private parts. She then licks it off her fingers and your, you know," I said while shifting my eyes to his crotch. "Could make for an interesting afternoon."

Just then Clarise and Jonathan returned. I noticed that, except for Phyllis, who mingled freely with everyone, the wealthy members of the group were pretty much keeping to themselves during the breaks. I put the thought out of my mind, but made a note to observe if this trend continued. My hope was that everyone would get to know each other, and discover something they shared in common, despite the fact that some were worth several million while others couldn't even afford the gas money to make the trip.

"OK everyone. It's time to move on. We have less than an hour, and I'd like to wrap up this subject. I'll give you the second question before you leave. When we reconvene next Sunday I'd like to hear your responses to your thoughts about that day's topic. But, getting back to where we left off, we were talking about sex. I must confess I chose this question first because I figured it would make you the most uncomfortable, so I wanted to ask it up front. If you brave this topic, then all my other questions will be a piece of cake. So, is there anyone having sex that feels that they are doing it for their partner, and in the process satisfy his or her own sex urges?" I asked as I looked out over the group.

"Sometimes I do," responded Jonathan. "Just like any other couple, young or old, sometimes we have sex even when we don't feel like it, to satisfy the other person."

"Please don't think me a sexist, Jonathan, but I never expected to hear a man say that he has sex just to please his wife. I think that is splendid. Anyone else care to comment?"

Beatrice raised her hand.

"Yes Beatrice."

"I'm not married, I'm divorced you might remember, but I have a boyfriend. We have sex often, except during the day when I'm keeping the children. I certainly don't feel old, and I know my man isn't just having sex with me because I want it, I know he wants me just as bad."

"How often do you have sex, Beatrice?"

"Oh, I'd say at least once a week. Fred, that's my boyfriend, would probably do it more if I would let him. But I'm busy mostly during the week, but every weekend we get together."

"That's great Beatrice. I think it's healthy to have a sex life, as long as it's not painful or anything. I understand that the moisture in a woman's vagina is not as plentiful once you reach a certain age. Can anyone tell me about that?"

No one seemed to want to approach that subject. Judith was squirming in her seat. I was afraid she'd pass out. I looked around the room, waiting for someone brave enough to step up to the plate.

"OK," loudly admitted Carmen. "Since you people act like you're embarrassed to tell it like it is, I'll have to speak up. Curie, there are so many products on the market that can help with that problem, that I would be surprised if anyone was going through painful sex, if that was the case. There are moisture gels on the market that you can buy at the grocery store that feel just like your own natural juices. David and me, well we don't need to use stuff like that most times, but when we do, I don't hesitate for a second using them. He likes it because I get to use it on him, and then he does the same for me. Even when we don't need it we use it sometimes—makes for good foreplay."

"Very good point, Carmen. Thank you. And since Carmen brought up the subject of foreplay, I'd be very interested in someone going through his or her foreplay routine, if it's different than what you did when you were say, 25."

"There's no difference in that," yelled out Phyllis, who, up until now, had yet to respond about her own sex life.

"What I liked when I was 25, I still like today. You know—everything. And the man I dated up until about six months ago liked it too. He wasn't shy at all," said Phyllis.

"What about oral sex? Anyone performing oral sex?"

Judith got so embarrassed that she jumped from her chair and ran out of the room.

"I have oral sex," declared Rachel. The words rolled off her tongue as smoothly as if she was confessing that she drinks coffee in the morning.

"Well, Rachel. Elaborate, if you will, for the group." I was happy that Rachel was commenting. Up until now she had been responding in her role as co-writer, and not as an interviewee.

"What's there to elaborate on, Curie? I still give and receive oral pleasure. It's as simple as that. I loved it when I was younger, and I love it even more today. I must confess; however, that most of my sex partners of late have been somewhat younger than I, not that has anything do with why I like oral sex. I just thought I'd share the fact that I don't care about a person's age, if I'm interested in them."

"How much younger, Rachel? And are you certain that you aren't choosing your partners because of their youth?"

"To answer your first question, the young man I'm currently seeing is 40. He's no child. And, to address your second question, no I'm not seeing him because of his age. I'm very much attracted to him because not only is he physically attractive to me, and vice versa, he's also a very interesting and talented man. We share a love of the arts. And as for the age difference, I really don't care what others think about that."

"Does Suzanne care?" I heard myself asking, although I hadn't planned to blurt out the question that way.

"She doesn't appear to. Quite frankly, Curie, we never talk about that sort of thing. You'd be surprised. We see each other frequently. She runs August House, as you're aware. I'm there at least one week out of a month. We catch up on everything that's been happening at the gallery, about upcoming artist exhibits, new art acquisitions, and the like, but we, for the most part, keep our private lives private. We know who each other is seeing, but that's about the extent of our discussion when it comes to men."

"That's interesting, Rachel. I'd like to come back to this topic at one of our other sessions."

I addressed the group. "It's important that we capture how other people view your lives, especially your adult your children, especially because you're their parents. Children don't tend to see their parents as sexual beings at any age."

Rachel looked uncomfortable discussing her relationship with Suzanne, and I was certain that we would not be returning to the subject. Although Rachel maintained her cool, regal bearing, I sensed some irritation in her clear blue eyes. I moved on.

"Who else would like to tell us about foreplay, or oral sex, or any type sex for that matter?"

"My wife and I don't have oral sex anymore," volunteered Andy. "We still play around though. We kiss, cuddle, you know—we're real close, even closer since the kids grew up and moved away. I love her in a deeper way now, too. It's funny. I don't remember exactly when it happened. We've always had a special love for each other, but now our souls love one another. Do you know what I mean?"

"I do," immediately said Clarise. You make love by looking at one another, when you walk past each other, or when you're just sitting in the same room. You don't have to be talking or doing anything special. Or you could be miles apart, and feel enveloped in each other's love. Is that what you mean, Andy?"

"That's exactly what I mean, Clarise. I could have never explained it the way you just did, though."

"That's very special, Andy. I hope everyone realizes what you and your wife have," I softly said, then moved on to Frank.

"What about you, Frank?"

"My wife and I are getting along just fine. If I am doing those things with my wife, I'm not going to tell you about it. Some things a man just has to keep to himself."

"All right Frank. What about you, Clarise?" I readily moved on since Frank was being rigid.

"Well, Curie," began Clarise. "I do sometimes, have oral sex, that is. Other times I don't. It all depends upon the moment, or how I feel about myself. Some days I don't want to be aroused sexually. I just want to be by myself, to reflect and get in touch with my spirit. I travel a lot, so I'm not always with my partner. But we have a very loving and committed relationship."

"Thank you everyone, It's almost 5:00 o'clock," I announced while glancing at my watch. "Why don't we wrap up today and next Sunday we'll pick back up then move on to the next question. I want you to think about this one and really share with the group your candid thoughts. I appreciate how open everyone was with today's sticky subject. I think it was a good idea to get the sex question on the table right away. With that almost a closed issue, or maybe not, depends upon if any of you want to continue the topic, we'll move on. Next topic, how do you feel when you see young, vibrant people? Like when you're watching television and you see young people playing sports, just fooling around, kissing, and making love, or whatever, on television or in person? How do you feel when you're at the mall, and you see 16 or 17 year olds having a good time, laughing and being sexy, like you used to do? Do you get sad sometimes, or feel old? Are you happy that you've matured, and achieved some goals? Do you still act like those younger people do? Bottom line, how do you feel about yourself at your current age when surrounded by youth?" That is our topic for next week."

"You trying to depress us, Curie?" asked Frank.

"Of course not Frank," I responded. "I just want to know what you're thinking and feeling when surrounded by young people. This will give our readers some validation for their own thoughts if they share your feelings. Then, there are some younger people who want to really know what you feel about them, not what television tells them in special reports and the like. So, with that in mind, discuss it with your friends, relatives, partners, or whomever you feel comfortable with. Really dig down deep so that you can share your innermost feelings about this most important topic."

"I'll do my best," said Judith.

I hadn't noticed when Judith returned to the room. I was happy that she would try to tackle our next subject. She seemed so sheltered in both her thinking and in her daily existence. I hoped that she would feel more comfortable in our next meeting.

"And Sarah," I whispered, stay behind for a little bit, OK?" She nodded yes.

The group dispersed. Some moved into little groups to discuss the day, others to the bathroom to freshen up, and Andy left right away to catch a televised football game with some friends.

I walked over to talk with Sarah.

"Sarah, are you OK?" I asked. "I hope that you weren't offended by any of the questions today."

"Oh no, I knew what to expect. You had warned me, remember?" she said and managed a faint smile.

"Oh yes. I did warn you. Thank you so much for helping me out with this project. I want you to know how much your participation means to Nova's Arc, and to me."

"Thank you for allowing me to be here. It may not seem like it now, but I was happy the day you called to ask me. I thought you'd long forgotten about me. You even kept my phone number. That made me feel good. I don't get out very much. This is my way of repaying you for being so nice to me that day I ran into trouble with my car. I best get going. I'll see you next week, same time?"

"You bet, Sarah. Drive carefully." I escorted her to the front door.

"Wait a minute," I heard Carmen's voice blare through the room.

"Nobody can leave just yet. I have a special treat for Nova's Arc. I'm going to perform one of my famous numbers for you. I'll be hurt if you leave now. And nobody walks out on Carmen Santiago."

"We'd be delighted to hear you sing, wouldn't we Sarah?" I said while tugging at Sarah's arm.

"Oh, I guess a few more minutes won't hurt," she said and stepped back inside the door.

"Ladies and gentlemen, may I have your attention please?" broadcasted Clarise. Carmen walked to the glass room and took a seat at the grand piano.

"Carmen is going to perform a private show just for us. Could you all please return to Nova's Arc?" requested Clarise.

"Andy's already left," said Phyllis, as we all returned to the glass room for Carmen's performance.

"Ladies and gentlemen," said Carmen in her lively, professional stage voice. "I'd like to close our first meeting with a number I prepared just for the occasion. I hope you like it. And if you don't, keep it to yourself. I'll be performing the same time after every meeting."

We all applauded. Carmen curtsied, and then sat back on the piano bench.

As she played, everyone, including me, had a look of pleasant surprise on our faces, as Carmen sang a beautiful song, which she had written. It was more like a concert piece. I had assumed that she would play a festive, dance song. Instead, it was a beautiful love ballad about a man and a woman deeply in love, one from a distant land, and the other from America. The lovers overcame the barriers of language and race, and experienced a deep and passionate love. Her song was entitled "Love Assure."

The piano solo was slow and melodic, a sonata that was easy to imagine being played in a large concert hall. Carmen finished her number, stood, and took a bow in front of the piano, like famous maestros do.

The captivating number had us all spellbound. We applauded, and Clarise cried out "Bravo".

"Carmen, that was brilliant," declared Rachel. "That's an absolutely enchanting song. Did you write it?"

"As a matter of fact I did. My husband helped me with a few of the words, but the musical composition is all mine. Does this mean you like it?"

"Oh yes, very much, Carmen," beamed Rachel. "In fact, I liked it so much that I would like for you to perform that number this coming Monday night. I'm having a small dinner party for some investors, and my guest will be just as enchanted with your song as we were. If you have other songs, similar to that one, I'd like to hear them, also."

"Next Monday? You mean tomorrow?"

"Yes. That's right. Tomorrow is Monday."

"Well, I guess I could squeeze you in. You see—Monday is one of my days off. I don't get too many of those and I usually just relax with David on Mondays. But for you, Rachel, as a member of Nova's Arc, I'll make an exception. It'll be like performing in Carnegie Hall," she said as she spread her arms to demonstrate the size of Rachel's home.

"And I'll pay you well. You perform just like you did tonight. And begin by playing the song you just sang. Be here at 8:00. We'll be having dessert by then."

I was happy for Carmen. I could see bringing the positive effects of bringing us all together, already.

I noticed that tears were streaming down Sarah's face. It was apparent that the hypnotic song had struck a sensitive chord with her. She approached Carmen.

"Thank you Carmen, for such a beautiful song," she said, wiping away the tears with the back of her hand.

"You're welcome sweetie. There's no need to cry, though. Take care, and I'll see you next Sunday."

"Yes, I'll see you next Sunday, for sure," said Sarah.

I watched as Sarah grabbed her purse and left.

I recalled the day I first met her. I felt sorry for her then, and I found myself feeling even more sorry for her now. She looked so lonely. There was something about her that I couldn't quite put my finger on. Her usually sad, but beautiful hazel eyes lit up when Carmen sang her song.

The loneliness I assumed she felt living all alone in that tiny apartment in National City must be unbearable. I wanted to run out to her before she got in her car—hug her, tell her that whatever hurt her was over, and to forgive herself or whomever had caused her such pain in the past. But I decided to keep my nose out of Sarah's business—for the time being. I knew that sooner or later I would ask Sarah more about her life, and I hoped that she would confide in me, or anyone in the group.

Bradley walked up to leave, also.

"Wait just a minute, young man," I teasingly said. "Rachel and I have to get your romance pack together, remember? Excuse me. I'll be right back. Don't you go away, OK?"

"Oh yea, no problem. I'll be right here," responded Bradley.

I spotted Rachel, who was talking with Clarise and Jonathan.

"Rachel," I called out. "Shall we get Bradley's romance pack together? He's about to leave."

"Certainly, dear," she said, and turned to Clarise and Jonathan. "Could you please excuse me?"

"Of course, Rachel. I have to go anyway, said Jonathan."

"Me too, I'm afraid, but I'll see you tomorrow morning," said Clarise.

Rachel bid Jonathan and Clarise good evening, and confirmed her breakfast plans with Clarise. Then she walked into the sitting room and gathered up a big bouquet of exotic flowers. She asked Gertie to wrap them in shiny white paper and tie them with lavender, silk ribbon. She then removed two long, white candles from a drawer in the kitchen, and took a bottle of champagne from her refrigerator. She placed the champagne, glasses, candles, some gourmet jelly and thin wafers, and a small box of Swiss chocolates into a metallic gold gift bag.

"Here Bradley," she said. "If this doesn't rev up Rhonda's motor, nothing will. Spread that jelly all over your lips before you kiss her. She'll lick you clean from head to toe trying to get another taste."

Bradley blushed. "Thank you kindly, Miss Maxwell. That sounds dangerous." He hurried out of the front door. Everyone else left, too. Rachel and I stayed behind to discuss our first session.

"They're all wonderful, the group is great," exclaimed Rachel. "But it's plain to see that we'll have to work on Sarah and Judith. They seem to be a bit, well, stuck. Judith might just be a little easier to pry loose than Sarah; however. Sarah appears to be in her own little world, a sad little world at that. I wonder what on earth could have happened to her to make her feel so downhearted? She emits such unhappiness. This group is probably the best thing that's happened to her in a long time—maybe in her whole life, poor thing."

"I don't know, Rachel. There's something about her that just keeps nagging at me. It's not just that she seems unhappy. There's something much deeper going on with her."

"Where on earth did you find her? And please, don't think I'm being a snob. It's just that she's just so fragile. I thought you wanted to interview people who were candid, witty, honest, interesting."

"That's true, but I also want to interview people who have something worthwhile to say that others will find helpful and enlightening. People like Sarah, and Judith, who don't talk a lot, their thoughts can sometimes be of more value than those of the people who talk all the time. They've had time to really think about life, and although they may or may not have lived as full a life as some of the others in the group, I'll bet their imaginations are pretty fertile. As far as we know, they may have lived an even fuller life. And besides, people who don't talk much usually spend more time listening to others. They end up being smarter than we big mouths are because they've really observed and contemplated the world around them. Just give them a chance to get comfortable. They'll open up more, I'm sure."

"I suppose you're right. You have an interesting way of complimenting two of the dullest people I've ever met. But, you're right. I shall not judge. I shall accept them for what and who they are. If you hear or see me doing otherwise, you have my permission to yank my hair."

I couldn't believe that this cultured and wealthy woman was telling me to yank her hair if she showed disrespect to the two lonely and unassuming women. The more time I spent with Rachel, the more I liked her. Incredible was becoming too commonplace a word to describe her. And with all her qualities, she still loved performing oral sex, too. That was fertile fodder for my imagination."

Just as I was pulling open the heavy front door to leave, I came face to face with Suzanne, who had stopped by to drop off some papers for Rachel's signature.

"Oh my God, you startled me!" I exclaimed.

"Curie. Hello. I'm sorry if I startled you. You startled me too. Is my mother here?

"Yes. She's in what I call the glass room.

"I know which one you're talking about. It was good to see you again. Goodbye."

"Yes, you too Suzanne. Goodbye."

I though Suzanne's greeting was rather curt, but guessed she was in a hurry to see Rachel. I left to return home and organize my notes.

Chapter Six

"Interlude"

Rhonda could hardly wait for Bradley's return from his first interview. She peered out of the living room window every time she heard a car drive by. Finally, Bradley pulled their white Toyota into the driveway. Rhonda ran to the door and swung it wide open.

Bradley wanted to surprise Rhonda with the romance package Rachel had prepared for him, so he left it in the car and walked up to her.

"Is everything OK?"

"Yes, everything's just fine. You know I've been dying to hear all about the rich woman's house. What did you do over there?"

"Hold on Rhonda. Let me get settled first. Then I'll tell you all about it."

Bradley and Rhonda walked into the house.

"Oh shoots, I left some papers Curie gave me out in the car. I want you to read them. I'll be right back."

Bradley walked out to the car to retrieve the gold bag and bouquet of flowers. He hurried back up the drive and stepped through the door proudly displaying the flowers.

"Happy Sunday evening, Rhonda! These are for you!" he enthusiastically said and placed the exotic bouquet in Rhonda's arms.

"Bradley, where one earth did you get these flowers, from that rich woman?"

Bradley didn't answer.

Rhonda beamed with excitement. "Rachel knows her flowers. These are beautiful, Bradley. Thank you baby, now come on over here and let me give you some sugar."

"Wait a minute. That's not all," said Bradley as he held out the gold colored gift bag.

"What's that? For me too?"

"Yes. It's all for you, or should I say us."

"Did you get this from Rachel, too?"

"Curie started this mess…"

"Wait a minute Bradley. I like it. I don't care where you got it; this is some expensive champagne. And look at these chocolates. I'm glad you'll be going over there every Sunday!"

"I can't say that I'll be bringing home something every Sunday, Rhonda, but I'm sure glad you like what I brought."

"I love it Bradley. Now where's my sugar?"

Joe returned to his apartment after leaving Rachel's. He didn't discuss the evening with his wife or his daughter. He walked right to the refrigerator, opened a beer, sat in front of the television, and fell asleep.

After returning from Rachel's, Judith joined her sister, Moira, in the kitchen for tea.

"How did you like the group?" asked Moira.

"Actually, the whole thing was rather vulgar. If I hear the word sex one more time I think I will explode," said Judith as she poured her tea.

"Sex? Was the entire evening spent talking about sex?"

"Yes, I think so. I wouldn't go back at all if Curie hadn't told us what next Sunday's topic will be."

"Oh, what's that?"

"Let's see," said Judith as she grabbed her purse and rummaged through it to find the topic she had written down from the meeting.

"Oh yes, here it is. Next week we'll be discussing how we feel about getting old. That's not exactly how Curie phrased it, but that's what it means. She said we'd talk about how we feel when we see, or are around young people. Do we still act young, want to be young, wish we were young, or just feel like washed up old people?"

"Judith, you make it all seem so negative. I'm sure Curie didn't put it that way."

"I said she didn't use exactly those words. I think what she's looking for is whether or not we're happy with the way our lives turned out."

"Well, are you?"

"Now you sound like Curie. I'll think about it, try to talk about it at next Sunday's meeting, and I'll let you know if I'm happy when I come back from the meeting. Right now, I'm tired. I think I'll go to bed early."

Judith finished her tea and left the kitchen.

Moira sat at the table alone. She thought about the questions that Judith had given as part of next week's topic.

"I could be happy," she muttered to herself, "if I didn't have you depressing me all the time," she muttered to herself. She gulped the last remaining drops of tea, switched off the kitchen lights, and sat in the living room listening to Vicki Carr records.

Sarah had spent her evening alone, and by dusk had fallen asleep in her tattered, green recliner. The sun set, and the street light near her apartment cast an eerie glow through her tiny living room window. She began to have a recurring dream of when she was a critical care nurse at Valley Hospital.

Sarah's dream was always the same. She is checking on a patient who in recovery from surgery. Her fiancé, a handsome and very successful doctor, walks in. They leave a patient's room, and enter a stairwell.

"I love you, and I can't wait until we're married," whispered Sarah.

53

That's the moment when Sarah's dream always turns into a nightmare.

The doctor tells Sarah that he can't marry her, they argue, with Sarah protesting his decision, and crying out that she loves him.

"I just can't marry you, Sarah, I'm sorry," adamantly says the doctor, and walks away.

The heavy metal door slams shut, leaving Sarah alone in the stairwell, which is as quiet as a tomb.

Suddenly, Sarah hears the distressing cries of a baby. She struggles with the heavy door, but has difficulty getting it open. Finally, the door swings open and Sarah runs down the hall to look for the baby.

As she turns a corner, she comes face-to-face with her fiancé and a beautiful, blond woman. She freezes. She can neither move nor speak. The doctor and the woman join hands and walk away, disappearing into a corridor. The hospital seems empty, except for her fiancé, the woman, and Sarah. Sarah runs to the corridor.

"Is that the reason you broke off our engagement?" Sarah screams out, her voice echoing through the deserted corridor. "Is this the reason our engagement's off? Talk to me, answer me. Are you in love with this woman? What about me? Come back, don't leave me, come back," she pleads, but the doctor and his female companion walk out of the hospital and up to his car, which is parked right outside the hospital door.

At this point in Sarah's dream, the images become distorted.

Sarah runs up to the doctor's car, which is parked right outside the hospital. Just as Sarah puts her face up to the passenger window to get a closer look at the woman, the car takes off, and Sarah runs down the street, chasing after the car. The face of the mysterious woman never comes into focus. Although her face was distorted, Sarah sees pity in the woman's eyes. "No!" she screams then wakes up.

Sarah has been plagued by the same disturbing nightmare for many years. She ran to the bathroom and slumped to the cold linoleum floor of the dimly lit bathroom, crying and reliving her nightmare. She pulled several sheets of toilet paper from the wooden spool and wiped her eyes. She cried until she fell back asleep on the dingy little bathroom floor.

In one of Sarah's talking moods, she told me she began having the recurring nightmare when she was released from the psychiatric hospital. After her fiancé ended their engagement, she suffered a mental breakdown, and was sent to Serenity Hospital for the mentally disturbed.

Before her breakdown, Sarah was the best critical care nurse on her floor. The other nurses were happy that she was marrying the rich, handsome physician, and were devastated when he broke their engagement. Sarah had told them all of their plans to build their dream home in beautiful La Jolla once they were married, and had invited them all to the grand wedding that she had spent months planning.

She never discovered who the woman was that had stolen her fiancé's heart. By the time she was released from the mental hospital, Serenity, she had lost the will to find out who had taken her love away, and became a recluse.

The doctor didn't see or talk to Sarah after he broke off their engagement. It was after two failed suicide attempts that she was sent to Serenity Hospital. She spent more than five years in the mental institution, and had tried on several other occasions to take her life, but each time she was discovered by a hospital worker and revived.

Five years later, Sarah no longer showed signs of wanting to end her life and was released. She never returned to nursing.

Before she awoke the next morning, Sarah had dreamed the agonizing nightmare again. She was awakened by her own screams near sunrise.

"I'll have to tell the group one day what it feels like to be old, and totally alone," she sadly told herself. She stood and looked out of a little window in the bathroom. The sun was rising.

Later that morning, Clarise and Rachel were having breakfast in a restaurant near Clarise's home in Sunset Cliffs.

"Wasn't Carmen fantastic last nigh, Rachel?" asked Clarise.

"I never would have suspected that Carmen was so talented. Her robust manner defies her delicate touch with the piano. And that song was simply magnificent. If I hadn't heard it with my own ears, I would never had believed that she performed it."

"She is a professional performer, Rachel. I'm sure the crowds that she performs for aren't interested in that type of music. She probably doesn't get the opportunity to play it for very many people."

"Well she will now. I plan to engage her to perform every time I get the chance. I'll be helping her get exposure and she'll be helping me entertain my clients. We both win this way, don't you think?"

"Yes, of course. I get good feelings about her, Rachel. Just think. You two would never have met her if it hadn't been for Curie. By the way, when you first told me about Curie, I had this feeling that it was by providence that you two met. When Curie announced that you would be assisting her in writing the book, I felt certain then that your meeting each other was fated."

"Yes. Curie and I discussed it the other day. I was so taken with her project that I wanted to be a part of it—well, more than just being interviewed."

"Where on earth will you find the time, Rachel? You're already so busy now that I'm surprised that you are having breakfast with me."

"Clarise, I'll always have time for you. And, I'll make time for Curie's book. I always make time for the people and things that are important to me. And this group is important to me."

"You must admit that this is an unusual group. There's something about some of them that I can't pinpoint, but I get this feeling when I'm in the room with everyone. I can't explain it just yet, but I'll work on it. I'll do a tarot reading on the group."

"You do that Clarise."

Rachel and Clarise had been friends for some time, but Rachel didn't put too much stock in tarot cards.

"Clarise you're probably feeling a little unnerved because of the extreme mixture of people in the group. After all, how often do you spend time with an elderly grocery bag boy, a baby sitter, a sheltered soul like Judith, and a strange bird like Sarah?"

"Not very often, I admit. Frank is not exactly Mr. Personality either, is he?"

"God, I forgot about Frank. How could I forget about Captain Frank Johansen? He's some character."

"You called Sarah a strange bird, but I'll bet she's the one that will end up being the most popular one of the group. Curie seems drawn to her. Didn't you notice how Curie took the time to walk her to the door, and to make certain that everything was OK with her?"

"Yes I did. But Curie is just that way. She's very caring, and she could plainly see that Sarah needs a boost to her self-esteem. She told me how she met Sarah. She became Sarah's savior one hot day in Downtown San Diego. Apparently Sarah's car had stalled, and Sarah became a damsel in distress. Curie decided to rescue the poor woman. I was touched by that story when Curie told it to me. I could never see myself doing what Curie did, but I admire her sensitivity and concern for the woman."

"Curie's actually quite clever. Think about the group that she's assembled. There's people there of means, some middle class people, and then there's those who can hardly afford the shirt on their backs. But think about everyone individually. What do we have?"

"I don't know. What do we have, Clarise?"

"We have people who may not be wealthy in the material sense, but are rich by any standard. There's Carmen. She probably makes a pretty decent living singing in the nightclub, but with her talents she could make all the money she wanted. So in all actuality, she's richer than many wealthy people I know because she knows uses her special gifts to make others happy. Then there's Jonathan. I like Jonathan, please don't misinterpret what I'm about to say, but he's rather smug. After the group's first break, he made some rather disparaging comment about some of the members of the group. I'd rather not repeat what he said, but it was not at all complimentary. Hopefully, over time he'll come to realize that everyone there has a beautiful soul and is blessed with a very special gift. There's no difference between any of us. He's talented when it comes to banking, high finance, but I think Carmen is richer. You get what I mean? She gives to the world great music, and she infuses it with a part of herself. My hope is that Jonathan one day realizes the true value of people."

"I won't ask you to repeat what Jonathan said about the group, or maybe about Carmen," said Rachel. "As far as I'm concerned, everyone in that room is an equal; we're travelers on an exciting mission. In my book, that's more valuable than high finance."

"I'm sorry, I shouldn't have mentioned that about Jonathan, but since we were discussing the group…I hope you understand."

"Clarise, forget about it. Excellence beats out prejudice every time. We'll just have to make sure that Curie has the right material to produce a best seller. But getting back to Carmen's talents, I can't wait to hear her perform again. My little party will help to expose her to the right audience. Once we have her performing in Madison Square Garden, Jonathan will be begging her to become one of his bank's valued customers."

Both women burst into laughter.

"That's what I meant about Curie being clever," said Clarise. "She knows that it makes no difference who we are on the outside. She's merging us into this melting pot to show that it doesn't matter. No matter who we are, or how rich or poor some of us may be, or where we come from, we all need attention, care, to be paid some attention…to be loved."

Clarise and Rachel talked long after breakfast, then hugged goodbye.

"Don't forget to read those tarot cards about the group. Let me know what they tell you."

"Sure thing, Rachel. See you tonight."

The two women hugged again then departed the restaurant.

Chapter Seven

"Carmen the Virtuoso"

It was Monday night.

Carmen arrived at Rachel's to perform her one-woman show dressed in an elegant, long white evening dress. Normally, Carmen, although 61, performed in glitzy, somewhat revealing outfits. But tonight, she looked refined and elegant. She moved in graceful, small steps to the door.

Gertie, dressed in a formal maid's uniform, answered the door and escorted Carmen into the glass room, which Rachel had filled with beautiful flowers and an exquisite ice sculpture of a woman sitting at a grand piano.

Carmen was at a loss for words when she saw the fascinating sculpture. She slowly scanned the crowded room of tuxedo-clad men and-diamond draped women. She had performed before crowds most of her life, but as she studied the room full of powerful and influential people, she got a little nervous.

One of Rachel's guests, Julianne, a socialite and heiress to an international department store chain, was sitting at the piano playing around with a show tune. Rachel was anxious to replace her with Carmen.

"Carmen, I'm so glad you're here, Rachel said as she walked up to greet Carmen. "Ladies and gentlemen, this is Carmen Santiago," eagerly announced Rachel. "Everyone is excited to hear you perform, dear. I've told them all about you."

"Gracias," Mrs. Maxwell," said Carmen.

"Would you like something to drink…get comfortable before you begin?"

"Yes. I'd like some white wine if you have it. Who are all these people? It's hot in here?"

Just then Clarise walked up with a glass of Chablis and passed it to Carmen, as if she had read her mind.

"Hello Carmen. I'm glad you're here," said Clarise, and kissed Carmen on the cheek.

"Julianne's playing is OK," she whispered, but I'm getting tired of her show tunes."

"Well, I've prepared a list of some songs I hope you like."

"Remember, first, we want to hear the one you performed for the group. I simply loved it, and I know that everyone here will too."

"That's my plan, Clarise. Is everybody ready?"

"We're ready when you are. Wait, I'll introduce you."

Clarise and Carmen walked to the piano together. Julianne looked at Carmen and smiled, then stopped playing and stepped away.

Suzanne, who looked stunning, and very different dressed in a short black strapless dress, approached the piano.

"I don't believe I've had the pleasure. I'm Suzanne Sullivan. You're in Curie's group, right? My mother tells me you play the piano."

"Yes. You're the one who run's Rachel's art gallery. She told us about you yesterday."

"Did she also tell you I'm her daughter?" asked Suzanne, who was irritated at the way Carmen had referred to her as a worker in her mother's gallery. Carmen noticed her irritation.

"Oh, yes. She said that you were her daughter. She's very nice, your mother. I'm Carmen Santiago. It's nice to meet you."

Carmen was ready to get started and didn't want to spend more time on small talk with Suzanne. Beads of sweat had formed on her brow, and she took off her gloves and slung them on a chair near the piano.

She sat on the piano bench and played a quick warm-up tune. Everyone stopped talking and looked at Carmen.

"Ladies and gentlemen," said Rachel, as she moved closer to the piano. "It is my pleasure indeed to introduce Carmen Santiago. As you will hear, she is a talented composer, singer, and pianist. Mrs. Santiago will be performing some of her extraordinary original compositions for you tonight. And Carmen, I hope I don't make you nervous by saying this, but keep in mind that just about everyone in this room is a filthy rich investor in one project or another."

Many in the room laughed, and everyone applauded.

Carmen smiled, but didn't respond. She was no longer nervous. She closed her eyes and took a deep breath. She slowly opened her eyes, adjusted her position on the piano bench, stretched her fingers, and began to play the hypnotic song that she had played the Sunday before.

Everyone's eyes were transfixed on Carmen, as her fingers lightly stroked the piano keys, like butterflies dancing across the keys.

A tall German man leaned in and whispered to Rachel.

"This song is incredible. Did she write it?"

"Yes," Rachel whispered back. "She said she composed it, with a little help from her husband. Exquisite, isn't it?"

Everyone applauded, and many yelled out, "bravo" before Carmen had finished.

The noise from the crowd almost broke her rhythm, but Carmen kept on playing. When she sounded the last note of the mesmerizing song, the crowd broke out into thunderous applause.

Carmen stood and bowed to the audience, and the overwhelmed group raised their glasses in a toast to her. Rachel beamed with pride. She was happy to see that the talent she planned for the evening was receiving such heartfelt acceptance from her guests.

59

Everyone in the room was awestruck at Carmen's performance. Rachel had told her guests that Carmen was an exceptional composer, but no one expected the intense and dramatic show that Carmen was providing.

The eager group anxiously awaited another song from Carmen, the virtuoso. Most were so moved by her first song that they approached the piano, crowding Carmen before she began her second number. She took another slight bow, and drank a sip of white wine.

"Ladies and gentlemen, I'd like to speak to you, if I may," she said and rose from the piano. Her white gown blended in with the grand piano.

"I am Carmen Santiago. The beautiful Rachel asked me to come here tonight and play for you. It is my privilege, as I have been performing for many, many years. This distinguished group makes me feel good, because you seem to love my music as much as I do. It makes me feel very, very good inside. I perform at Santistiban's, a fabulous place here in San Diego Tuesday through Sunday. But there, I play a different kind of music for a different type of crowd. Who knows, before the night is over maybe you'll want to hear some of the music I play for the group over there. And what about this beautiful ice sculpture? I think the woman at the piano is me," she said, and Rachel raised her glass to confirm Carmen's comment.

"Thank you, Miss Rachel," said Carmen. "Now, let me play for you another of my original compositions, which, by the way, I wrote just last night. This one's for you, Clarise" she said as she smiled and blew a kiss in Clarise's direction.

The room was so silent in anticipation of Carmen's dedication that you could have heard a pin drop. Even Gertie peered in the room to observe the great Carmen perform.

Slowly Carmen started to play. The intro began soft and slow, then, built in intensity. The music softened again, and Carmen began to sing…

"I had a perfect start, it was just a word, dreaming one night of Sunset Cliffs, your beautiful name I heard. The name was haunting, came to me, a loving whisper, bringing peace. Saw deep red lips and flame red hair, an angel named Clarise. Brought light from heaven meant for me, was like a bright sunray. When I awoke, I saw your face, and the word you spoke was 'Pray'. Pray for touches from a friend, smiles on rainy days, for the broken hearted, reach out your hand, and touch God back, always."

The people in the room were spellbound.

Carmen sang a chorus and three other versus to her tribute to Clarise, then ended… "and God touches back, always".

"Remarkable," said Rachel, as she put her hands to her face and tears streamed down her cheeks.

Carmen's piano solo was a rhapsody, and all of Rachel's guests were in awe of the lone, dark-skinned woman who played unnerved, as if in another time and place, at the beautiful, white grand piano.

The swell of the Pacific Ocean created a perfect backdrop for Carmen's riveting performance. Gertie tipped out of the room to instruct her help to bring in more hor'duerves, as if the last note of Carmen's song signaled it was OK to enter. She didn't dare allow the servers to interrupt the spell of enchantment that Carmen had cast.

As Gertie walked through the crowd, checking on the food, and giving orders to servers that Gertie had hired for the evening, she overheard a conversation between Rachel and one of her guest.

"Rachel, where on earth did you find this magnificent woman?" said a man named Dan from Dallas, who was dressed in full Texas gear. The eccentric man puffed rings of smoke into the air with each word.

"Carmen came to me through a project I'm working on with a local writer named Curie Nova, a rather talented woman."

"I'll tell you one thing, Rachel. That old gal sure's got a lot of passion in her. What would you say if I told you I'd like to steal her away from you? Hell, with talent like that she should be performing...and don't take this the wrong way cause you know I love you Rachel, but she should be performing on some stage before a much larger crowd that this, or some little local joint, like that Santistiban's. That woman's a walking gold mine."

"Well Dan. You don't have to steal her. I'll give my permission for you to walk on over there and tell her that yourself. How about I introduce you."

Gertie smiled and left the room.

"Fine, let's go," said Dan as he crushed his cigar in a porcelain saucer then grabbed his cowboy hat, which he had placed atop the glass table.

Rachel escorted Dan to the piano. Carmen was walking away towards the restroom to freshen up.

"Carmen? Carmen? May I have a moment to introduce you to one of Texas' most distinguished cowboys? This is Dan Cook of Dallas. He is quite taken with you and your beautiful music."

"Ah, Mr. Dan Cook, It's a pleasure to meet you, Sir." said Carmen as she extended her hand.

Dan grabbed Carmen's hand and gave it a feathery kiss.

"Miss Carmen, I have to tell you that I'm usually no fan of fancy music, but what I just heard from you tonight is pretty damn fantastic. Rachel here tells me that you wrote those songs yourself."

"Yes, I did. Well, the first one my husband David helped with a few of the words. The others I wrote all by myself."

"What about the song about Clarise? That was a real pretty one."

"Yes, I wrote that one just last night. I am happy that you liked it, Senor Cook."

"Call me Dan. Carmen, I want you to take my card here," he said as he dug into his jacket pocket and retrieved his business card. "Call me at my office this coming Wednesday—I'll be back by then. My secretary's name is Elaine. If I'm not there when you call, just tell Elaine the best time to reach you, and leave your number so I can call you back. I want to talk to you about your singing. I have a friend who's in the music business and I can pretty much bet the ranch that he'd love to have you sign on with him once he's heard you sing—if, of course, that is what you want. For the next few days, you just think about what you want, and then you and me'll talk. How's that sound?"

"Senor Dan, that sounds simply fantastic. I look forward to talking with you next week. I'll call you on Wednesday, for sure."

"Good thing. Now if you ladies will excuse me, I have to find your restroom, Rachel."

Dan walked away, and Rachel winked at Carmen. She beamed a look of satisfaction, knowing that she was responsible for Dan and Carmen meeting one another.

Carmen was ecstatic and contemplated her upcoming phone call with Dan—her new, tall, Texan friend with the booming personality. She could hardly wait to tell her husband all about him. Had the offer of assistance come from anyone other than one of Rachel's guests, Carmen would have been suspect of such a forthright gesture to help her. But Rachel had already announced that everyone in the room was a wealthy investor in one project or another, so she figured that she was soon to be one of Dan's projects.

Carmen returned to the piano and played two more of her original compositions. The group gave her a resounding applause after each song. She ended her set with a Spanish version of Frank Sinatra's, "I Did It My Way."

The evening was winding down, and several of Rachel's guests were biding her goodnight. Most made a point of speaking with Carmen before leaving, especially Dan.

"Now you don't forget to call me. Goodnight Carmen," he said, then, gave her a kiss on the cheek.

"Goodnight Dan. I appreciate everything, and I will call on Wednesday, for sure," responded Carmen as she bid him Goodnight.

Gertie and her hired assistants entered the room and began clearing the multitude of glasses and other dishes from the room. Rachel and Clarise escorted two remaining guests to the front door, then returned to the glass room.

"Carmen, you were smashing tonight. Thank you for your lovely songs and for sharing your astonishing talents with us," complimented Rachel as she walked over and took Carmen's hands in hers.

"Thank you, Rachel, for your flattering words and for the opportunity to be here and meet Dan tonight. I think I have found a new friend in Dan. He said that he would help me with my music, you know."

"Of course, Carmen. I was standing right beside you, remember? I knew that if you performed tonight something magical would happen. Dan's one of the wealthiest men in all of Texas, probably in the whole United States, and I want you to know that he has the biggest heart, too. If Big Dan says he's going to help you, believe it, because he will. He's never gone back on his word with me, and he'll keep his word to you, too."

"Ah, that's so good. I cannot wait to go home and tell my husband. He will be so excited for me."

"Yes, of course, Carmen, go home," Clarise chimed in. "You must be exhausted after performing all those songs."

"No, I'm not tired. I perform a lot longer than this at Santistiban's. But I am ready to see my David."

"Certainly," said Clarise. "Carmen," she hesitated. "Before you go I just want you to know how beautiful it was of you to write a song and dedicate it to me. I was speechless as you sang your song about the angel named Clarise."

"I wrote that song specially for you, Clarise, because I had this dream last night. It was a sign. When I woke some little voice inside my head said 'write it down,' before I forget the dream, you see. So, I get up first thing and I wrote everything down that I could remember from that dream. Even the melody of the song was stuck in my head, don't know where it came from, but I wrote it down, too. This song was easy to write because I didn't really compose it. It was composed for me. All I did was serve as the tool to capture it, and bring it here for you. Thank you for coming into my dream."

"I'd like to hear more about this dream someday soon."

"Yes. There was more to the dream than I put in the song. I want to tell you about it sometimes. Goodnight, ladies. I see you next Sunday."

"Goodnight Carmen. Drive carefully," answered both ladies in unison.

After Carmen left, Rachel and Clarise stepped out onto the balcony to get some fresh air.

Rachel turned to Clarise.

"Tonight was very special, wasn't it? Carmen was extraordinary. Can you believe she wrote that song about you just last night, and from one of her dreams?"

"Yes, I can, as a matter of fact," said Clarise, as she took a deep breath of the mist-filled air.

"It's so beautiful out here, Rachel. You had a great party. Everyone enjoyed themselves immensely."

"Yes, I'm happy. And thank you Clarise, very much, for being here tonight."

The two women talked for a few minutes more, and then Clarise left for her home in Sunset Cliffs.

Chapter Eight

"Feeling Old Yet?"

It was Sunday again. Robert was leaving for Washington D.C. for three days so we rose early to have breakfast together before his flight.

We dressed and went to our a little restaurant near our home. I told him all about how the group was progressing.

"One day I'd like to meet Rachel," he said.

"I want you to," I said as the waiter stepped up to our table.

"She's a fascinating woman. I'll ask her to dinner soon. Maybe even Diana would like to come along."

Robert had been so busy traveling that I hadn't had the chance to give him the details of Nova's Arc until now. We stayed at the restaurant long after we finished our breakfast to catch up on each other's lives.

After driving him to the airport, I rushed back to get things ready for the next round of interviews. I could hardly wait to hear of Bradley's romantic overture to Rhonda.

Sunday's had become especially exciting to me, and I hoped that the others were enjoying our sessions as much as I was.

I made it to Rachel's by 2:00 to help her get set up. Gertie answered the door.

"Hello Miss Nova. Mrs. Maxwell stepped out for few minutes. She come back soon. Come in."

"Thank you Gertie."

Gertie, a very friendly Mexican woman whose family still lived in Tijuana, was improving considerably in speaking English, but she still had a way to go. She once told me that she could speak it better than read or write it.

"May I get you something while you wait, Miss Curie?"

"No thank you Gertie."

"I was arranging the chairs, back here, for your group. I'll finish," she said and walked away."

"Gertie, may I help you with that?"

"No thank you. I almost done," she replied then left the room.

I looked around the big living room, noticing things that I hadn't seen before. Rachel's house was so massive that I was not surprise that I hadn't seen many of her things before.

I picked up a little porcelain statue of a robin, which sat atop the fireplace mantel. I was sure I had seen one like it before, but I couldn't remember where. I closely admired the delicate little porcelain bird, then placed it back on the mantel and walked onto the patio, just outside the living room. It was filled with flowerpots of beautiful greenery and blooming flowers. Although I had visited Rachel several times since meeting her, I could still hardly believe that I was standing on her patio, taking in the view of the Pacific Ocean from her balcony.

It was obvious that Rachel trusted me, and I was grateful that she had placed such confidence in me and in our project.

I walked into the glass room and see if I could help Gertie, even though she told me she was almost done. I saw Rachel walk in.

"I see you're getting set up. I've had a hell of a day, already. I have an exhibition next week, and the artist is telling me that he may not be able to get all of his works here on time. That's just not acceptable. I'm sorry Curie. I don't mean to ramble on. How are you?"

"I'm fine Rachel. Hope you feel like the group today."

"Believe me, Curie. I am looking forward to the group. It will take my mind off Andreas, my temperamental, excuse-giving artist."

"Good. I think we'll have a more relaxed group today, I can just feel it. Now that I've shaken them all up asking the sex question, I think they'll be more relaxed today with their homework done."

"I sure hope so. I'd like to hear just a little more honesty this time, Curie. There was some skirting your questions last Sunday. Perhaps they'll open up more today. Let's hope, anyway."

"Yes, let's."

Clarise was the first to arrive. She brought along a tape recorder so that, if Carmen kept her promise to sing after the interview, she would be sure to capture it on tape this time.

The group assembled in the glass room, eager to begin the day's session.

"I hope everyone thought about the questions I posed last Sunday. What we'll do is let Bradley tell us all about how Rhonda liked the romance package Rachel and I put together for him, and then we'll go right to today's discussion."

Bradley blushed when everyone turned to look at him. The group applauded.

Bradley stood and flashed a big smile.

"You women are geniuses," he began. "You should do this for a living—putting love in a neat package—that is. At first I felt a little nervous about showing her the stuff you gave me, cause I thought maybe Rhonda wouldn't like me bringing home that bag that she would know came from Rachel's. After all, I ain't never done nothing like that before. But she loved it, especially the candles and flowers. We didn't drink the champagne, cause we don't drink, so Rhonda gave that to a woman next door who does. But anyway, I ain't got so many kisses and hugs from Rhonda in one night in a long time like I got last Sunday evening. We didn't do anything, you know, sex, if that's what you waiting to hear, but I wouldn't trade the joy I saw in my wife's eyes for anything. Made her feel real special. Thank you ladies for last Sunday. I really appreciate it."

"You're welcome, Bradley," said Rachel.

I didn't respond, as I was busy visualizing the old black woman I'd seen many times while visiting the Johnson's. I was sure they gave the champagne to her. I could see her sitting in a lawn chair on her front porch, guzzling that $150 Dom Perignon, right out of the bottle. I snapped out of my daydream to address the group.

"That's great Bradley. See I told you that your wife still wants romance. Just because you both are getting on in years doesn't mean that she has lost the desire to be treated special. Bradley, that's a very sweet story. Thank you very much for sharing it with us."

I looked at Rachel.

"If you need your love life spiced up, please feel free to consult with Rachel. I've already put in an order for some of those chocolates."

"I'll take three boxes," joked Phyllis.

"OK. Let's get started with today's discussion. Who remembers today's topic?" I called out to get the meeting on track.

All hands went up. I was impressed with the group's enthusiasm. "OK, that's terrific. I see you put some time into this one. Beatrice, why don't you tell Nova's Arc what today's topic is."

Beatrice stood proudly to deliver the topic of today's interviews. "Today, we will be discussing how we feel about ourselves and things when we're surrounded by a lot of young people, or when you see a lot of younger people walking around half naked on the television."

"Very good, thank you Beatrice. I must say that you certainly spiced it up a bit from the way I described it last Sunday. I like the way you put it. I might add. Now, who would like to open the discussion?"

Andy raised his hand and stood without waiting for me to call his name.

"I spent a good part of the week with your questions regarding today's topic lodged in my head. What I soon realized is that what you asked I had already asked myself a million times already. Your asking us to think about it just made the thoughts grow more intense. I talked about it with my wife, with a few friends we had over for dinner last night, and I thought about it a lot when I was alone," said Andy, who then took a deep breath.

"Yes, go ahead Andy," I said, then nodded for him to continue.

"I'll be honest with everyone. This topic sort of got to me. You know how I feel when I'm surrounded by a lot of young people? I feel like a young man trapped in an old man's body, that's how I feel."

Andy put his hands to his face, and then slid them down. "I feel like I've cheated myself. I'll tell you what I mean by that in a minute, but I digress. You see—I've achieved great things in my career, and helped a lot of people. But there's something that I still wrestle with today. This may sound foolish to you all, as old as I am, but I still have a lot of unresolved issues with my father, may

67

he rest in peace. When I was young, and growing up, I never got much in the way of attention from my father. My dad was a very serious and busy man. By the time I was a budding young athlete, I had lots of people telling me how great I was, but I needed something from my dad. He was a strict disciplinarian, and although I'm sure he was proud of me, I never felt like he supported me. I needed someone to support me..." Andy's words trailed off into silence, and then he started talking again.

"I had four brothers, and it seemed I was treated just as a common person, and that my brothers were treated special. He seemed more interested in my brothers' lives than in mine. I felt if I had that kind of support from him, like he gave my brothers, that I could have achieved something special. Now that I'm older, I see that those feelings were a crutch, and that I was already special. But at the time, my dad's support would have made all the difference in the world to me. I was hoping for him to push me, to walk up to me, and say, 'you have potential,' I needed someone to say that. I don't even think I was really injured when I was playing for the Bears. I used that injury as an excuse, too. I was told by the coaches, and everyone on the team, and countless others, that I had the quickest hands in football. I fought that, told my doctors that my knee was worse off than it really was. Deep down I know I told myself that I didn't really have what it took, and I needed someone to tell me that I did. I couldn't look myself in the mirror and tell myself that. It just wasn't in me at the time. And now, when I look in the mirror, I still get frightened, because I've never given it, you know, this subject, and how I feel and all, a real voice before now. What I realize is that I don't feel wise, or like the older, sophisticated lover you see getting the young, beautiful girls, like you see in the movies. I've been lying to myself for years, saying that I feel pretty good about myself, about my age, and what I've accomplished, but in all actuality, and after thinking about myself all week long, like you asked us to do Curie, I acknowledged that I have a lot of insecurities."

"What type of insecurities, Andy?" I was shocked at Andy's revelation. He was the most positive and optimistic person I'd ever met. "What about all those go-getter quotes in the memos?" I asked myself. I turned my attention back to Andy.

"Insecurities. Well, I used to be a football player, with the NFL. I spent all my high school and college years being just that. That's all I wanted to be. I was a damn good football player, too. The time finally arrived for me to really shine, in the pros, and before I could play out the first season, I blew it. At the time, I think I handled everything pretty well, but now I see these hotshot young players, running in a blaze on the football field, and I know that could have been me. I know it sounds pretty foolish. But if I could go back in time for just a little while, and do some things differently, I wouldn't let that injury become my crutch, then I could be a hall of famer—I just know it. Ridiculous, I know that's what you all are thinking, but that's how I feel about it."

"Describe the feeling, Andy, not what gives you the feeling, if you can."

"It's anxiety, like time is running out before I will get to do something that made me feel as powerful as football did. But there I was looking to my father to validate me, and all my power went down the drain. I was so intimidated by my father that I didn't want to bring up anything to him. I was scared I'd be chastised or criticized as not being able to do it on my own. I've done a lot of interesting things in my day, don't get me wrong, but nothing as elevating to the senses as being on top of the world when you're rushing 120 yards past some of the fastest and fiercest men alive. I've been there, and I miss the feeling. I shouldn't have let the fact that my father was too busy with a lot of other stuff, and my other brothers, deflate my confidence and rip away my glory."

"Do you miss the game too, Andy, or do you just miss the power?"

"I guess you could say both. I miss the glory. I used to tell a lot of people that I didn't miss that, but honestly I do miss the glory. I liked being before a crowd doing things that many couldn't. And, I liked hearing about it later—people coming up to me and showering me with accolades about how incredible my game was. I've spent a lot of my life beating myself up about it, and it makes me sick right in the pit of my stomach. I've been successful in business despite all that, because most times I just push it down—deep down."

"What about when you see a lot of young people on television shows, or staring in the movies? How does that make you feel?"

"If the show is good, then I feel good about seeing the young people. If it stinks, then I feel the same way about them as I would about a rotten older actor. But one thing that separates the way I feel about so many young actors having the limelight today from actors from my generation is that the actors' today haven't really worked hard to earn their day in the sun. Either their relatives boosted them, or they slept their way to it, but they have not, in my eyes, achieved the title of 'star' like in days before. As far as I'm concerned, there are no movie stars anymore, just a lot of actors. But I mostly watch sports on television. I live in their shoes and tell myself, they're doing it for me. It's really sad, because I gave up on myself, so now I root for them."

"Now you're just not being fair to yourself," jumped in Bradley. "Those old days of glory and fame can't take away from who you are now. You may not have your name in the football hall of fame, but you seem to have risen to the top in the investment field. You shook off that ghost long enough to climb that mountain."

"But it wasn't easy," said Andy. "It took all I had to pull myself away from what I used to be. That ghost whipped the hell out of me. Gave me bellyaches, ulcers, and I lost my way for a number of years. Hell, I drank, drugged, escaped from my friends and family by staying away for weeks at a time, and all kinds of other crazy stuff, just trying to do anything but face myself."

"What brought you back, Andy?" I asked.

"I did. Yes, I still feel empty, sometimes, which I've just admitted to you, but I had to put all my energy into pulling myself out of the hell I found myself living in, and decided to throw the passion of that whole thing into my work. And I worked hard, and then worked some more. I used all of the philosophies I learned that molded me into a football player, and executed the plays on Wall Street. I wasn't running 120 yards anymore, but I had built more than $820 million in profits for the firm before I was 40. And in those days, that was a hall of fame accomplishment. But enough about that. I'm depressing everyone. Bradley, you go next, tell us what you think about the fine young actors out there today."

Bradley walked up to Andy and shook his hand.

"Andy, you've got a lot of guts. I respect that, and anybody that can make $820 million dollars is a hall of famer in my book. Now, as far as these so called actors of today, in the old days actors did the same thing they do now? A lot of them probably slept their way to the top too, and you don't have to look too far to find a relative with most of the older star's last names. I do agree, that the stars seemed to work harder to make it years ago, but it doesn't mean that they got there in different ways than young people do today."

Jonathan stood up.

"Now that's where I beg to differ. Many years ago a true movie star never showed her breasts, and everything else, to capture attention. Her mystique engaged the audience, or her talent, even her feistiness…take Kathryn Hepburn, for instance. I don't remember ever seeing her, if you'll excuse my French, her ass, but I do remember her face—the look in her eyes when she spoke with such conviction in 'Look Who's Coming to Dinner.' Her emotions seemed real when she pleaded with Spencer Tracy to accept her daughter marrying outside her race. And what about Sidney Poitier's performance? I haven't seen acting like that from any of the current popular young actors of today. There was no sex, or violence, or nakedness in that particular movie, and it's a classic. That's it. No one makes what can be called a classic, anymore."

I had not intended for our discussion to turn into a group movie review, but the passion Jonathan had inspired was raw, and everyone seemed to be engaged by the subject, so I let it continue.

Phyllis was chomping at the bit to get a word in while Jonathan was speaking. So, I called on her to share her views.

"Now that you've opened the floodgates, let me tell you what I think," said Phyllis very matter-of-factly. "Half of those anorexic girls are walking around with fake breasts. In fact, it's probably the majority of them. I've always had ample breasts so I never had to resort to anything phony like that," she said while outlining her body with her hands. "I don't feel insecure when I'm around young folks, it's they who should feel insecure around me. I may be old, but I still look mighty good. Sometimes I do miss being able to do some of the things I used to do, but it's not an everyday feeling. When I get an ache or two, then I begin to resent my body for letting me down, and for getting in my way of dancing all night long, like I used to. But I never resent other people for having a beautiful young body."

Phyllis returned to her seat. I was happy when I saw Judith raise her hand.

"Yes, Judith," I acknowledged.

"Well," she said, then stopped talking.

"Yes, go on Judith."

"Well, I didn't discuss the topic with anyone. My sister Moira was around, but I really didn't want to go into it with her. So, I spent a lot of time alone in my room just thinking about things. The first thing I felt was panic. I looked around at the four walls of my bedroom, the same four walls I've seen for many, many years, and it terrified me, to tell you the truth. I even realized I hate that damn flowered wallpaper Moira had put up in my room. But the frightening thing is that, as I sat on my bed, I felt like I was shrinking, like Alice in Wonderland. I felt like I was going to disappear in that flower papered room. It was if I suddenly realized just how alone I've been for most of my life. I'm surprised I'm even here with you all. I'm surprised you even want me here. This wasn't my idea. It was Moira's. She said I'd make some new friends. And I'm glad she talked me into it."

"How so, Judith?" I asked her.

"Because Nova's Arc is the only group I've ever been a part of. No one ever asked me to be a part of anything before, and I never approached anyone, you know, to become a part of another's life. I have Moira, but half the time I don't think she even likes me. I used the excuse that I wasn't interested in talking with others about life and such, but what I'm finding is that's not true. I like hearing about how everyone feels about this stuff, even the sex," she added, then blushed, and continued. "I find myself getting angry at Moira for the way my life has turned out. She's been everywhere, done everything, and I have accomplished absolutely nothing. At times I hate her for being so confident. But I know it's not her to blame for what I've become. It's me. And I don't know if it's too late, but I'm going to take one day at a time and get out of my house. I even signed up for one of those computer classes. Just think, I'm gonna learn how to surf the worldwide web," Judith proudly stated. I was proud of her, too.

Judith stopped talking. Her face was flushed, but she had a smile of satisfaction that she had purged herself and shared with the group. I was happy for her, and I could feel that others in the room shared my happiness.

"Thank you very much, Judith."

I was surprised when I saw Sarah raise her hand.

71

"Sarah, I'm delighted that you are ready to share with us your opinion on this topic. Go ahead, please."

"Thank you, Curie. I don't own a television, so I don't get to watch actors. And I haven't been to a movie in years, even ages. I wouldn't recognize any of today's movie stars. But, I can tell you how I feel when I'm around young people, you know, in person. Quite frankly, I don't even think I notice who's young and who's old. I see a lot of youngsters at the apartment complex where I live, and I hear them outside at all times of the night. But you know, I don't think I could recognize a single one of them if they were standing right here in this room. Where I live, it is not uncommon for me to hear 12, 13, 14 year olds standing around at all times of the night, saying real bad words. And some even carry guns, I'm sure. But I haven't paid that part any attention, either. So, I don't feel old when I'm around young people, I realized that I don't feel at all. I got to thinking about it all last week and I realized that some of these children might be just as lost as I am. They come from homes where's there's no direction, no love, and maybe even no hope. Others wander around aimlessly, never attending school, doing all sorts of things, like taking drugs and drinking alcohol. I feel helpless to help myself so I truly feel unequipped to help them. It's a scary feeling to walk around so many people and to feel so alone at the same time."

"That's insightful, Sarah."

"Thank you Curie. And another thing. I know what it feels like to be scared. Not every day is miserable, but there are some days when I've just wanted to end my life. I hope that if any kids read your book that they'll understand you don't have to be old to feel the way I do. I've felt this way a long time. I was very young when I began to feel this way."

Sarah had brought up a very important point, and that was that the things which she and Andy had shared were not only the feelings of older people, they were feelings shared by others who were going through whatever crisis was happening in their lives.

Although Sarah had stated that she had thought about suicide, I didn't want to go in that direction with the group, but made a mental note to bring it up to Rachel. Sarah was scaring me. I shifted the topic a bit to move away from what I knew everyone was thinking.

"Would everyone agree that there are a lot of bright, extremely smart young people today? After all, they can do things with computers and other hi-tech equipment that we only dreamed about," I said to get the group moving in another direction.

Mostly everyone nodded in agreement.

"You have blocked out a lot Sarah, it seems, by not noticing people, young and old. I'd like to elaborate on that at a later date. But tell the group, if you can, how do you feel about being older? What have you missed out on, Sarah," I asked.

"I miss my fiancé, and…" Sarah said without finishing her sentence, then sat down.

Clarise interrupted the silence left by Sarah.

"I feel rather hopeful for today and tomorrow. I don't compare myself to the young people I see. Depending on the day, sometimes I feel just as young as they are. I still see the world as a place of constant wonder. The young people remind me of that wonder when I find myself getting bottled up about trivial things. I remember the wonder in the world and move beyond being stuck in the past of triviality."

Rachel stood.

"Sometimes I feel resentful when I see a new wrinkle, the damn things," said Rachel and laughed. "But I don't see myself as an old woman, but in reality I'm aware that there will come a day when I can no longer go from country to country, meeting with people at all times of the night to discuss the latest art acquisition. There will come a time when I will have to pass the reigns to someone else. I don't like that idea. I'm sort of a control freak, but I know that the time will come when I can no longer do for myself will surely come. So, I don't resent the young people, I resent no longer being one of them anymore, at times."

Bradley waited patiently for Rachel to finish to give his commentary.

"I feel pretty lucky whenever I see young people today," he said. "For the ones who are headed in the right direction, staying out of trouble, I feel inspired and undisturbed inside. When I see young people who are going in the wrong direction, getting into all sorts of trouble, doing drugs, going to jail, I feel good that none of my children went that way, and pray that none of my grandchildren end up that way. So bottom line, I feel OK any way it goes. There are some things I would have like to have accomplished, but that doesn't matter now. So there's nothing I want to do about that now."

"Talk about your bullshit!" shouted Jonathan. "I'll bet every one of you in this room, who haven't admitted it like Rachel did, are resentful as hell about getting old. You act like nothing has changed, and that you feel and act the same way about life as you did 30, 40, even 50 years ago. You're lying through your teeth if you're saying that you don't mind seeing your body shrivel up. You know you miss the feel of a young body against your flesh, and having terrific, all-night-long sex. And you sure as hell can't say that you don't miss trying to conquer some portion of the world, if not the whole damn thing. I'd be willing to bet that if any one of you could turn back the hands of time you'd pick right back up where your dreams went astray and chase them down like a crazed lion. You men would beat your chest like Tarzan and grab every young female thing that moved. Who's brave enough to tell me I'm wrong, or better yet, that I'm right.

Who feels like crying their bloody eyes out right now because every time you look in the mirror you see your facial features fading into some indistinct blob, have accomplished absolutely none of your real dreams, and know that you'll just die unfulfilled, unappreciated, and full of unrealized ambitions?"

"Damn, Jonathan, that's cold," remarked Beatrice. "And who you calling a broken down old has-been who ain't never done a thing with their life? Not everyone in this room feels the way you do. Speak for yourself."

I was actually enjoying the dissension Jonathan had created. Until now, Nova's Arc had been very cognizant not to step on each other's toes, like they were part of some social tea party.

While their politeness showed good manners, it made for dull discussions. I wanted action, passion, emotions, and that is exactly what Jonathan was serving up.

"Please forgive me if I sounded a little harsh, but since you've spoken, Beatrice, why don't you tell the group all about all of the amazing dreams you had when you were a young girl and how you accomplished them," challenged Jonathan.

"Well, I'm doing exactly what I set out to do. I own my own business, live in a real nice apartment, and I raised my children."

"Are you sure that's all you set out to do? Have you forgotten anything?" chided Jonathan, trying to get a reaction from Beatrice.

"Yes...well, almost. I wanted to be a movie star when I was a little girl, but all the girls in my neighborhood wanted to be a movie star. That was just a childhood fantasy. My mamma told me to forget about that foolishness, cause in the days I was growing up the only parts in the movies for black women were maids. Mamma said if I wanted to play a maid, I could begin right there in her house, by helping her to clean up. She said I didn't have to go all the way to Hollywood for that."

"But you would have had a lot more fun perhaps in Hollywood. But you'll never know that because you didn't try. And you could have tried to break the stereotypes that were forced down your people's throats by Hollywood. But you didn't try that either. That would have involved putting yourself on the line, right?"

Phyllis looked up at Jonathan with a look of disbelief that he would put Beatrice on the spot that way.

"Jonathan," snapped Phyllis. "What's gotten into you? And to think I had a crush on you. Why on earth are you being such a butt hole today?"

"I'm being an asshole because I'm asking some challenging questions? Curie can't ask you these questions. That's why she asked us to be here, to ask each other tough, riveting questions, of each other. Curie doesn't want a bunch of namby, pamby, and politically correct hogwash—a bunch of boring old coots captured in her book, I'm sure. Let's give her some excitement, some real feelings, some honesty about how we truly feel about what we know is terrifying the hell out of most of us."

Not a sound was heard after Jonathan finished his appeal. I saw Carmen stand, but she sat back down.

"Don't everyone jump in there at the same time," I joked.

Carmen stood up again.

"Jonathan may be on to something, although he could try to use less hurtful words and scare the hell out of everybody. As a singer I have lived a lot of my dreams, and you be quiet Jonathan," she chastised. "I thought I was petty satisfied with the way my life had gone so far, until I became a part of Nova's Arc. You see—if Curie hadn't asked me to join the group, I would never have met Rachel. It was Rachel who introduced me to a friend of hers named Dan Cook, one of the nicest men I've ever met. He talked to me about my music, and said that he has a friend in the music business. This friend can help me get signed to a recording contract; something of which, at my age, I would never had dreamed possible. What an opportunity, huh?"

"You have a beautiful voice, Carmen. I'm very happy for you," said Judith.

The rest of the group congratulated Carmen on her good news. Then they applauded.

"That is great news, Carmen," said Andy. "You know, Jonathan, I was being totally honest about my not being able to play football, and all. You've accused us of not being on the level, but what about you? We haven't heard your response to today's topic."

"I was wondering when someone would notice that. For Christ's sakes, some of my response was in my questions to the group. I'll be 60 next month. I must say, that sounds old compared to what, I don't know. My daughter brings home all of her beautiful friends. They're in their 40's and to me that's young. Now, my granddaughter's friends make me feel ancient, because they're in their 20's. Some of them invite me to some of their trendy spots. And I take them up on it once in a while. It feels good to be asked, but when I get winded from dancing too fast, it depresses me. I can't do that anymore, if I want to go on living. I get tired and need a nap. I accomplished many of the professional things I set out to do in my life, but personally I would have like to have achieved more. I have all the money I'll ever need, and I've raised a successful family, but I would give up almost all of my wealth to be in love."

"Be in love?" shouted Phyllis. "Is that what this is all about? Are you shouting at us because you're not in love? You mean to tell us that after all these years and all your accomplishments, all you have to fret about is not being in love?"

"Phyllis, don't trivialize what I just said. I didn't say that I was fretting about it. I just meant that it would be a wondrous thing. Are you in love, Phyllis? I guess I shouldn't ask you, you sound like you're in love with life, and that's good. I'm asking someone else, any of you."

Sarah cleared her throat. I could feel the tension in the room as she stood and faced the group, a protocol that had been abandoned earlier in the evening.

Sarah nervously spoke. "I don't have your money Jonathan, but I have experienced great love."

"I don't want his money," yelled out Beatrice.

"Oh, get real, Beatrice. You'd pull off your left arm and toss it over there on that glass table to have the money I have in my wallet right now."

Beatrice looked embarrassed, and I felt bad that Jonathan had spoken to her in such a crude manner. I told myself that I would have to intervene and let Jonathan know that if he continued his disrespectful style of communicating, that he would no longer be welcome in the group.

Just as I was about to speak, Frank, who hadn't said a word the entire evening, stood up.

"Now hold on there, Jonathan," he said with authority. "Some of the points you've made have been pretty valid, while others have been completely out of line. You're acting like some of those smart asses I used to tame in basic training. You're a grown man, not a young recruit away from home for the first time."

"Now you're being insulting, and…"

"And what?" Frank asked, cutting Jonathan off. "I have something to say. Let me finish and then you can have your say again."

Frank's military background was coming in handy, but I had a feeling that it wouldn't be enough to stop Jonathan, who was in rare form tonight.

"Now like I said, son," continued Frank, who was 72, and the oldest in the group. He sounded like he was speaking to an army recruit. "First of all, you should never make assumptions about others. How do you know that this lady here would give up just about anything to have your money?" he asked while pointing to Beatrice. "If the woman says she's happy the way her life has turned out, then accept that. She's the only one who knows for sure, not you, me, or anyone else in this room. Your bullying, although probably quite effective on Wall Street, isn't necessary here. With your vicious attitude, you would have done well as a military officer. You probably were in the military. I'll bet you were highly decorated. It takes that kind of merciless, take no prisoner's alive way of attacking people, to command a troop in a time of war. But what we have here is a collection of old civilians, and not one of them look like a perilous threat or dangerous enemy to me."

"Yeah," was all that Beatrice could think of to proclaim she was in agreement with Frank.

"I'm Air Force Captain Severied, retired. I respect what you said, Frank, and I'll try to tone it down a bit. Beatrice, I apologize if I made you feel uncomfortable. I didn't intend to single out your comments, but I want to encourage you to be honest with this group. It won't do you or Curie's book any good if you don't come clean."

Beatrice didn't respond, although she did smile. I was glad that Jonathan humbled himself enough to apologize to her. I was also happy that Jonathan challenged her, and that maybe she would think before commenting the next time.

I looked around the room to see if anyone else wanted to say anything before our break. I looked over at Joe, who was the only one left who hadn't commented on today's topic.

"I'll be next," said Joe. "I know why you're looking at me. But first I have to go to the restroom."

"It's a deal. Why don't we take a fifteen-minute break, and then we'll come back and pick back up with Joe."

The group dispersed. Jonathan walked towards Beatrice, but she pretended not to see him coming, and walked the other way. He moved on to talk with Frank.

I figured Jonathan and Frank were reliving military memories, so I didn't approach them. I walked over to Clarise instead.

"A little more fire in the group today, huh?" I asked Clarise.

"Fire is not the right word—it's more like a volcano eruption. Jonathan is clearly frustrated with his life, and he took it out on poor Beatrice. Although I don't agree with his choice of words, I must admit that he brought up some pretty good points, though."

"Yes he did. If it wasn't for the fact that he hurt Beatrice, I would have enjoyed his bantering."

"Jonathan has spent so much time making money that he forgot to spend time falling in love. Now he's afraid that he'll die without ever knowing the splendor of that emotion. That's why he was so mean spirited. Jonathan doesn't intend to sound so harsh, it's just that he's feeling panic, like his time is running out. Look at him. He's sixty, but he is still quite a handsome and powerful man. But he's so busy trying to recapture his youth, going out with his granddaughter's friends and all, that he's forgetting all about his wife. What do you think she'd say if she knew her husband just admitted to us all that he's not in love with her?"

"He'll definitely need an anonymous name that's nowhere remotely similar to his own when this book is published," I responded.

"Everybody's returning. I'm going to use the restroom, then I'll be right in," said Clarise.

I walked back into the glass room to begin the second half of our session.

"I trust everyone feels refreshed. OK Joe, I'd like to get right back into our discussion of today's topic. How do you feel about where you are in life today?

And, how do you feel when you're surrounded by young people, and see them dominating the television and movie screens?"

Joe, who was still clutching the red Cardinals cap he had been holding all evening, stood up.

"I have no feelings most of the time, at least none that I can put a finger on. I'm kinda numb, I guess you could say. I love my wife, so I guess I do have some feelings left. But I don't talk to her too much. Mostly, I come home after working at Von's, settle in a chair, watch TV, mostly sports, and go on off to sleep. I don't like working at my age, but I have to. There just ain't enough money coming in to live on. I listen to folks like Jonathan, who says he has all the money he'll ever need, and I feel like I should just get up and leave. I can afford food, and get back and forth to work, but I don't have money to have fun with. Probably wouldn't even know what to do with a lot of money, but it sure would be good to be able to afford to take better care of my wife. She don't feel good most of the time now. I'd like to buy he something special, cheer her up, and make her feel real special once in a while. It's frightening at my age to not have anything after all these years. Most of you are probably thinking that I've just wasted my life, but I didn't waste nothing. I've been working all my life. Worked as a mail clerk at an insurance company till they forced me to retire. I liked that job, I felt important. Everybody was nice to me, and said good morning to me when I came by with their mail. The girls would even flirt with me. That really made me feel good. Oh, I knew they were just being nice, but it felt good anyways. Now at Von's I don't even notice if someone's being nice. I just use all the strength I have in these arms to push that food basket out to people's car, unload their stuff, and make the trip back into the store. Then I repeat that all over again all day. Not like in the mailroom. There, there was different things to do after the mail was sorted. And I had a lot of seniority, so I didn't have no snot-nosed kids telling me what to do, like they do at Von's," growled Joe, then he returned to his seat.

Joe's confession did not elicit an outpouring of emotional support from the group. It wasn't that Joe did not deserve the same tender mercies that were extended to Andy, or Beatrice, but somehow Joe's story was predictable. The sad feelings that engulfed me as Andy spoke were not invoked after hearing Joe's tale.

I was surprised to hear Andy admit that he was still struggling with childhood wounds, as he had given no indication before now that he was living with the agony he so passionately described. Andy was always bright, optimistic, and full of cheer. The side of himself he chose to show the group today was quite unexpected.

However, Joe, on the other hand, had worn his aggravations and regrets on his shirtsleeve for all to see since the first time the group met.

There were sighs of pity for Joe, but heartfelt empathy for Andy. The different levels of respect were evident, and Joe had opened the door to receiving only pity for his confession. Like I suspected the other members of the group felt, I viewed Joe as a casualty of his own mind, and Andy as a man who, as a child, had been damaged by the careless handling of his young soul by it's protector—his own father.

It was obvious to us all that Andy never reconciled with his father, who had been dead for over 15 years now, and that his pain stemmed from a nonsupportive and intimidating parent. His heart-wrenching story caused my emotions to rise and fall—like the waves I saw swelling in the Pacific Ocean, just outside of the glass room. The group was also astonished at Andy's highly emotional outpouring.

Some of the members of Nova's Arc displayed obvious signs of discomfort when Sarah and Joe spoke. It was also noticeable when, during the break, most walked up to Andy and Judith to remark that they had shown great courage in exposing their deepest feelings and thoughts, but only Rachel expressed to Sarah and Joe that she appreciated their honesty. Rachel gave Sarah's hand a gentle squeeze, then looked over at Joe.

"Hang in there, Joe. Life isn't over yet?" she declared, and politely excused herself.

I was hoping to hear more from Bradley, who I noticed had tears rolling down his cheeks while listening to Andy's confession. While he silently nodded in empathy as he listened to the outpourings of the gentle, usually confident Andy, I could sense that Bradley, too, had begun to think about some of his own shattered dreams.

"OK, everyone. I'd like to move on," I said, trying to pry loose even more emotion from everyone. I turned to look directly at Bradley.

"I'd like to go back to Andy's commentary for a while. Bradley, would you please tell us what you were thinking when Andy spoke about the pain he felt in having to give up one of his dreams?"

Bradley stood.

"Well," he hesitated, and then continued. "I was just thinking, my thoughts swirling around in my head about something that happened a long time ago. You see—I was stationed in France while I was in the Army. And keep in mind that was before I got married to my precious Rhonda. I had plans to stay in France after my tour was up. The reason was because I met this beautiful, young girl named Simone. Me and this young French girl fell deeply in love. But at the urgings of my mother, I returned to the United States. It tore me all to pieces to leave that girl behind. But my mother kept pushing me hard to come home; said that I had no business fooling around with that young girl, and that I'd get myself in a lot of trouble if I just left everything and everyone at home. Now, I loved my mother and she didn't ever say anything of a serious nature to me unless she had thought long and hard about it. So, I listened to her. But when in comes to Simone, I wish I had just been a man and told my mother what was in my heart. I wish I had stayed in France with Simone. Don't get me wrong, I love my Rhonda, but I've thought about many times what my life would have been like had I followed my heart."

"Do you resent your mother for interfering, and coercing you to return to the states?" I bluntly asked.

"No, I could never resent my mother, may she rest in peace. It was my ultimate decision to return to the states. I should have listened to myself on that one, is all I'm saying."

Rachel chimed in. "Bradley, have you ever seen or spoken to Simone since you left France?"

"I did for a few years, then the calls got less and less, until one day we just stopped talking all together. I kept promising Simone that I'd bring her to the States. But that never happened."

Bradley abruptly stopped speaking and sat down. The mood was somber.

Rachel wanted to know more, and continued to question Bradley.

"Bradley, would you mind telling us if you ever compared Rhonda to Simone, when she was young? Did you ever resent that she wasn't Simone?"

"Honestly? At first I did resent Rhonda. Every time I looked at her I thought of Simone and regretted that she wasn't her. After Rhonda and me started dating, I thought about Simone more than ever before. But that's when I stopped calling Simone. I started liking Rhonda, and I figured it was time to let go. Me and Rhonda were married about two months after we started seeing each other. I remember me and Rhonda's first fight. The first thing I thought was only if I had stayed with Simone. But I'm OK. I don't know what happened to Simone. She probably got married and is having a good life. I hope she is."

Bradley chose not to share everything about Simone with the group, but he said he understood very well what Andy meant by pushing his agony down— deep down. I watched as he wiped away his tears with the back of his hand.

At that point I wanted to run up to everyone in the room and start giving out hugs. Bradley had openly wept; Sarah had shared her fears and how desperate she gets sometimes, and had even talked of suicide. Judith was liberating herself from her sister's control, and I was so proud of Andy having shared the story of his relationship with his father. I felt that what they had said might touch other people somewhere who may be having similar feelings of inadequacy, fear and regret.

Andy's story especially touched me. I had held my breath almost the entire time he spoke, and listened carefully as his heart broke, healed, and then broke again. And although Andy tried to change his mood by switching the topic to movie stars, it was obvious to me that Andy had survived the dysfunction of his early home life, but had not yet overcome it. I wondered if he would ever forgive his father, or himself.

Although I was not moved immediately by Joe's confession, the pity that he had induced lingered. I wasn't certain if he was trying to elicit pity, as Joe was not an easy man to get to know. He mostly talked about his old days in the insurance company mailroom, which was boring after the first few minutes. And there was bitterness to his plight that did not endear the group to him.

The feelings of pity that lingered reminded me that Joe, too, had very real issues that shouldn't be dismissed just because he did not achieve the level of financial success that Andy had, or the heart-wrenching tale of love lost that Bradley shared.

I started to question my motives, and why Joe's declaration of uncertainties had a different, even less, impact on me than Andy's or Bradley's.

I made a note to give serious thought to this issue after the session and to further examine why Joe did not engender group support. "Perhaps the group decided to withhold their comments," I thought to myself. I didn't ask the group how they feel about Joe's admissions. I decided to go with the conclusions I had drawn from my own observations.

"How about we take ten minutes. We'll then wrap up, and that will be it for the day," I eagerly announced.

The group was happy to have the break in hopes of a shift in the mood. The emotional discourses had been draining, and I wanted to end the evening on a high note.

I watched Joe as he nervously clutched his cap, nearing rolling it into a tube. I pretended not to notice and walked into the restroom to freshen up.

The group reconvened a few minutes later.

"You know, guys, why don't we call it a day. I think that we've delved pretty deeply into some hurts and fears today, and I know that by sharing yourselves this way we will be able to help others who may have similar hurts. Sometimes when people know they're not alone, that is enough to help them feel better about themselves."

I was beginning to sound like an armchair psychiatrist. Before I could formally dismiss the group, Carmen was already seated at the piano; ready to play her promised closing number.

"Thank you Carmen," I said and nodded her way. "Listen up everyone—next week's topic will be one that I'm sure you'd rather avoid, or maybe you wouldn't. But anyway, we will delve into the topic of death and dying. I know, it's a downer topic, but it is an important one, and I would like to capture how you feel about this subject. Until next week. I now turn you over to Carmen Santiago."

"Thank you," said Carmen, who performed a beautiful song from the set she had sung at Rachel's the previous Monday night. After a round of applause and compliments, the group disbanded.

"Wanna join me for a drink," Jonathan asked Frank.

It appeared that Frank and Jonathan were becoming friends. Until Frank realized that Jonathan was in the military, the two men hadn't spoken a word to each other. Now they were meeting for drinks, and who knows, maybe Jonathan would even invite Frank to his country club. I was happy to see that Jonathan had found a common bond with someone in the group. Although my intent was not to forge new friendships, but to write a book, I sincerely hoped that rich and poor would find a common bond, and that somehow all would be enriched by the experience of knowing, and sharing with each other.

This was happening for others in the group as well. I noticed that Phyllis was friendly to everyone in the group, and during breaks spent a lot of time talking with Jonathan and Clarise.

Judith and Andy talked during breaks, and Carmen and Clarise were becoming close. Rachel was a gracious hostess to everyone, but she maintained a certain distance as project writer. She and Clarise, of course, continued their close, personal relationship. Rachel and I had developed a close, but still, professional relationship. I saw Beatrice and Joe often chatting. Sarah was the only member of the group who had yet to connect with anyone, and I wondered if she ever would. My attempts to engage her in conversation were bleak, at best. Whenever I saw her standing alone during the breaks, I made it a point to walk up and initiate a conversation. But our talks were often strained.

Everyone left Rachel's shortly after Carmen's number. I headed home to go over my notes of today's session.

Diana dropped by as I was listening to Joe's commentary.

"God, who is that depressing man? Sounds like he's mad at the world."

"Oh, that's who I've called #9. I'm going to give them real names soon, but for now I keep track of everyone by number so I don't slip up and use their real names."

"I know three of the real names," bragged Diana. "Which numbers are my dad, Clarise, and Rachel?"

"None of your business, Diana," I said and smiled at her.

"That man, the one who was talking when I came in, why is he sounding so down? What we're you all discussing?"

"We were discussing fading youth, and dreams lost. It was a very sensitive topic, and several of the members cried before the evening was done."

"Did my dad cry? What am I asking? My dad never cries. How did he do on this topic?

"Actually, your dad was the hit of the evening. I can't go into what he said, but he certainly stirred up the group."

"That's my dad. He's good at that. You should hear him getting under mom's skin sometimes."

"Diana, the man who you heard speaking, #9, would you listen to his tape with me? I'd like to get your opinion of some of the things he's saying. If you hear me call out some of the people's names, ignore it. Besides, you don't know most of them anyway, but I promised to keep them anonymous."

"Sure thing. I'll ignore the names. Play it for me."

I rewound the tape to the place where Joe began speaking. When he finished his remarks, I turned off the recorder and waited for Diana to speak.

"Well," she began slowly. "That's Joe from the mailroom. You don't have to care that I know who he is; after all, I helped you find him for your interviews in the first place. God, I feel sorry for Joe. But it sounds to me that he is feeling even sorrier for himself. I know I heard him say it on the tape, but he really resents having to work at Von's, sounds like. He's stuck on that mailroom job he had. He didn't make a lot of money there, but I guess it was home to him. He worked there for over 30 years. I can't imagine how someone could work in the mailroom for that long and not get promoted to something significant after all those years. I figured he was just happy working in the mailroom, and that money was not his motivation. Now it seems that earning money is his only reason for working at Von's at this late stage in his life."

"Diana, the reason I wanted you to listen to the tape is that there was another man there who told a heart wrenching story about the shattering of one of his youthful dreams. He is still in conflict with his father, and everyone, including me, wanted to run over and hug him to make him feel better. But once Joe finished, I didn't sense the same sympathy. The other gentleman is wealthy, still looks OK, and is actually quite funny, except for today. While Joe, on the other hand, said he has been poor all his life, still has to work after being retired, and frets because he can't buy his wife pretty things. Shouldn't we have felt more sympathy for his situation than the other man's?"

"Well I don't know. I didn't hear the other guys speech."

"I won't play it for you, but believe me, it broke my heart. It was about psychological abandonment by his father and how it still affects him to this day."

"And you think Joe didn't have, or couldn't express the why's of his situation as well as the other guy?"

"Maybe that was it. Come to think of it Joe didn't explain why he was in his current situation, just that he was in it. We were left with assumptions. I assumed that Joe never had any ambitions to be something as lofty as the other guy, so his regrets couldn't be as meaningful. I let the fact that Joe was a former mailroom clerk, turned bag boy, color my empathy, or lack thereof, for Joe."

"Are you prejudice, Curie?"

"I never thought so before now. But I did have a different reaction to the other man. The wealthy guy took the time to invite us into his private world of thoughts, and shared sensitive things about him, which left him vulnerable. That's it!" I shouted. "The other man was vulnerable, child-like in his explanation, whereas Joe was like a bitter old man. It was natural for me to respond kindheartedly and more readily to child-like innocence than to embittered regret. Thanks Diana. It was all there, but I couldn't put my finger on it."

"You're welcome, Curie. Anytime Rachel decides she doesn't have time to help you with the book, let me know. Maybe I can give you a hand."

"I'll keep that in mind. Speaking of Rachel, I have an appointment with her on Tuesday. She wants to talk with me about the book, and about putting together the manuscript. She's still excited about this whole thing. I've got to get all my notes organized before I meet with her. God, I'm so swamped, I don't think I'll get to leave my house until next Tuesday."

"Want to have dinner with me?"

"Sure," I quickly responded. We both laughed.

"Didn't have to twist your arm. What was all that bullshit about not being able to leave?"

"Shut up and let's go. You're driving."

While Diana and I were enjoying lobster dinner at Snowboard's Restaurant, a casual seafood restaurant in Ocean Beach, Sarah had spent the evening sitting alone in her apartment, having a bowl of vegetable soup for dinner.

She sat in her tattered recliner, and after eating, fell into a deep sleep. Her dream quickly turned into the nightmare that she had so many times before. There was her young, handsome fiancé, and there was she, working as a critical care nurse at Valley Hospital.

The blurry face of the blonde woman who had stolen her fiancé's heart was clearer this time, but still indistinct. Sarah reached the part of her dream where she runs after Philip, screams, and wakes up, but this time she didn't scream, run after the car, or wake up. Instead, the mysterious blonde turned and looked at Sarah, and said "Oh, God!" then the car sped away.

Sarah woke up in a cold sweat, and strained to remember where she had seen the blurred faced woman before. Not only was she was certain that she had seen her before, but she was just as sure that she had recently heard the woman's voice, as replayed the woman saying, "Oh, God!" over in her mind.

After dinner, I went home to prepare for my meeting with Rachel. Working long into the night, I organized mounds of cassette tapes and notes for my first-cut manuscript. By Monday morning, I was back at it, and continued all through the day.

Tuesday arrived, and I excitedly left for Rachel's. I was anxious to hear her opinion of the how the project was going.

"Come in Miss Nova," said Gertie as she opened the front door. I tell Mrs. Maxwell you are here."

"Thank you Gertie," I said. "I'll just make myself comfortable back here," I said.

While waiting for Rachel, I walked around the living room, certain that I would see some things that I had not noticed before. It had become like a private treasure hunt for me. I had come to expect to discover something that I hadn't yet seen, although I had been in Rachel's living room on several occasions now.

I walked over to the fireplace and scanned the mantle. My eyes were drawn once again to the little porcelain statue. I was certain that I had seen the little bird somewhere else. Then, like a bolt of lightening, it hit me. An identical little bird was on Sarah's coffee table the day I met her and drove her home.

I found it rather odd that Sarah would own the same statue as Rachel, being that Rachel's home was filled with expensive works of art and Sarah's was virtually bare.

"Sarah must have a reproduction," I reasoned. I replaced the statue on the mantle just as Rachel entered the room.

"Ah, Curie. Do you have the manuscript?" she eagerly asked.

"Yes, Rachel," I said as I started walking towards the glass room.

"Good. I can't wait to see it. I tell you what...rather than keep you here while I read this, and waste your time, how about I read it this morning, then you can come back this afternoon, or if that's too soon for you, we can make it another day this week. I'll call you later and we can discuss it over the phone."

"That's a good idea. My afternoon is pretty jammed, so I prefer later in the week. I'll schedule it when you call."

"That's fine. I'll see you later this week."

As the door closed behind me I started to feel more like Rachel's employee. I blew it off by justifying it as her business style. Rachel had already made it clear that she didn't like wasting her time, or anyone else's. Rather than resent her direct way of communicating, I reasoned I should appreciate the fact that she wasn't beating around the bush. And I had to admit that I rather liked her style. After all, I had read several stories about how Rachel took her late husband's fortune, and her own, and multiplied it many times over with her shrewd business savvy. Rather than resent her, I decided it best to learn from her.

I was surprised when Rachel called later that afternoon.

"Curie, there's very little that I could add to what you have already written. Your style of writing is excellent. The characters just walk right into your heart and into your living room. I know that I'm one of the characters, but while I was reading, I pretended not to be. I read this as if I had never met a soul in the room. If a stranger were reading this book, they'd see the faces, hear the voices, and welcome Nova's Arc into their home, too. Everyone will want to have group interviews after we publish this book. I made a few nit-picky notes in the margins, but other than that, bravo!"

"Thank you Rachel."

With praise like that coming from a woman as well read and as world traveled as Rachel, I couldn't wait to hang up and yell "hallelujah." Rachel was not the type of woman to sing false praises, so I was ecstatic that she liked my work enough to say, bravo.

"So there's no need for us to meet?" I asked her in a feigned calm voice.

"No, you've done all the work that needs to be done so far. If you don't start writing sloppily, I'm not going to have anything to do in this partnership," she chided.

"Oh believe me, you are doing more than your share. Every Sunday you roll out the red carpet for the group. And it was your idea to hold these group sessions. I don't know how to thank you for being so kind."

"That is thanks enough. Enjoy the rest of your week, Curie. Get out of the house and have a good time. You've earned it."

"I will, and thank you again."

"Goodbye Curie."

When I replaced the receiver I shouted, "Yes!" followed by a little celebration dance. Ecstatic, I ran over to the phone and called Robert at his office.

"Robert Prisco," he answered.

"Robert, let's go out to dinner tonight."

"What's going on? Boy, do you sound happy. What's going on?"

"I just feel fantastic, and I'd like to have dinner out tonight, maybe do a little dancing afterwards. We going out or not?"

"I had planned to have dinner with my dad, but he called earlier to say he'd have to cut it short. He'll be happy if I rearrange dinner with him for another day. You're on. How about 7:00?"

"I'll see you here at 7:00 sharp. How about we go to Jim Croce's?"

"It's a date."

I couldn't wait to tell Robert about my telephone conversation with Rachel. I felt extremely fortunate that Suzanne was not at the gallery that day I walked into August House. Not only did I not have to sell my art, but also I had one of California's wealthiest women working with me on my book.

During dinner, I told Robert all about my Rachel's reception to my draft. Afterwards, we celebrated by going to a little Jamaican club near Jim Croce's and danced the night away to the pulsating sounds of a Ragae band.

The remainder of the week, I didn't work on the book. Instead, I took a mini vacation to visit some friends in Los Angeles. By Saturday I was headed back to San Diego for Sunday's session on *death and dying*.

Although I felt rested, I didn't feel excited about talking about death.

"The show must go on," I told myself, and prepared for the upcoming afternoon at Rachel's.

Chapter Nine

"A Lesson in Life"

Are we ready for today's topic? I'm sure you all remember what the topic is."

"Death and dying," yelled out everyone.

The group looked anxious. "OK Nova's Arc. I know that death and dying is not exactly anyone's favorite topic, so we'll try to keep the discussion as light as possible, if that's possible."

"Yes, the unavoidable dying game," mused Jonathan.

"Today's session has come to order," I announced. "OK, why don't we just jump right in. I know it's not the most popular subject, but inevitably, we must all come to terms with this mysterious subject. I say mysterious because no one really knows what's going to happen once you die. Or maybe some of you have an idea. Who wants to be the first to tell us what you think is going to happen to you when you die? Does anyone have any hypotheses or beliefs?"

"I have an idea of what will happen," Joe immediately responded.

"Yes, Joe. Let's hear it."

"I believe that when you die you don't feel a thing once the last breath has been taken. I don't believe in the heavens, I think you just rot, if you're buried, and if you're cremated, then you're just ashes. That's what I think."

"That sounds pretty final, Joe," I said. "Does anyone have a different view?" I asked, wanting to move away from the faithless way Joe had addressed it.

"Yes, I do," Clarise said while waving her hand. "I think you move on to another life. I believe that everyone is reincarnated, recycled, as is everything in nature. Just because the body is useless once dead, the soul never dies; thus, it must enter another body to continue the work it was sent to earth to do. Since the world is not yet complete, and won't be until there is perfect harmony, the soul must return to earth to continue its mission."

"I tend to agree with Joe," chimed in Frank. "I don't believe in this reincarnation business. I don't have anything against others thinking that they'll be back, but as for me I intend to live this life as if it is my only one, and that is to the fullest before it's lights out."

"There's nothing wrong with living this life fully, Frank." responded Clarise "In fact, it is your responsibility to do so. However, it doesn't mean that what you're doing is enough. As long as there are unfulfilled desires in your heart, you will return as many times as is necessary until the mission of awakening is accomplished. As long as you have attachments to this world, longings—

meaning you see nothing but the material, and ignore your soul's growth, then you will return until you realize just what and who you are."

"Who am I?" flatly asked Beatrice.

"You're not just a woman who has a daycare business. You are walking on this earth with the true God in you, and you have the power to manifest great and powerful creations that will help mankind awaken to that great fact. As long as you see yourself as just a body with a skeleton and a brain, you will miss the true beauty that is God. You will miss the power of Love. Thus, you must return until you find it. That is the true desire of your heart, and a void will exist until you realize that. You will return again and again until you find that great Love."

"That's pretty heavy stuff," interrupted Andy. "I never really thought about it that way, but it makes a lot of sense. What do the rest of you think?" he asked, wanting to hear others validate Clarise's perceptions.

"I don't know about this reincarnation thing either," hesitated Bradley. "Sounds more like a fantasy or fairy tale to me. I believe in going to heaven or hell when you die, like my father taught me."

"So you actually believe that you will be walking around in heaven, floating on some cloud, doing nothing all day?" sarcastically asked Frank.

"Well, I don't know exactly what I'll be doing," said Bradley. "I won't know that until I'm dead. But I do believe in Jesus Christ, our Lord, and I do believe in heaven."

"As long as it gives you peace of mind, there's nothing wrong in believing that," remarked Jonathan.

"Jonathan, I sense that maybe you don't share Bradley's view. Would you share with us what you believe?" I asked.

"Like Joe, I believe that the worms will eat our faces, and we'll turn into dust," he responded.

Beatrice yelled out. "I believe the devil will be jabbing you in your butt with a hot poker, then again, he'll probably cut you some slack since he and you are probably such good friends." The group roared with laughter.

Beatrice had found an opportunity to get back at Jonathan for what she perceived as rudeness and snobbery the Sunday before.

"That was pretty juvenile, Beatrice, but I guess I had it coming," Jonathan said smugly.

"OK everyone," I said, while laughing. "Let's get back on track. Rachel, what do you think about this topic?"

Rachel, who too was still laughing from Beatrice's comment, stood. But before she could respond, Clarise jumped from her seat, her face was ashen like she had seen a ghost, and she looked like she would faint at any second.

"Clarise, are you all right?" I said while rushing up to her. "Clarise...Clarise, what's wrong?"

"Oh," she said after I grabbed her by her shoulders and gently shook her.

"Curie, oh, I'm so sorry. I don't know what happened. I'm OK."

"You sure? Would you like a glass of water?"

"Yes, please. Thank you."

Joe hurried over to the refreshments table and returned with a glass of water for Clarise.

"Thank you, Joe," said Clarise. "Please, everyone, I'm OK. I just felt a little light-headed. Please, Rachel, go ahead."

"Goodness Clarise. Here we are discussing death and dying, and now you've scared the hell out of me. I've forgotten my point. Oh yes," she stammered. "What I was going to say is that I think once you die you still roam the earth, a body-less soul. I'm not talking about some chain-dragging, bone-rattling ghost like portrayed in Dickens's 'A Christmas Carol,' or ones like in the movies whose only purpose is to scare people to death. I'm talking about turning into pure energy—power, like electricity, lighting up people's houses. We help get astronauts to the moon. We're streaks of lightening. We're flickers in a flame. Some souls help humanity, some hurt. Some are like angels who sends moonlight to a lost and weary traveler, others are like tornadoes, who tear down—destroy."

Frank couldn't wait to comment. "Rachel…is that you talking? I never would have suspected you to think that way. You seem so grounded and down to earth, but you're sounding more like Clarise. Have you been reading tarot cards too?"

"Frank, we all have our beliefs. Just because you don't agree with mine is no reason to be rude. Besides, it's a much nicer thought than just rotting in a casket, like you and some of the others seem to hope for."

"You have a point there, Rachel," yelled out Phyllis. "It's certainly a different way of looking at things. I rather like your explanation, Rachel."

Carmen stood up and placed her hands on her hips. "Why do we have to talk about this stuff? This is depressing me."

"Carmen, I'll address that," I said. "Please be seated." Carmen's scowl disappeared as she sat.

Why does this subject depress you, Carmen? After all, sooner or later, it's something that we all must face. How about you tell us how you personally feel about the fact that you're eventually going to die?"

"I know it's going to come," she said. "But I don't want to think about it now. After all, I'm getting ready to sign a music contract."

"Well, tell us anyway. I'm sure you've thought about it at one time or another."

"Since you seem intent on dragging it out of me, I'll tell you. I'm 61 yeas old. I think I look pretty good for my age, and I have only a few wrinkles, which I wear quite well. But let's face it, I know I won't live forever. When I'm performing, I feel like I could, though. I'm not scared of death itself; it's the thought of no longer breathing that bothers me. Sounds silly maybe to some of you, but I get scared when I think of not breathing. I have been to funerals of family, friends, and co-workers, who have passed on. Whenever I am alone after the funeral, I get so scared cause I can't get the faces out of my mind. Then I think of them not breathing anymore, I feel like I'm suffocating."

"Are you afraid of death, Carmen?" I bluntly asked.

"I don't think I'm afraid of death itself, like once you're cremated. It's the part when you first die, and your soul leaves your body, and you can no longer breathe. I guess it because I'm a singer, and breathing is very important to me. I'm also enjoying this life tremendously. And when I think that I'll be signing a recording contract soon, after coming so far, I just thank God every day I wake up, because I want to live long enough to record some of my songs. I am thankful for every day that I've had, don't get me wrong, but after coming this far, I'm not ready to go yet. Society just casts aside older people, and they think that all we think about is death. But that's not true. There are the same things in our hearts today as there were when we were younger. We have just experienced more. But that doesn't change the fact that we still enjoy our lives just as much as younger people, and have desires and needs just the same."

Everyone nodded in agreement. "I agree wholeheartedly with you, Carmen," I responded.

Carmen walked up to where I stood to continue addressing the group. I was taken aback by her blatant assertiveness.

"What I think is that we don't need to talk so much about dying. Let's talk about life. We're alive here now, so let's enjoy what we have, and not live in the past, nor grieve for a death that hasn't come yet. We're alive, doesn't everyone agree? Isn't that why we're here…to share our lives, to make new friends, and enjoy these new relationships? What good is talking about death going to do us? We know it's going to come. We have to make something of our lives, celebrate each new day. Look at us, we're sitting here discussing death, ignoring the beautiful new beginnings of friendship that we all share. Get the magic back. Look out of that big window; see the ocean, feel the breeze, look at those waves, surging with life. Let's go outside and take a deep breath of life. Who wants to join me?"

At that moment, Carmen walked out of the room and on to the patio.

As I listened to Carmen and watched the faces of the others, I was happy that Carmen had incited the group to action. She had never seemed like the type who would go out with just a glimmer. I imagined Carmen either fighting it tooth and nail when death came for her, or eagerly submitting to its seductive, mysterious call. And she had said something that I'm sure many people say every day. "Just because you're a certain age doesn't mean that you don't treasure life the same as when you were younger."

Carmen didn't look 61, but more importantly, she didn't act 61, whatever that was. I hadn't a clue how 61 year olds were supposed to act, or who developed the chart that tells us, according to age, how we're supposed to behave?

The rest of the group was also happy that Carmen had brazenly stated that she wasn't afraid of death.

Carmen admitted that she thinks about death, and that her thoughts sometime scare her, not death, itself.

"I love being alive, so I choose not to dwell on death, but life instead," she yelled from the patio.

"Why don't we take a fifteen minute break," I said as I watched Carmen out on the patio inhaling and exhaling lungs filled with ocean air.

"We'll ask a couple more of you about this topic when we return, and then we'll have a free form conversation. I agree with Carmen, that we shouldn't dwell on this subject, however, I'm glad that you've shared your opinions with me. Many of you have given us food for thought, and theories that I want to explore in more detail, one on one, like yours, Rachel and Clarise."

"What about mine?" asked Frank?

"There's nothing to explore there, Frank. Yours and Joe's seem pretty cut and dry. But thank you, too, for sharing your ideas. OK, let's take that break."

Sarah didn't seem interested in today's session, although I though she'd be the first to participate. After all, it was she who brought up suicide in the previous meeting. I saw her walk off alone into Rachel's living room. I decided to join her, but stopped when I saw Beatrice approaching.

"Curie, I hope you don't call on me today. I'm a little tired, and I really don't feel like thinking too much about this. Besides, after thinking about it all week to prepare for today, I found myself feeling that all the effort I was putting into living was all for nothing. I got so depressed when a good friend of mine died last year that I wondered what was the use in working all your life. My friend, she finally got a chance to retire, and then she just died. She could have lived her life as a gypsy, doing whatever she wanted when she wanted to, instead of working like a dog all her life, just to die before she could get to enjoy herself. She died tired and broke after working for over 35 years as a hotel maid."

"Oh, I'm so sorry, Beatrice. If it's going to upset you, you don't have to address the group. I'm sure your friend is resting in peace. And thank you for sharing your feelings with me."

"Thank you, Curie," she said and walked away.

I had lost sight of Sarah and decided to return to the glass room.

But Sarah was still in the living room alone, looking at Rachel's paintings and other works of art. Among Rachel's many treasures, sitting on the fireplace mantle, Sarah spotted the little porcelain bird.

"It's my bird!" she gasped. "It's little robin, the little robin. He gave me the little robin," she exclaimed to herself.

The little bird triggered all kinds of confused emotions in Sarah, and she became extremely nervous and confused. Her hands shook as she picked up the bird to get a closer look. It was identical to the bird that was on her coffee table, the one that her fiancé had given her many years ago.

Beads of sweat formed on her brow as she looked around the room to see if anyone was watching her. She unzipped her purse, slipped the little bird into the open pocket, then hurriedly walked out of the living room and joined the group.

"OK everyone, let's get started again," I called out. The group reassembled in the glass room.

"I've been thinking. Carmen has the right idea. How about we end today's session early. I have plenty of interesting comments for my book, so there's no need to belabor this topic.

Rachel stood. "How about those of you who want to, stay here a while and we'll turn today's meeting into a cocktail party."

"That sounds like a good idea," said Jonathan. Most of the others nodded in agreement.

"Then that's what we'll do. Meeting adjourned," I declared.

Rachel asked Gertie to set up the bar on the patio."

"Everyone, let's move to the patio and drink beer and margarita's, look out at the ocean, and marvel at the wonders of nature," announced Rachel.

"Make it scotch and it's a deal," said Joe.

"Scotch you want, Scotch you shall have, Joe," playfully responded Rachel.

"Excuse me Curie," Sarah walked up to me and said in a shaky voice. I thought she was going to faint.

"I have to go home."

"Oh Sarah," I said distressingly. "Are you OK? You don't look so good. Would you like me to have someone drive you home?"

"No, I'll be fine. I just need to get some fresh air," she said and headed for the door. I followed after her.

"I'm terribly sorry you're not feeling well, Sarah. I was hoping that you could stay here with us and enjoy yourself. After depressing everyone with all that death talk, it may just what you need."

"No, Curie. I really have to go."

"I understand. Maybe next time?" I asked.

"Sure. Thank you Curie. Really, I appreciate your kindness, but I have to go."

"OK Sarah. You take good care of yourself and I'll see you next Sunday. You sure you don't want me to drive you home."

"I'm sure."

"Goodbye Sarah," yelled out Beatrice as she strutted towards the patio with a beer in her hand.

Sarah looked like something had upset her. But I let it go, and joined the rest of the group on the patio.

Sarah got in her car and carefully took the little bird out of her purse. Tears streamed down her face as she cranked her engine and sped away.

Everyone except Sarah stayed to enjoy Rachel's impromptu patio cocktail party. Carmen ran out to her car and brought in several tapes that she had recorded from her nightclub act.

The lively Latin dance numbers instantly brightened up the once somber group. Carmen sang and danced along to her tunes, entertaining the group amidst the breathtaking backdrop of the Pacific Ocean.

Phyllis approached me and whispered. "I'm sure this party is unlike any that Rachel had ever had. Look at Joe, drinking expensive Scotch, laughing and trying to keep up with Carmen's wild dance steps. Even Frank seems more relaxed, smoking that cigar. And look at our girl Judith, listening to Jonathan's every word. He over there telling stories about some of his celebrity friends."

Phyllis walked away to join Andy. They sipped champagne, and leaned over the balcony, taking in the splendor of the ocean waves.

Beatrice felt special while Clarise read her palm, telling her all about her long lifeline and even predicted that she would marry again.

Rachel was enjoying just watching everyone have a good time.

Carmen and Joe stopped dancing. Joe hadn't understood a word of the Spanish song, but had kept up with the rhythmic beat.

Clarise walked over to where Rachel and I sat.

"Rachel, could I speak with you for a few moments?"

"Certainly Clarise," she said. "Excuse me, Curie." I'll be back in a few moments. Enjoy, get up and dance."

Clarise and Rachel passed Gertie as she was on her way out to the patio with a tray of sliced meats. She was humming a song, and enjoying seeing Rachel's friends having a fun time.

Rachel led Clarise into the sitting room. After they sat, Clarise wrinkled her brow. "Rachel, I hate to bring this up while everyone's having such a splendid time, but I just have this dreadful feeling."

"What's the matter, Clarise? Don't you feel well?"

"I feel fine, Rachel. It's you I'm worried about?"

"What ever on earth are you talking about, Clarise. I feel better than I have in years?"

"Listen to me, Rachel. I know you don't believe in this psychic, paranormal stuff, but remember when I almost passed out earlier, when we were assembled in the room?"

"What about it?" Are you feeling better?"

"Rachel, I feel fine. It's just that, back then, I saw danger around you. I didn't see any particular danger—I just saw a flash of something that disturbed me. I couldn't make it out very clearly, but it was scary. It involved you somehow, and I saw broken glass all around."

"For heaven's sakes Clarise. You're scaring me. I don't believe in this stuff you're talking about, but you look scared, and that is what's scaring me. Now, I can take care of myself. There's no danger. Look at everyone. They're having such a good time. Can you imagine anything dangerous about that?"

"No. I don't feel anything anymore; I just had to tell you what I felt earlier. I'm sorry if I upset you."

"Don't fret about it. I feel fine, the group is having a fantastic time, what could go wrong?"

Clarise didn't push her point. She smiled at Rachel.

"I suppose you're right. But nonetheless, I still want you to call me tomorrow. Tomorrow's Andrea's exhibition, right?"

"Yes. He's the next Picasso. I'll be leaving for the gallery very early in the morning so I'm going to get to bed early. It should go very smoothly. We've invited people from all over the world. Suzanne has taken care of just about everything already. I'll call you later tomorrow so that you can see that everything's fine. I'll tell you all about it."

"Promise?"

"Promise. Now, let's get back out there and enjoy this beautiful evening."

Rachel and Clarise returned to the patio.

"I'd like to propose a toast," happily announced Rachel.

"May we live every day with a song in our heart, our friends by our side, and a long life filled with cheer and good thoughts."

"Salute," said everyone as we raised our glasses high.

"What a splendid Sunday evening," declared Judith. "Here's to you, Sarah, wherever you are."

Sarah had returned home. She took the little bird out of her purse and sat it next to the one on her table. They were identical.

Flashes of her nightmare popped into her head as she stared at the little identical birds.

"Oh, God," she said, as she held her head in her hands. When she removed them, her face was distorted, and she had a wild look in her eyes.

"Oh, God, oh God," she kept repeating.

To her horror, she remembered where she had heard the voice of the woman in her dreams. Then she envisioned the blurred face of the woman that she saw near the end of her nightmare.

All of a sudden, she stood up and screamed. "It's Rachel!"

Fear combined with Sarah's anger, and she became completely enraged. She started sobbing uncontrollably, pounding her thighs so hard with her fists that she left massive bruises.

"All along it was Rachel. Rachel. Why didn't I realize that all along it was you who had walked out of the hospital with Philip?" she sobbed.

She ran over to the table and grabbed Rachel's little porcelain bird and violently crashed it against the wall. The little bird's decapitated head rolled against one of the table legs, wobbled, and stopped. She began angrily muttering to herself.

"She invited me into her home, she stole my Philip, she ruined my life. Took away my life. I hate, I hate her, I hate her," she ranted as her anger boiled over. "God, help me!" she pleaded, and fell to her knees.

Exhausted, Sarah stood up and walked in her bare feet over the shards of broken porcelain. She slumped into her tattered green recliner—talking to herself again, as if Philip was in the room.

"How could you do this to me? You loved me, Philip. We we're going to be married. How could you abandon us and love another? You said you loved me. Then you met that woman and tossed me aside, taking away everything that I was. I'll bet you never even told Rachel about me. She probably didn't even know that you were engaged. I'll bet you didn't tell her, you coward, you lying bastard coward."

Sarah cried herself to sleep.

Meanwhile, at Rachel's, the cocktail party was winding down. By 7:00 P.M. everyone had left.

Sarah was still sitting in her green recliner, where she slept all night. She awoke at 6:00 A.M. the next morning and immediately looked underneath the table to see if the little robin's head was still there. She hoped that the evening had been just another nightmare. Still nudged against the table leg was the little porcelain robin's head.

For the first time since leaving the mental hospital, the past night Sarah did not dreamed the agonizing nightmare of Philip breaking their engagement. She picked up the little porcelain head and held it gently in the palm of her hand.

"I'm sorry little bird," she said through tears, stroking the decapitated bird's head as if it was real. She placed it on the table next to her bird. It's face rolled over. The bird's little brown hand-painted eyes stared blankly at her.

"God what have I done?"

She suddenly realized that for the first time since leaving the hospital that she had been trapped inside that nightmare. She didn't know how she'd ever be able to look at Rachel ever again, and was worried how she would react when she saw her.

She placed the robin's head on the table and grabbed a broom. She swept the broken pieces of the little bird into a pile, brushed them into a dustpan and tossed them into a trashcan. She reached over to the table, grabbed the little decapitated head, and tossed it into the trash, too.

Almost in fast motion, Sarah grabbed her bird from the table, shoved it into her purse, and left the apartment, slamming the door hard behind her.

Meanwhile, in La Jolla, Rachel had slept soundly. But when she awakened at 7:30 that morning, she had a slight headache. Slowly, she got out of bed to dress for a meeting with Jonathan at 9:00. She had just completed a sale worth more than $5 million dollars, and wanted to finalize the paperwork before the art exhibition later that afternoon.

"Oh God," she said. "Gertie, would you get me some aspirin?"

Rachel showered and dressed, then took the aspirin that Gertie left on her dressing table.

"Gertie," she called out. "Would you please come in and help me with this necklace?"

Gertie entered the room and hooked a beautiful gold necklace with a sparkling, perfect emerald, around Rachel's neck.

"This is such a beautiful necklace, Mrs. Maxwell. You look wonderful!"

"Thank you Gertie, it's my favorite. I have to rush. Sorry about the big mess on the patio from last night."

"No worry, Mrs. Maxwell. I'll clean it all up for you."

"You're a sweetheart, Gertie. I'm heading to the bank to visit Jonathan. I'll be back in about an hour. Get my black dress ready; you know the one with the long sleeves. When I return, I'll have to change quickly to meet Suzanne at August House."

"Yes ma'am," said Gertie.

Rachel finished dressing and left for her meeting with Jonathan.

"Good morning, Mrs. Maxwell," said Jonathan's secretary, Alice.

"Good morning, Alice. I have a 9:00 o'clock with Jonathan."

"Yes, Mrs. Maxwell, he's expecting you."

Jonathan walked out of his office and warmly greeted Rachel. "Good morning Rachel. You look absolutely ravishing today, as always."

"Cut the bull, Jonathan. I look like hell, and you know it. You party hounds really tied one on yesterday."

"Sounds like you tied one of your own, but you still look gorgeous. I had a fine time yesterday, Rachel. Most of that group probably don't get to go to parties in La Jolla very often."

"I'm glad everyone enjoyed themselves. Now, let's get down to business. I have to meet Suzanne."

"Of course Rachel," he said. He held up an index finger, and then buzzed Alice.

"Alice, I'm expecting Mel Abraham. I have some papers for him to sign. Would you let me know when he arrives?"

"Sure thing, Mr. Severied," said Alice.

Minutes later, while Rachel was spreading out her papers on Jonathan's conference table, Alice buzzed back.

"Excuse me, Mr. Severied, but Mr. Abraham is here."

"Thank you Alice. Rachel, could you please excuse me for one minute? I've been trying to get Mel down here for days. It'll only take a minute, I promise."

Jonathan walked out of the office and closed the door. He led Mr. Abraham into a nearby conference room.

Rachel walked over to Jonathan's phone to telephone Suzanne.

"Rachel, I'm so glad you called," said Suzanne. "Your cell phone must be turned off. I've been trying to reach you. I tried calling Gertie to find you, but your answering machine picked up. I need you at August House earlier than I thought. Could you possibly come down at 11:00?"

"Suzanne, I'm at the bank with Jonathan. Can't you handle whatever it is?"

"Ambassador Fredricks will be arriving at noon. He wants to meet with you before the exhibition because of a personal emergency. He won't be able to attend, but insisted upon seeing you before he left."

"OK Suzanne. I'll see if I can cut this short with Jonathan. I'll have to swing by the house to change, but then I'll be right there."

"Thank you, Rachel. I'll call the ambassador and let him now."

Rachel looked at her watch. She wondered what was keeping Jonathan. After waiting ten minutes more, she decided to leave. Jonathan was still in the conference room with Mr. Abraham.

"Alice, tell Jonathan something's come up. I have to leave. Tell him I'll see him at the exhibition."

"Yes, Mrs. Maxwell," said Alice.

Just when Rachel reached the elevator, Jonathan emerged from the conference room. Mr. Abraham looked upset, mumbled some angry words at Jonathan, and stormed off.

"What's the matter with him?" asked Alice.

"He's angry at the world all the time, but this morning he's angry because his portfolio took a dive. I was just the messenger."

"Poor man," exclaimed Alice.

Jonathan walked back in his office.

"Where's Rachel?" he asked while running back out to Alice.

"Oh yes, something came up and she had to leave. She said she'd see you at the exhibition."

Jonathan rushed into his office and closed the door. He walked over to the window and spotted Rachel on the front steps of the bank, talking on her cell phone. He was about to turn away when he saw Mr. Abraham charge out of the front door of the bank and run right into Rachel, knocking her briefcase and cell phone to the ground. Her briefcase flew open, and her papers spilled onto the steps.

Mr. Abraham helped Rachel retrieve her papers, then stacked them and placed them into her briefcase.

"What is he doing?" Jonathan asked himself. He ran to the phone and placed a call.

Rachel was shaken, but not upset with the bungling man. He passed her cell phone to her, and rushed off.

Rachel got into her car and headed home. The rush-hour traffic had faded, and Rachel was soon back home.

"You back already?" asked Gertie.

"Yes, I've got to get to the gallery early. Did you lay out my dress?"

"Yes, everything all laid out for you."

"Thank you, Gertie."

Rachel raced upstairs. She slipped into her dress and pulled out a string of pearls, but changed her mind about them and tossed them to the bed. She decided that the emerald necklace looked perfect. She took a quick peek into the mirror, freshened her lipstick, and then headed downstairs.

"Bye Gertie. I'll be back around 6:00 this evening."

"Yes ma'am," acknowledged Gertie, then shut the door as Rachel stepped into her car.

Just after pulling beyond the gate, Rachel realized that she had a flat tire.

"Damn, damn, damn," she shouted, and hit the steering wheel hard with her palms.

"I'm in too big of a hurry for this," she grumbled and stepped out of her car, leaving the car door open. "Now I'll have to have Gertie bring a car out to me. Damn, damn."

She leaned into the car for her phone to call Suzanne first to let her know she was on her way.

Suddenly, and out of nowhere, a hand grabbed her by her collar.

Rachel let out a loud scream, but not a soul could hear her from the secluded, densely landscaped area. Her attacker violently swung her around. The grip loosened and she slipped to the ground. Furiously, she scampered against her open car door, trying to lift herself from the ground. Her attacker panicked and grabbed one of the bricks that bordered the drive. Before Rachel could stand, her attacker savagely struck her twice, shattering her car window on the second blow. She fell and slumped to the ground, her blood flowing freely from an open head wound.

Gertie, who was out on the patio clearing the remains from the cocktail party, didn't hear a thing. As she entered the kitchen with a tray of glasses, she noticed the blinking red light on the security box, indicating that the entrance gate was open.

"Mrs. Maxwell didn't close the gate?" she asked herself. She walked out to take a look. She stood on her tiptoes from the steps and peered down the drive. Suddenly, she heard a blood-curdling scream. "Rachel's in trouble," she nervously told herself, and dashed down the steps and towards the gate. Gertie ran as fast as she could. Up ahead she could see Rachel's car.

"My Rachel. My Rachel's in trouble!" she cried out. Her heart pounded heavily as she ran faster and faster. She heard the sound of a car engine, and saw a faded brown car driving away.

Gertie finally reached the gate. She spotted Rachel slumped below the passenger car door, blood spilling freely from an open head wound. She frantically dashed around the side of the car and strained to look down the winding path, but the car was out of sight.

Gertie quickly ran back to attend to Rachel. "Help me, God, help me!" She scampered back up the drive to call 911. Halfway up the driveway, she stopped when she heard the sound of a car pulling up. She didn't know if she should keep running to the house or run to see who was coming. Gertie was panic-stricken. She turned around and ran back down the drive to see who was in the car, but stopped suddenly.

"What if that's the killer, mad man or something?' She asked herself. She was about to turn back again, when she recognized a familiar woman stepping from the car. It was Sarah.

"Miss Sarah!" she called out, and ran back down the driveway to the gate.

Completely out of breath, Gertie ran up to Sarah. "Miss Sarah. I glad you here. Something terrible happened to Miss Rachel."

But Sarah didn't acknowledge Gertie. Instead, she began to mutter to herself incoherently. Gertie watched in horror and disbelief as Sarah picked up the brick that had been used to strike Rachel and banged it forcefully several times against Rachel's car.

"Madre Santa de Cristo!" screamed Gertie. She ran fast to the house, looking back and forth at Sarah, who was almost hidden by the shrubbery. Gertie made non-stop signs of the crucifix, nearly falling several times. She was speaking non-stop in Spanish, and let out a series of blood-curdling screams, all the way to the front door. Almost out of breath, she slammed the door shut and clutched her chest. She pushed herself from the door and ran to grab the phone. She punched in 911.

Sarah was still walking around at the gate. Confused and bewildered, she paced in jagged circles around Rachel's car.

"Rachel, Rachel. Look what what's happened," she sobbed. She reached into her purse, took out her little bird, and in a rage, hurled it to the pavement.

The police arrived within minutes after Gertie's call and discovered Sarah slumped over Rachel's body, her dress drenched with Rachel's blood. She was muttering incoherently to herself.

An officer removed her from the ground. She was covered from the pool of blood that had spilled from Rachel's temple, incoherent, and in a daze.

"Oh God, Rachel. Look what's happened to you," she mumbled, as blood dripped from cuts on her hands and arms.

Blood was smeared on her face, as she repeatedly grabbed her face with her bloody palms.

The arresting officer placed Sarah in the back of the patrol car and called for backup. He walked over to Rachel's body, and said to himself. "Holy Christ, what happened here? It's Rachel Maxwell."

A swarm of patrol cars and detectives soon arrived, followed by hordes of newspaper and television reporters. The responding officer walked over to a sergeant who was kneeling over Rachel's body. "This lady's comatose, sergeant. I've read her her rights, but she won't respond. Should I take her in?"

"Yea, take her in," responded the sergeant. "Take someone with you."

The officer, accompanied by another patrolman, took Sarah into custody. She was taken downtown for booking. While enroute, Sarah began mumbling to herself."

"Do you understand that we're taking you downtown for booking, Miss?" asked the officer.

Sarah didn't respond. She just stood there, unable to speak. She was placed in the patrol car. She stared out of the window as the officers sped away.

Enroute, Sarah mumbled to herself.

"Little robin, little robin," she said repeatedly.

Puzzled, the officer who had accompanied the arresting one, looked at Sarah, then shrugged.

"She's off her rocker," said the arresting officer, and the other agreed.

The press descended on the murder site like flies. Local, and some national, television stations interrupted normal programming to immediately broadcast the story of the wealthy socialite who had been viciously murdered in front of her La Jolla estate. Her name had not yet been released.

Two other officers, McFeeney and Richardson, were dispatched to the home of Suzanne Sullivan. After they rang the doorbell, Suzanne's housekeeper, Frances, opened the door.

"Ma'am, I'm Officer McFeeney and this is Officer Richardson. We're from the La Jolla police department."

"Miss Sullivan is at August House. She has a meeting with her mother. What's this about?" asked Frances.

"Miss, did you say Miss Sullivan is at August House?

"Yes. She's there with her mother, Rachel Maxwell."

"Thank you," said officer Richardson. They headed for the gallery.

When McFeeney and Richardson arrived, Stephen led them to Suzanne, who was in her office, dialing Rachel's cell phone number.

"Miss Sullivan. I'm Officer Richardson, and this is Officer McFeeney. May we speak with you privately?"

"Yes," said Suzanne. "Come on in. What's wrong? Has something happened to Rachel?" she asked as soon as Officer Richardson closed her door.

"My mother was due here hours ago to meet with Ambassador Fredericks. I can't find her anywhere. I can't even reach her housekeeper. Has something happened to my mother?"

"Miss Sullivan, there's been a terrible accident. Your mother is Rachel Maxwell?" asked Officer Richardson.

"Yes, what's happened to Rachel? What's happened to Rachel?" she repeated, fearing the worst.

"I'm afraid Mrs. Maxwell is dead, Miss Sullivan."

"Dead? What are you saying? What happened to Rachel?" she screamed.

"We don't have all the details just yet, but it appears that your mother has been murdered. She was discovered by her housekeeper around 10:00 this morning." said officer Richardson.

"How did it happen? You said she was murdered. How was she killed?"

"I can't be sure of murder at this time, and I can't answer too many questions right now, Miss Sullivan. The coroner pronounced her dead about 30 minutes ago. I'm afraid we can't tell you much more than that."

"Where did it happen? Can you at least tell me that?"

She was obviously on her way out, I understand to see you here, but she got no further than her front gate. That's all I can tell you, right now," said McFeeney.

Suzanne stood up, but then slumped back to her chair.

"I knew something bad would happen with her hanging around all those strange people. But Rachel had her own way. When she wanted something, she didn't care about the risks. Who killed my mother?"

"We don't know that. There has been an arrest. A woman was discovered at the crime scene."

McFeeney looked at Richardson after making that statement. He knew that she would want further information, but both men knew they could provide none.

"What woman?" shouted Suzanne.

"I'm afraid you'll have to ask those questions of someone downtown, Miss Sullivan. You can ask for detective Folson. Jack Folson."

"Give me his number. I'm calling him right now. Where's my mother? Where did they take my mother?" she demanded.

"The morgue, Miss Sullivan. Would you like us to take you downtown? You'll have to come and identify the body," said Richardson.

"Do you have this detective's number?" Suzanne asked.

"Yes ma'am," said McFeeney, as he pulled a card from his top pocket. "You can reach him at this number." He passed the card to Suzanne.

"What about the woman who killed my mother?"

"We didn't say that the woman has been charged with killing your mother, Miss Sullivan. Only that a woman was found at the scene."

"Where is this woman now?"

McFeeney cleared his throat.

"She's been taken into custody. They'll want to talk to you. I'm very sorry about your mother, Miss Sullivan."

Since Suzanne had not accepted their offer to drive her downtown, the officers departed, but reminded her that she would have to come and identify Rachel's body.

Suzanne remembered that Ambassador Fredricks was still waiting for Rachel. He had grown impatient and was preparing to leave.

Suzanne composed herself and walked out of her office. Still in shock, she didn't know what she would say.

She picked up a photograph from her desk of her parents. Philip and Rachel were smiling and waving from a sailboat that Philip had named "Magnificent Lady Maxwell." Suzanne wept openly as she clutched the photo of her dead parents.

She held the photo before her and brushed a finger across the face of the two, thinking of how she and Rachel were so different.

Rachel was headstrong, impulsive, witty, and aggressive. Suzanne was reserved, humorless, and all business, and had never carried herself in the manner of a typical wealthy woman.

Now Suzanne was even wealthier. She was the sole heir to Rachel's over $800 million dollar estate.

She called the front desk. "Stephen, can you please come into my office?"

"Yes, Miss Sullivan," he responded. "Ambassador Fredericks is getting pretty impatient. I think he's leaving."

"Would you ask him to give me just a few minutes. I'll come out and talk with him right after I speak with you."

Stephen convinced Ambassador Fredericks to wait for a few minutes more and rushed into Suzanne's office.

"Stephen, I'm afraid I have some really dreadful news. Rachel is dead," she blurted out and began to sob again.

Stephen gasped and took a seat in front of Suzanne's desk. "How dreadful, Suzanne. What happened?"

"I'll bet she was murdered by one of those people that she was involved with on Sundays?"

"Oh, good heavens, Miss Sullivan. What people?"

"You know, Stephen. That group of Curie Nova's. There was a woman found at the murder scene, at my mother's house. Oh Stephen, someone killed her right in front of her own house. They've arrested this woman."

"That's simply horrifying," he responded. "Poor Mrs. Maxwell."

Stephen despondently walked out of Suzanne's office. He stopped at the doorway.

"Miss Sullivan, I'll tell your guests that the exhibition is canceled."

"Oh no, Stephen—I'll do it."

She wiped the tears from her eyes, and walked out to speak with the ambassador. After hearing the news of Rachel's demise, he offered Suzanne his condolences and departed the gallery.

Suzanne watched as he and his entourage silently walked away. She thought about the several hundred guests who were on their way to August House for the exhibition of artist, Andreas Vandiver. Rachel had invited influential and wealthy people from around the world to view his work. Members of the press, some who had been invited to cover the event, were joined by countless other reporters, all hoping to get a statement from Suzanne. It was now public knowledge that it was Rachel who had been murdered.

Stephen rushed to lock the gallery doors. Outside, the press grew in numbers by the second.

"Wait, Stephen," said Suzanne. I need to tell them something." She walked to the door and peeked her head out.

"Excuse me, ladies and gentlemen. I'm afraid Rachel will not be attending the exhibition. You see there's been a dreadful accident. As most of you are probably already aware, there's been a horrible incident."

Tears fell down her face as she tried to inform her guest, and the press, that the exhibition was cancelled due to her mother's death.

"My mother…my mother. I don't know anything more. I'm sure you'll understand why I have to cancel the exhibition. And for those of you who have come a long way to view the works of Andreas Van Diver, I do apologize," she said as she looked out over the sea of faces, many who had arrived for the exhibition.

"I know you've come a long way, but as I'm sure you understand…" Suzanne's words trailed off.

Stephen stepped up and pulled Suzanne back inside before the press could begin asking questions. A gallery employee led her back to her office. Stephen stuck his head outside the gallery door.

"For those of you who have come for the exhibition, I apologize. For the press, there is nothing more we can say." He closed the door and locked it.

Suzanne didn't want to accept the news that Rachel was dead. Stephen walked in to comfort her.

"Thank you Stephen."

"Suzanne, there's no need to thank me. I'm so terribly sorry for what's happened. The ambassador wanted to know more about what happened to Rachel, but I didn't give any details. I don't know any details to give."

A young female employee knocked on Suzanne's door. "Excuse me, Miss Sullivan, but there's a group of people from the TV news and newspaper reporters out front, and they want to speak with you."

"I'll take care of this," Stephen told Suzanne and walked out to address the press again.

Stephen opened the door and several reporters tried to push their way through. Stephen managed to shut the door, all the while shouting that Suzanne was not available for comment.

"Can you speak with us, sir? Who are you?" shouted a male reporter.

"I work for Miss Sullivan, and I cannot give you information because I don't have any details. Even if I did I wouldn't be at liberty to share them with you."

Suzanne was trying to reach Detective Folson. Stephen walked into her office.

"Thank you again, Stephen," she said with a sad smile.

Her hands shook as she punched in the last number. She picked up a cigarette, lit it and took a long draw. A female officer answered.

"I'm sorry, but Detective Folson is not in. Shall I have him call you upon his return to the station?"

"No. This is Suzanne Sullivan. I'm coming down to see him. See if you can find him. Tell him I want to know who killed my mother."

She hung up the phone before the officer could respond.

"Stephen, cancel all my meetings for the next two weeks. Place a sign in the window saying that August House will be closed until further notice out of respect for the late Rachel Maxwell, would you please? And, one more thing, I'm going home, then I'm going to the morgue, and then to the police station to see a Detective Folson. If the press harasses you while I'm gone, just tell them you don't know anything and have no comment."

"Yes, ma'am," he said and stepped out, closing the door behind him.

When Suzanne emerged a few minutes later, the flood of reporters had grown ten-fold. Stephen placed the sign he had made with a black marker in the window and walked away, ignoring the screaming horde of reporters outside.

"Suzanne, I wouldn't come this way, if I were you. The press will hound you relentlessly. You may want to slip out of the back. There's a sea of reporters out front waiting to get a statement from you."

"Thank you Stephen, I'll leave out of the back."

Stephen escorted Suzanne out to the back of the gallery. They squeezed between crates and statues, inching their way to the back door.

"Oh, Miss Sullivan. Your car's parked out front. How will you get home?"

"I'll walk. I'll run," she yelled out, pushed the back door open and took off.

Suzanne lived only a couple of blocks from the gallery. When she got near her house, she saw several reporters standing outside her security gate.

"Oh God," she said in Rachel's familiar tone. She walked to a little flower shop less than a block away to call her housekeeper. She pulled out her cell phone.

"Frances, I'm at the corner. Go out front and tell those reporters that I'm at the gallery."

"Ma'am? OK, but they're all waiting for you."

"Just do as I say. I'll be there soon," she snapped and clicked off the phone.

Suzanne waited a few minutes while Frances got rid of the reporters and many others who had gathered at her gate. She called August House and asked Stephen to meet her at the flower shop. When he arrived, she jumped into his car.

"Take me home," she ordered, and Stephen took off.

Frances had successfully gotten rid of most of the reporters, but a few remained, with microphones in hand.

Stephen pushed through them, shielding Suzanne from the onslaught of questions that were being shouted at her.

"Miss Sullivan, how do you feel about the cult member who's been arrested for killing your mother?" rang out the voice of a loud-mouthed female reporter.

Suzanne didn't respond. She stopped for a second and gave the reporter a contemptuous look. She and Stephen ran inside the house and slammed the door.

Chapter Ten

"A Different Nightmare"

Sarah was taken into custody and booked on suspicion of murder. The contents of her purse were laid out for property identification. An officer picked up her faded brown purse and held it from its tattered straps, which were so worn that they looked like they would soon snap. The desk Sergeant, Hector Garcia, read aloud the contents.

"Small black hair comb, one change purse, one dollar and twenty five cents inside, one driver's license, a key ring with three keys, a half eaten package of salted peanuts, a locket with the picture of a young, white male—looks like an old picture, and a business card."

Detective Folson, a tall, square jawed black man with short, curly black hair, picked up the white business card with black lettering and read it aloud.

"Curie Nova, Writer. I wonder who she is, and why this woman has her card, and not much else? Call and find out if this Curie Nova knows anything about her." He passed the card to officer Garcia and walked away.

Sarah was strip searched, fingerprinted and photographed, then led into an interrogation room wearing a prisoner's uniform.

Detective Folson and another Detective, Johnny Dumont, entered the little, confining room ready to take Sarah's statement.

"Do you know you're being held on suspicion of murdering Rachel Maxwell?" immediately asked Detective Folson.

His deep, baritone voice echoed throughout the little room and reverberated off the walls.

Sarah didn't respond. She continued to stare straight ahead.

"She's comatose. Has a doctor looked at this woman," he asked Detective Dumont.

"Yes, she was seen by a doctor. He dressed and cleaned the wounds on her arms and hands. Look at her," he responded.

"I can see that, smartass. I'm talking about a psychiatrist. This woman is somewhere else. She's in shock, for Christ's sake. We're not gonna get anything out of her. Has she said a word since she was taken into custody?"

"I don't know, I don't think so."

"Has she tried to call anybody?"

"No. She didn't respond when she was asked her if she wanted to make a phone call. She acted just like she's acting right now, staring straight ahead, not saying a word."

"Did she say anything when she was in the patrol car?"

"The officers who brought her in said she mumbled a lot of stuff in the car, but nothing that made any sense," said Dumont.

"Well we're not going to get anywhere with her now," said Folson.

"Wait a minute," Dumont suddenly said. "There is one thing the officers mentioned. She said the name Philip, and kept calling some name...robin, yeah, she kept saying, little robin."

"Little robin, what the hell does that mean? And who is Philip?"

"I don't know."

"Where's the maid that discovered Mrs. Maxwell's body, the one who saw Sarah Jenkins at the murder scene? What's her name?"

Detective Dumont was drawing a blank. "The housekeeper? She's out front."

"Gertie, isn't that her name? Go get Gertie and bring her into my office. I'll talk to her. Maybe I can get something out of her," he ordered as he rushed towards the door. He stopped before leaving the room. "And try to reach this Curie Nova and get her down here, too. If Sarah Jenkins won't talk, maybe this writer can tell us something about her," he added.

He passed the business card to Dumont, who left the room to get Gertie.

"Garcia, get Sarah out of here," ordered Folson.

Officer Garcia escorted Sarah back to her cell.

Dumont brought in Gertie, who was visibly shaken and still crying. After discovering Rachel's body, her English had all but disappeared, and she was speaking non-stop in Spanish.

She sat across from Detective Folson's desk, making the sign of the Crucifix and saying the same Spanish words repeatedly.

"Madre Santa de Cristo, Madre Santa de Cristo." She tugged relentlessly at rosary beads that she had wrapped around her left hand.

"You're Gertie, right?" asked the stern Detective Folson.

Through sobs, Gertie looked up at Folson and responded in a string of Spanish.

"Esa mujer mató a mi Rachel. She went on and on, telling how she found Rachel's body and about Sarah kneeling over her, with blood dripping from her hands and arms, but it was all in Spanish.

Folson didn't understand a word she said.

"For God's sake, what the hell is going on? First I get a mute who won't say a damn thing, now I got you."

He sprang from behind his desk, frustrated and angry. He ran over to the door and jerked it open.

"Garcia, get in here, now!"

"Officer Garcia is in booking right now," bellowed the voice of an officer from down the hall.

"Damn it, get me someone in here that can speak Spanish. And bring me some aspirin."

Officer Hernandez, an officer who was on his way out, turned around and reported to Folson's office.

"Tell me what she's saying. And, tell her we need to record this."

Officer Hernandez spoke to Gertie in Spanish. She nodded at Folson and wiped her eyes.

Hernandez asked Sarah what happened? They spoke, then he turned to Folson.

"She said that Rachel left to go to the gallery, and didn't close the front gate behind her. When she went to see why the gate was still open, that's when she found Rachel's body, and then a few minutes later discovered Sarah Jenkins kneeling over Rachel, with a bloody brick in her hand. She ran back into the house and called 911. She said this Sarah Jenkins was part of a group of people, who called themselves Nova's Arc."

"Stay with her and get her full name, if she has a house other than living at Rachel's, get that address, and any other information. Let her know we'll be questioning her again," commanded Folson.

Folson left his office and walked up to Dumont. He was hanging up the phone when Folson reached him.

"Did you reach Curie Nova?"

"Sure did. She's coming down now. She lives in Scripps Ranch, so she should be here in about an hour.

"Did someone get ahold of a psychiatrist to try to communicate with Sarah Jenkins? Does she have an attorney?"

"Nobody knows. She won't talk to anybody."

"After we talk with this writer, make the rounds and find out who's in this Nova's Arc group."

"Do we have a number on how many were in the group?" asked Dumont.

"I don't know yet. Ask the writer."

"What was this group, a cult?"

"The hell if I know. According to the statement from the officers who spoke to the daughter, Suzanne Sullivan, they were just a group of old people helping this Curie Nova write a book. According to her, they met every Sunday at Mrs. Maxwell's house. A strange group, too. She said some of those people were wealthy, and others were as poor as a church mouse. Miss Sullivan said this Curie Nova formed the group specifically for the purpose of writing the book."

Dumont shook his head. "I don't understand why Mrs. Maxwell would be involved with a group like that."

While both detectives went back to Folson's office to talk about the case, Sarah sat alone in a cell. She was mumbling. The guard heard her, and walked close by, but couldn't understand much of what she said, and walked away.

Sarah's speech became clearer as the guard moved farther away. "Gotta go to Rachel's, Nova's Arc. Gotta get my robin. Want to go back to the Arc. Philip, is that you?" she asked herself, looking and pointing to the corner of the cell. She stopped talking and started staring straight ahead again.

Meanwhile, I was headed for downtown. Just before I closed my front door, I heard a television reporter talking about Rachel's murder. I stepped back in to listen.

The reporter's voice was intense.

"Rachel Maxwell, millionaire heiress and the owner of August House Art Gallery, was discovered by her housekeeper at 10:00 a.m. in front of her La Jolla estate."

A photograph of Rachel flashed across my television screen. I froze. The reported continued.

"Mrs. Maxwell, a 62-year old socialite, was viciously murdered and a woman who police have identified as Sarah Jenkins, has been arrested in connection with her murder. Sarah Jenkins, a former member of a group called 'Nova's Arc,' was identified at the scene of the murder by Mrs. Maxwell's housekeeper, Gertie Ortiz."

"Nova's Arc? How in the hell did they find that out already?" I asked myself out loud. "What the hell!"

I ran out of the house without locking my door and jumped in the car. I arrived at the precinct disturbed and distraught over the death of my friend, Rachel, and shocked to hear the news that Sarah had been arrested on suspicion of her murder. All sorts of crazy things ran through my mind. Although I felt sorry for Sarah, I was angry that she had murdered the woman who had opened her heart and her home to us.

I pushed my way past the crowd of reporters and into the precinct.

"Who are you?" yelled out a male reporter.

I ignored him, pulled open the door to the precinct and stepped inside.

"I'm Curie Nova. I'm here to see Detective Dumont," I said to the first officer I saw.

I was led down the hall and into Folson's cluttered office. Dumont was there, also.

"Please sit down, Miss Nova. I know this must be a distressing time for you. Thank you for coming right down," said Dumont, and he stood and motioned for me to sit in a chair beside his.

Detective Folson sat behind his desk. Still in a state of shock, I wasn't sure if I should be talking to the detectives, but I talked anyway.

"Yes, this is extremely shocking and unbelievable. Rachel was the kindest woman I'd ever met. She treated us all so wonderfully, made us feel special. I can't even begin to understand how this could have happened to her."

"That's what we're trying to find out," said Folson. "Would you like some coffee, Miss Nova? Dumont, go and get Miss Nova some coffee," he said without waiting for my response.

"What happened?" I asked Detective Folson.

"We can't answer that right now. But we hope that you can answer a few questions for us."

Dumont poked his head out of Folson's office and asked a clerk to bring in some coffee.

Folson leaned forward, clasping his big brown hands on a stack of papers.

"According to Miss Sullivan's statement," said Folson, "you are writing a book, and to do that, you and Mrs. Maxwell were interviewing people at her home every Sunday, is that correct?"

I took off my shades and revealed my bloodshot eyes. I had been crying ever since I heard the news that Rachel had been murdered.

"Yes, that's correct. But I'd rather not answer any questions right now."

"Can you at least tell us what you know about Sarah Jenkins?" asked Folson.

"I guess I can. I met Sarah several years ago, her car was stalled downtown and I helped her to get home," I began.

I told the detectives all about my visit to her apartment that day, and about her sparse, little, darkened place in National City. That was all I wanted to tell them, but I found myself answering more of their questions.

Folson moved from behind his desk to sit in the chair that Dumont had vacated. Dumont was now sitting on the edge of Folson's desk.

"Can you think of any reason why this woman would want to kill Mrs. Maxwell?" Folson asked.

"Honestly, no. Sarah was always a quiet woman, but she was extremely kind and gentle. She seemed to enjoy being a part of the group. To be honest, I didn't think she'd say yes when I asked her to join the group."

"Why is that?" he asked.

"Because she just didn't seem like she would ever leave that apartment unless she had to, you know what I mean? When I walked into her apartment, I sensed that she was a recluse. I felt sorry for her. So when I started assembling the group for my interviews, I thought that by asking her to join, it would help to bring her out, and at the same time, add some interesting insights to the book."

My brain told me to stop answering questions, but my tongue wouldn't obey.

The clerk entered the room carrying a try of coffee. Dumont moved from Folson's desk and took the tray.

"What made you think having a recluse in your book would be interesting?" asked Dumont, as he passed me a cup of black coffee.

I preferred cream and sugar, but drank the black coffee without telling him that.

"Mr. Dumont, there are many old people living alone, scared, worried, depressed, and think that nobody cares about them. Lots of them are poor and have no family to help take care of them. I'm sure that hearing from someone like Sarah would not only be helpful to a lot of people in her shoes, but would open others to her world, make them aware, and maybe reach out to be kinder, and more understanding of their situation, if nothing else," I defensively told him. "Besides," I added. "Just because Sarah is getting old, is lonely and poor doesn't mean that she has no valuable thoughts to share. I didn't think of Sarah's opinion as any less valuable as anyone else's in the group."

"I didn't mean to infer anything to the contrary," justified Dumont. "It's just, you have to admit, Sarah Jenkins doesn't look like the sort of person that would mix well with a group."

"I disagree, Mr. Dumont. I'm sure the others thought her different, but they didn't treat her with any less respect. It wasn't a social club, anyway. Everyone understood their role."

"What do you think about her role now, Miss Nova? All the evidence indicates that the last role she played was bludgeoning Rachel Maxwell to death," Dumont crudely snapped.

"You sack of shit," I thought to myself, but I didn't say anything. I was too upset to worry about the manners of the offensive detective.

I began to cry again. I refused to believe that the gentle Sarah had committed such a heinous crime.

"You know your tape recordings of the group may become evidence?" advised Dumont.

"No. I don't. Those people spoke with me in confidence. There's no way that I'm going to share their comments with anyone. What these people said was between them and me. I'll speak to my lawyer and demand that it remains that way. I'm not talking to you anymore."

Folson and Dumont looked at each other. Folson spoke.

"Miss Nova, I'm sure your attorney will advise you, but writers have gone to jail for contempt of court on numerous occasions for failing to reveal their sources. Your tapes are not privileged communication. That's all for now. I'm sure you probably would like to be alone right now, anyway, so your statement is sufficient. Here's my card," he said while reaching into his jacket.

"Call me if you can think of anything that you think will help."

"Help who?" I asked. I wasn't sure if they thought I'd be helping to convict Sarah or save her.

"Goodbye," I said, then put my shades back on and walked out of Folson's office.

Detectives Folson and Dumont acted like they were convicting Sarah right there in his office. I wasn't looking forward to testifying, but I knew that the day to do so would surely come.

Reporters crowded the front of the precinct. Nova's Arc had made the front pages of the newspaper and the lead stories of the national news.

"How in the hell am I supposed to write a book using anonymous names now?" I asked myself. "Everybody will find out who the group is, and these information hungry buzzard reporters are gonna hound me to the depths of hell for everything I know. They won't stop until they've plastered every one of the group's pictures and names in the newspapers, on television, and all over the Internet," I counseled myself.

Microphones were shoved in my face, some so close that I was afraid I'd chip a tooth. It was obvious that they all had discovered who I was.

"No comment," I kept repeating, as I disappeared into the sea of people, mostly reporters. I also noticed a lot of others crowded outside the precinct; some looked like homeless people.

They were swarming the front of the jail in support of Sarah. The implications of this tragedy were more serious than I had imagined. "Will this turn out to be rich versus poor?" the thought flashed through my mind.

It certainly was more than I could handle right then, so I walked faster to get to my car, almost running, pushing the reporters aside.

A young, African American man continued to chase me, and was far more aggressive than the other reports.

"Excuse me, wait a minute," he yelled out. But I continued walking as fast as I could.

"Miss Nova, please. I'm not a reporter," I faintly heard him say. I didn't care who he was; I wasn't about to slow my pace.

"Please, Miss Nova. I need to speak with you."

He pressed his face against my car window, and placed his business card on the windshield so I could read it.

"Michael Anthony Clark, Attorney," it read.

"I have to go. Please excuse me," I yelled, and cranked my engine.

"Five minutes. Just five minutes. Meet me at Broad Street Cafe. Will you meet me there?" he pleaded.

"OK, I said, as I pulled forward.

I was afraid that if I didn't say yes, I'd have to run him over just to get out of the parking lot.

I drove to the coffee shop to hear what the brazen, young man had to say. He looked too young to be an attorney, but I didn't want to make assumptions based on his looks. He walked into the coffee shop minutes after I arrived.

"OK, Mr. Clark. What is it you want? I already have an attorney, you have five minutes," I said before he could sit down.

"I don't want to be your attorney. And thank you for meeting me. I'm Michael Anthony Clark."

The good-looking young attorney extended his hand. We shook hands as the waitress stood over us to take our order.

"Just coffee please," I told the waitress.

"Me too," said Michael.

The waitress walked away without saying anything.

"I'm Curie Nova. What can I do for you, Mr. Clark?"

"Call me Michael, and I already know who you are. I want to talk to you about Sarah Jenkins, the woman being held for the murder of Rachel Maxwell."

Michael Clark was blunt and to the point.

"What has that got to do with me?" I wryly asked.

"Please, Miss Nova. You know it has a lot to do with you. I already know about your group. I also know that Sarah won't talk to anybody. They're gonna fry her, you know, if they don't send her to some mental hospital for the criminally insane for rest of her life. I want to help her. I'd like to represent her."

His intentions surprised me.

"Represent her?" I loudly exclaimed, as the waitress arrived with our coffee.

"Will there be anything else?" she asked.

"No. Thank you," I said, and she walked away, looking back as she rounded a corner.

"Why do you want to represent Sarah?" I whispered, looking at him like he was just a little, confused boy.

"Because she needs someone to do that. They'll assign her a public defender if I don't. You know that. I don't know how you feel about this woman, but she was a part of your group. Whatever you may believe she's done, she's going to need someone who will care about her. I talked to one of the officers, who said that Sarah hasn't spoken a word since she was arrested."

"Yea, that's what Detective Folson told me, too. How long have you been an attorney, and why do you care about her?"

"To be honest, I just passed the bar about six months ago. Now just wait," he said before I could interrupt, as if he was reading my mind.

"I know what you're going to say. But I graduated from Harvard Law School, top of my class. After passing the Bar, I was courted by firms from all around the country. I have written more law briefs than others have who've practiced for years. Believe me, I can help this woman. Besides, I've been poor, as they say, dirt poor. I know what it's like. I can get inside her head. If Sarah gets some public defender, you know what'll happen to her. She'll just be another poor person who killed a rich person. Somebody's got to help her, find out why or if she killed Rachel Maxwell."

"You're acting like I have the authority to appoint you as Sarah's attorney. It's not up to me."

"But you can help me. Maybe she'll talk to you. She's got to talk to someone."

"I don't know. I'm not sure how I feel about Sarah right now. Look, Rachel was my friend. I loved her. She was one of the nicest women I've ever met. On the other hand, I've grown to love Sarah, too. I'm afraid for her. But I get sick at the thought that she may have killed Rachel. How am I supposed to divide my feelings this way? How am I supposed to split my heart apart, and neglect my feelings of abhorrence for what Sarah did, even if I do still care about her?" I questioned in a rush of words.

"I'm not asking you to champion for her, I'm asking you to do the right thing!"

I didn't say anything for a while as I sipped my coffee.

Michael watched me in silence, trying to read my face for any indication if I was having a change of heart about helping him. His big, brown eyes followed my hand as it moved the coffee cup from the table to my lips and back again. The silence magnified the clinking noise made by the cup every time I placed in on the saucer.

Michael, who looked like he could be Wesley Snipes' younger brother, just sat there, waiting for a sign from me.

"Well?" he finally spoke. "Are you going to Precinct 22 with me or not? With or without your help, I'm going to find a way to get Sarah to talk to me?"

"Why is this so important to you? Are you trying to make a name for yourself, or something?"

Michael looked indignant at my implication that he was trying to capitalize off Sarah's misfortune.

"You know what I think?" he asked. "I think you'd like to just wash your pretty little writer hands of this whole thing. But you can't. And you know what else? You know deep down that if you don't help Sarah, you'll never forgive yourself. Sarah is a real person, Curie, not a character in your book. You can't turn your back on this woman, cause you know that most of society will. What's she got? She's poor, she's old, hell, she might need psychiatric help, but what kind of care do you think she's going to get left at the hands of the system? Sarah will end up being just another crazy old woman. The media will have a field's day with her. Rachel Maxwell was loved by everyone, and not just here in San Diego. This woman has helped every cause you can think of all around the world. Many will be out for Sarah's blood. Do you want that on your conscience?"

"If she killed Sarah, it won't be on my conscience. It'll be on her conscience," I snapped back.

"If that's the way you feel, Miss Nova. I'm headed back to see Sarah. You can come with me, unless you'd rather go home and agonize about how, if you hadn't involved Sarah in your project, she might not be in this mess."

"You bastard, that's low. Now you're hitting below the belt, Mr. Clark. Now it's my fault, is that what you're implying?"

"I didn't say that, you did," he said as he tossed three dollars on the table and stood to leave.

"Wait a minute."

I reached across the table and grabbed his hand.

"OK, I'll go. But don't ever do that to me again. I don't like guilt trips. I never had a guilty bone in my body before, now you've created one. I'll talk to Sarah, but I can't guarantee she'll talk to me, or you."

"All you can do is try. Let's go."

Michael and I left the coffee shop. I wasn't looking forward to plowing back through the crowd of reporters, and hoped that the mob had dispersed. When we arrived at Precinct 22, the crowd of reporters had multiplied, and a mass of Sarah supporters had assembled.

Many had jumped on the "Save Sarah" bandwagon. The homeless were mixed with people from all walks of life. Most were there in support of Sarah, but a few anti-Sarah supporters were there, too, as well as some media-hungry representatives from various social organizations.

We made our way through the crowd and into the station. Detective Folson was walking out of the door as we entered.

"Miss Nova. Did you think of something you want to tell me?" he asked.

"No, Detective. I'm here to see Sarah."

"Nobody's allowed to see Sarah just yet."

"This is Michael Clark," I said while I pointed to the young attorney. "He's going to represent Sarah. I think she can see her attorney, can't she?" I poignantly asked.

"Does Sarah know that this is her attorney?"

"Of course she does," I lied.

The detective gave me a "I know you're bluffing" look, so I decided I'd better tell him the truth.

"OK, I'm retaining him for her. She doesn't have any family that I know of, so I'm her family right now."

Folson looked at me with surprise at my obvious assertive stance on Sarah's behalf.

"Miss Nova, and whoever you are," he said while glaring at Michael, "you cannot just barge in here saying that you are Sarah Jenkins' attorney."

"I am very well aware of that," said Michael. "Look, let's both save some time here. Miss Jenkins will obviously need counsel. If I can't see her now, I'll petition the Court for an Order appointing Curie as guardian-ad-litem, and then she could hire a lawyer, me, for Sarah. What do you say? Could we just see her for a few minutes?"

Detective Folson gave us both a once-over.

"You've got ten minutes," he sternly said.

"Thank you," quickly said Michael, as if he were afraid the detective might change his mind.

We were taken to see Sarah, and my heart pounded like thunder with every step I took.

"Let me go in first," I cautioned Michael. "She doesn't know you and it might frighten her."

The sight of Sarah in a prisoner's uniform broke my heart. I tried to push back the thought that she had killed my friend, Rachel, but my mind was flooded with the feelings I felt for both women.

"Sarah?" I softly whispered. "Sarah, its Curie."

She looked straight ahead. I knelt down, and the guard peeked in through a little square window.

"Sarah, this is Michael Clark. He's an attorney. He'd like to help you. You've got to talk to me, Sarah, so that we can help you."

I stopped talking and looked at Sarah. Her eyes met mine. I wanted so desperately for her to say something. She looked over at Michael, who had taken a seat across from us.

"Hello Miss Jenkins," he said in a tender voice.

"Sarah, you're going to need an attorney, you know that. Now we can't help you if you don't talk to us," I pleaded.

Just then a single tear ran down Sarah's cheek. Tears began to well in my eyes, but I fought them back.

Michael reached into his pocket and gave Sarah a napkin he had taken from the cafe. She didn't take it, so I did, and wiped her tear away.

Then suddenly she spoke.

"I loved going to Rachel's you know."

Michael and I looked at each other in surprise at the clarity of her voice.

I fought back my tears.

"Sarah, I loved going to Rachel's, too. I loved Rachel. I don't know what happened, Sarah, and I'm trying to deal with all this the best I can. But this is not about me; it's about you. Mr. Clark has told me that he wants to represent you. I know you don't know him, I don't know him either, so I can't say what's best for you. But, I do know that you will need an attorney to help you."

"Curie, what do you think? Do you think I killed Rachel?"

"Sarah, please don't ask me that. I don't know what to think. It doesn't look good. I don't want to ask you if you killed Rachel. I'm not sure I can take hearing anything about that right now. Would you like Michael, Mr. Clark, to represent you, Sarah?"

Sarah looked up at Michael. I don't believe that he took a single breath while the little, fragile woman stared at him. Then she nodded yes, and looked back at me.

"Good," said Michael, who breathed a deep sigh. "Sarah, I know you don't know me, but I promise you that I'll do the best I can to help you," he told her.

"Sarah can't afford an attorney—she doesn't have any money to pay you, Mr. Clark?" I declared.

"My time will be pro-bono—free. Let me worry about that, Sarah," said Michael.

"Michael, you're assuming a lot," I whispered. "Have you discussed this with your firm?"

"Yes," he whispered back."

It was done. Sarah now had an attorney.

I still had mixed emotions about helping Sarah. I wondered how Suzanne would feel about my helping Sarah retain defense. I worried what Nova's Arc would think, and if they would be divided in their feelings about Sarah, like I was.

I suddenly realized that I hadn't spoken to anyone in the group since Rachel's murder.

After we left the precinct, Michael made a public statement to the press that he was representing Sarah. It was like a feeding frenzy outside the station, and I didn't want to be captured on camera.

Chapter Eleven

"The Rich and the Poor"

When I returned home, I was happy to see Diana waiting there for me.

"Curie, I'm so sorry. I've been waiting on pins and needles. I was so worried about you."

She ran up and flung her arms around me.

"Diana, it's been one hell of a day."

Just then Robert pulled into the driveway. Both he and Diana immediately began questioning me. But I didn't answer them.

"Can you believe what they say, that Sarah murdered Rachel?

Why on earth do you think she did it?" asked Robert.

"I don't know? I don't even know if Sarah did it at all."

We walked inside the house.

They looked at me, waiting for me to elaborate. "I don't know. I just know that Rachel's dead. God, I feel so awful. I keep seeing her face, smiling at me, talking to me, sharing her private world with me. I can't get her out of my mind. Then, on the other hand, there's Sarah. If you could have seen her face in that jail…" my words trailed.

"I know this must be hard for you, Curie. I've made you some tea," said Diana as she left the room and walked to the kitchen.

"Thank you for being here, Diana," I yelled out to her.

I looked up at Robert. "Robert, I don't think that I can take many more days like I had today. This thing is really getting me down. I feel crazier than Sarah looked when I first saw her down there. And if I wasn't already upset enough, there was this attorney in front of the precinct who kept harassing me, who wanted to be Sarah's attorney. Well, he is Sarah's attorney, now."

Diana returned carrying a tea tray.

"What? Who was harassing you?"

"An attorney named Michael Clark."

"Why was he bothering you?"

"Because Sarah wouldn't talk to anyone. I had to go down to the precinct with him to get her to consent to retain him."

"You helped Sarah get an attorney?" Robert asked, surprised that I had gotten so intimately involved in everything.

"Robert, don't ask me like that," I angrily snapped. "I didn't help Sarah get an attorney, hell, what I mean is, he was going to represent her one way or another. All I did was go in with him to see her."

"Don't get mad, Curie. Even if you did help Sarah, there's nothing wrong with that. She needs someone, I'm sure."

"But what about Rachel?" chimed in Diana.

"What about Rachel?" I asked. "Helping Sarah makes me feel that I'm betraying Rachel. This is all so distressing, being caught in the middle this way."

"Have you talked to any of the others, any of your group? How do they feel? What about my father?" she asked.

I was surprised that Diana hadn't yet spoken with her father.

"I haven't spoken with any of them yet. I haven't even spoken with Suzanne. I'd better do that that right now."

Robert walked over and gave me a hug. "Curie. Don't worry, everything will be all right."

"Tell me that often, Robert," I said as I walked over and picked up the phone.

My fingers shook as I punched in Suzanne's phone number. Part of me hoped that she wouldn't be home, while the other part wanted desperately to tell her how sorry I was about what had happened to Rachel.

"Hello," answered a man whose voice I didn't recognize.

"Hi, I'd like to speak with Suzanne Sullivan, please. This is Curie Nova."

"Miss Nova, Suzanne isn't speaking with anyone right now. Would you like to leave your number?"

As I called out my telephone number, I heard Suzanne in the background. "Who is it?"

"She said her name is Curie Nova," said the man.

I heard Suzanne say that she'll take the call.

"Hello Curie," said Suzanne. Her voice was emotionless.

"Suzanne, I'm so sorry about what's happened. I don't know what to say, except I'm so sorry. How are you doing, Suzanne? Would you like me to come over?"

"No Curie. I'm here with my mother's brother, my uncle, and some friends. How are you doing, Curie? I want you to know that I don't feel any animosity towards you. It's that woman Sarah that I'd like to kill right now."

I didn't know how to respond. I instantly thought about how Suzanne would feel about me once she learned that I had been instrumental in helping Sarah retain a defense lawyer.

"Suzanne, if there's anything at all that I can do for you, at any time of day or night, please call me."

"Thank you Curie. Good bye."

"Goodbye Suzanne."

I let her hang up first. The dead silence left after she hung up was unnerving. I wanted to tell her that I had helped Sarah. I wanted to tell her that I loved Rachel. I wanted her forgiveness for involving her mother in my book. I replaced the receiver.

Although Suzanne had never been friendly towards me, I felt so badly for her. She and Rachel didn't have a close mother-daughter relationship, but I had never put much thought into it.

Rachel never got the chance to tell me how Suzanne felt about her involvement in Nova's Arc. She treated Suzanne more like a business associate than a stepdaughter, and I wasn't sure of the nature of their relationship beyond that.

I was relieved that I had made the telephone call to Suzanne. Diana brought me a cup of tea.

"Robert...Diana..." I hesitated. "What would you say if I told you I'm going to come out publicly in support of Sarah?"

"What?" they asked in unison.

"I know it sounds crazy. But Rachel's dead now. I can't do anything to make her come back. But Sarah's still alive, and I don't want this thing to kill her. I have such mixed emotions about Sarah. She's like a helpless victim of circumstance. I don't know what I believe. I can't see my way clear of helping her. Look at it this way. She has nobody. The sight of her in that jail broke my heart into pieces. She trusts me. She never would have let Michael Clark take her case without me being there. She won't talk to him unless she knows that I'm there for her. If she thinks that I've abandoned her, I just know she'll die. I have this feeling about her. I care about Sarah, and that's the feeling."

Robert walked over to me and knelt beside my chair.

"Curie, don't make any hasty decisions. Why don't you just sleep on this? You're still in shock. You've just lost someone you cared a great deal about. You were a part of Rachel's life, in a bigger way than you even realize. You were closer to her than Suzanne. Think about it. Suzanne probably knows that, too. I never heard you say anything about Suzanne being at her mother's house when your group met. In fact, I've never heard you say anything about Suzanne at all. But I have heard you go on and on about what you and Rachel did, what you talked about. The closeness you two shared was special. And I'm sure she loved you, Curie."

"You're right," I whispered while tears streamed down my face. "Maybe I should try to get some sleep."

Robert stayed up all night, watching over me. As I tossed and turned, I was comforted when I saw him, sitting in bed, reading a book, being my friend.

Finally, I drifted into a deep sleep. I awoke to the smell of breakfast cooking. I walked downstairs and heard Robert and Diana moving about in the kitchen.

"Thank you, Robert. Thank you, Diana. I don't know what I'd do without you?"

"I do," said Diana. "You'd sit around listening to tapes of Rachel and the group all day, getting more depressed than you already are."

"Yea," said Robert. "I'm going to get you full, then get you out of the house today. If you don't want to do that, then I'll sit right here with you."

Diana left the kitchen and returned carrying a bunch of flowers.

"Diana, you're priceless. Thank you. Have some breakfast."

"That's why I'm here. I didn't want to eat by myself this morning. Let's eat," she said.

"Have you talked to your dad yet?" I hesitantly asked, as I took a plate from the cupboard.

"Yes, I talked to him while I was waiting for you yesterday. You were so out of it that I didn't bring it up."

What did he say, how does he feel about this?"

"I asked him if he wanted me to come over, but he said that he and mother were OK. He sounded devastated to me, though. I talked to him for about an hour."

"What did he say about Sarah?"

"He didn't say a whole lot about her. He said he wasn't surprised that something didn't happen sooner, with people coming and going from Rachel's the way they did. He did say that he wished that I hadn't talked him into being a part of the group. And in all honesty, Curie, I wished I hadn't, too. What you were doing was good, don't get me wrong, but I wish that I hadn't involved my father in all this. The police are questioning him today. He's none too happy about that, but he said that he would tell them whatever they wanted to know. You can imagine what this is doing to him, being high profile like he is. God, Curie, his name is being mentioned all over television as a member of your group. They make him sound like some kind of experiment. And to make matters even worse, they're referring to your group as a bunch of old people. They're not using those exact words, but that's what it sounds like."

"What my group sounds like is the least of my worries. Detective Folson down at the precinct said that my tapes might be subpoenaed. How do you think the group will feel about me once their private thoughts are played in a courtroom?"

"I don't see the need to play their comments. Curie, the only comments the lawyers will be interested in will be Sarah's. Don't you agree?"

I was happy that Diana had said that. She was right. Why would anyone have to play the things the others said? They wouldn't be relevant.

"Thanks Diana. I feel much better now. You're right. Who gives a damn about how often these people have sex? Well, I'm sure some news journalists would like to get their hands on that kind of stuff, but there's no need for it to be released. And I'll make damn sure that it isn't. I've got to call the others."

"Would you like some privacy?" asked Robert.

"No. You guys can stay."

I made a list of everyone in Nova's Arc, and pulled out my address book. I dialed Bradley's number.

"Hello," answered Rhonda.

"Hi, Rhonda. This is Curie. How are you?"

"Curie, this is a mess, isn't it?"

"Yes, Mrs. Johnson, it's just terrible. May I speak with Bradley? Is he home?"

"No, Bradley is at work right now. The police was here this morning, though. Asked Bradley a lot of questions about that woman who's been arrested."

"Yes, I see. Would you please tell Bradley that I called?"

"Sure will, Curie. You take care of yourself. It's a shame that poor woman got killed like that, isn't it?"

"Yes it is, Mrs. Johnson. It's a shame. Goodbye. I hope to see you and Bradley soon."

I had forgotten what day it was. I realized that Joe, Jonathan, Phyllis and Beatrice would probably be at work, too. I decided to not call them at work. I hoped that I could reach the others who wouldn't be working. I decided to call Judith.

"Hello, Judith, this is Curie."

"Curie, I'm so glad you called. I've been a total wreck ever since I heard the news. I got a call from a Detective Dumont. Said he wanted to talk to me. This makes me nervous, Curie. What do you think he'll ask me?"

"Just answer his questions, Judith. I don't know what he'll ask. I'm sure every question will be about Sarah, though?"

"I don't know too much about her, Curie."

"Well, tell them that, Judith. I'll call you in a few days to check on you. If you need me, please call me, Judith."

"I will. What about the group?" she asked.

"In light of what's happened, I don't think we'll be meeting again. But I will keep in touch."

"Goodbye, Curie."

"Goodbye, Judith."

I decided to wait and call the others later.

Meanwhile, Detectives Folson and Dumont were making the rounds, interviewing all the members of Nova's Arc. I refilled my coffee cup and looked at Robert and Diana, who were staring at me, like they were waiting for me to break down and go into hysterics.

"Robert, Diana, you don't have to stay here with me. I'll be OK. And Diana, I appreciate everything you've done. How about we all go out to dinner tonight?"

"I'll leave for work only if you're absolutely sure that's what you want," said Robert.

"That's what I want. Both of you, go on. Diana, we'll see you back here tonight at 6:00?"

"OK. See you at 6:00."

I was thankful for my good friend, Diana, and was grateful to her for being so protective and sensitive to my feelings. I felt guilt over involving her father in the group, in light of what had happened, but I was glad that Diana had not tried to make me feel responsible for the tragedy in any way.

I lulled around the house for a while, trying to sort out my thoughts, when the phone rang. It was Michael.

"Hi, Curie. A couple of detectives, accompanied by the district attorney, are swiftly making the rounds and conducting interviews with Nova's Arc. Sarah's being arraigned at 10:00 this morning. Will you meet me at the courthouse at about 9:00?

"Yes, I'll be there," I said while looking at the kitchen clock.

By the time I dressed and drove downtown, it was 9:30. Michael was anxiously pacing in front of the courthouse.

"I'm sorry," I shouted as I ran up to meet him.

"Come on, let's go," he yelled. I followed his swift steps into the courthouse.

The Judge, The Honorable Richard Parker, was a distinguished looking silver-haired man who appeared to be in his sixties. He peered over his glasses and looked at Sarah. My mind wandered from Sarah to Rachel and back again. When I snapped out of my daydream, I saw Sarah and Michael standing before the judge.

"Sarah Jenkins, you are charged with the murder of Rachel Maxwell. How do you plead?"

"Not guilty, your honor," said Michael.

"Then bail is set at $1 million dollars."

Michael jumped up.

"Your honor, Sarah Jenkins has no record. She's no threat to anyone, and she will be under the care of a licensed physician until the trial. $1 million dollars seems exorbitant, your honor."

The prosecutor immediately disagreed.

"Your honor, Miss Jenkins has been charged with the murder of Rachel Maxwell. I have reason to believe that she might attempt to harm Mrs. Maxwell's daughter, Suzanne Sullivan."

Judge Parker looked at Michael and Sarah.

"Your honor, there's nothing in my client's history to substantiate that supposition. My client has no motive to want to harm Miss Sullivan. That's an unfounded allegation."

"Counselor, we're not trying your client's case here. Bail is set for $1 million dollars."

Michael looked at Sarah apologetically for the judge's decision. "It's going to be alright, Sarah. I assure you, I'll do all I can to help you."

Judge Parker cleared his throat to interrupt Michael and Sarah.

"Trial is set for two months from today," said Judge Parker and pounded his gavel. The Bailiff walked over to Sarah. I walked up and stood near Michael.

"Actually, Curie," he whispered, "I didn't want Sarah to be released, at least not until she's been examined for mental capacity. I'll get our firm to choose a renown psychiatrist."

After Sarah was cuffed, she turned and looked at Michael.

"Don't worry Sarah," he said.

She continued her blank stare—looking right through us. Michael gave her a faint smile and looked away.

"It's OK, Curie?"

"What?"

"I said, it's OK. I know you want to cry right now, go ahead…cry."

As Sarah disappeared form the courtroom, Michael and I looked at each other with pity and sorrow for Sarah.

"Curie, it's imperative that Sarah be examined as soon as possible."

"Then we can get her released?"

"No, Curie. It's not easy to raise that kind of bail money?"

"Not for a fancy firm like yours?"

"Look. I'm kinda going out on a limb with this case. My firm is behind me 100%, but there's only so much I'm going to ask for right now. What about you and your fancy friends?"

"To be honest, I'd be afraid to ask. I haven't even spoken with all of them since the murder. Can you imagine me asking Suzanne if she will help me with Sarah's bail? Get real, Michael."

"I didn't mean Suzanne, Curie. What about that rich banker?"

"He's mad at me for involving him in this in the first place. Let's just leave it alone for now, OK?"

"Calm down. Sarah will receive the best of psychiatric care. Even if my firm would spring for the bail money, I'm not sure I'd want them to. Sarah needs help right now, not freedom."

"Michael, that doesn't make sense. To help her is to set her free."

"And now you're a writer and a psychiatrist?"

I ignored his question. I watched as the guards lead Sarah away.

"Michael, I'm afraid for her. Why do you think that bail was set at $1 million dollars? What does the judge think, that Sarah will rampage the city and start killing rich people?"

"Calm down, Curie, of course not. This is murder we're talking about. Sarah's going to be tried for first-degree murder, and she showed no emotions during this hearing. No need for us to argue about her bail. With the evidence stacked up against her the way it is I'm surprised that the judge didn't set bail at $5 million. The prosecuting attorney is Nicholas Robinson. And he's good. He was a trial lawyer before I was born. We used transcripts from his trials as case studies at Harvard. I never thought I'd be standing toe to toe with him."

"Michael, forget about Harvard and your ambitions for a minute. What about Sarah?"

"I resent that. I'm not talking ambitions, here. I'm telling you he's a damn good prosecutor, and with evidence like he has, what lies ahead of me won't be easy."

"You volunteered. And now you have me worried. Who will call me to testify? Will I be a witness for the prosecution or for the defense?"

"I've already prepared to subpoena you, Curie. I want you to be a witness for the defense, although you'll be fair game for the prosecutor, not to mention the press."

"I'm not afraid of the press, or the prosecutor. I'm just going to tell the truth. It's you who'll have to figure out a way to save Sarah, not me. I didn't kill anybody?" I said with a trace of guilt.

I knew that it was I who had brought the two women together. I felt responsible in that way, but I tried hard to convince myself that I had played no part in the tragedy.

"Have you been able to get Sarah to talk to you, Michael?" I asked. "What does she say about what happened that day?"

"I couldn't tell you if she had said something, and I certainly wouldn't tell you here. But she hasn't said a lot. I'm going to see her now."

"Bye Michael," I said, and watched him leave the courtroom. He looked even younger than he did the first day I met him. He looked so serious, though, and I was moved at the young, assertive attorney's zeal to help save Sarah.

Chapter Twelve

"Those were the Days"

The following morning, Michael met with Sarah to start planning his defense strategy. Because Sarah wouldn't talk to him, he was becoming very frustrated, but didn't want to ask me to act as a mediator for him. So far, I was the only person that Sarah would talk to. But Michael was determined to break Sarah's silence. He was certain that his instincts hadn't been wrong about the mentally blocked, fragile, accused murderer that he saw on television the night Rachel was murdered.

Sarah was brought in to see Michael.

"Sarah, I can't help you if you don't trust me, if you won't talk to me," he pleaded. "I want to hear you say—I must hear you tell me—that you did not commit this crime, or if you did, I need you to say that, too. Then, and only then, will I know what to fight for, your guilt by reason of insanity or your innocence, because you've committed no crime. Guilty or innocent, Sarah?"

Sarah's eyes narrowed, but she didn't speak.

Michael's temper flared, and he snatched his briefcase from the table and yelled for the guard to open the door. He swung around and pounded his fist on the table.

"Sarah, if you don't talk to me I'm going to enter a plea of guilty by reason of insanity, and that's that. That will be easy to prove."

"No," whispered Sarah.

"What did you say?" asked Michael.

"I said, no," she spoke louder. "I don't want you to tell everyone that I'm insane. I'm not insane."

Michael looked at Sarah like he had just found his long, lost mother.

"Good, Sarah. Those last two sentences will help to save your life. Now, will you talk to me and please tell me what happened on the night that the police found you with Rachel Maxwell?

The guard stepped in, the back out and closed the door. Michael searched Sarah's face, waiting for her to speak again.

"Not yet," she said. "Let me tell you something else first."

Sarah spoke slowly and softly.

"I want you to know who I am, not try to figure out what I did, or did not do, just yet."

"OK Sarah. Tell me who you are?"

"First of all, my name is not Sarah Jenkins, it's Sarah Boyington. But you already know that, I'm sure. I'm also certain that you already know that I was a patient at Serenity Hospital for the mentally disturbed, true?"

"Sarah, yes. I put an investigator on your case right after you gave the nod to let me represent you. You wouldn't talk to me, and I had to do whatever it took to represent you properly. The fact that you were institutionalized doesn't help your case, but it doesn't necessarily hurt it either."

"What else did your investigator tell you?"

"He told me that you were at one time engaged to Dr. Philip Davenport, Rachel's late husband. That's kinda like a nail in the coffin, Sarah. I need to know everything you can tell me about what happened."

"Did your investigator tell you why I was locked away at Serenity?" she faintly asked. She stared up at Michael—her eyes were clear and penetrating.

"Yes," he said you suffered some sort of breakdown over a breakup with the doctor. Well, the investigator said more than that, but that's the gist of it."

"That's not totally correct, Mr. Clark. I did not suffer some sort of breakdown, and it was not just a love affair."

"Then, why don't you tell me why you were there?"

"It is important for you to know that the end of a love affair is not the reason I was committed, although it was partly to blame."

"How so, Sarah?"

"I fell madly in love with, and was soon to be married to, Dr. Philip Davenport. I was a critical care nurse at Valley Hospital, and Philip was there all the time, taking care of his patients. He was an OB/GYN. A very handsome gynecologist. Over the years, we developed a special friendship, and we fell in love. Philip asked me to marry him, and I was so happy. Some of the other nurses were jealous, but most were happy for me. Philip was a real catch, and although I looked pretty good, some couldn't see what the dashing young doctor saw in me. Six months before our wedding date, Philip broke off our engagement. I was devastated—not just over Philip, thought. You see, he and I had been through something very personal and very traumatic together, and I thought our love would last forever. One night, just as my shift had ended, Philip took me into a stairwell and told me that he was in love with someone else, and that our wedding was off. I humiliated myself by running after him, screaming down the hospital corridor for him not to end us. But he kept walking, not looking at me, or acknowledging that I even existed. When I reached him, Philip was escorting some woman to his car. I ran up to the car, begging, pleading, but the woman just turned and looked at me, pitying me. Then they drove away. I went home and tried to take my life. The next thing I knew I was in Serenity Hospital. I didn't discover who the woman was, and I grew worse over time. Finally, after five years, they released me from the hospital. But I still had no will to live. I didn't leave my apartment, except occasionally to buy a few things. I never watched television, or read the newspapers. I became a recluse."

After listening to Sarah tell her painful story, Michael spoke.

"Sarah, why do you say you was not at Serenity because of a failed love relationship? It sounds that way to me."

"I was in Serenity because I had lost more than just my life. I lost something far more precious than Philip, and I lost my will to live."

"Was the woman who stole Philip away from you Rachel Maxwell?"

"Yes. But I didn't know that. At least not until the night before she was murdered. I would have never known it if I hadn't been a part of Nova's Arc. You see Rachel's last name was not Davenport. I only knew her as Rachel Maxwell. I never knew what the woman who married Philip looked like."

Sarah stopped talking and started tugging on strands of her hair.

"When did you realize that Rachel was the woman that Philip was seeing when he broke off your engagement?"

"I've been having the same nightmare, almost every night, since I left Serenity. In every dream, the blonde woman who turns and pities me is there, but her face is blurry. The night before Rachel was murdered, I was wide-awake, but something clicked with the little bird I found in her house. I saw my nightmare playing out right before me. But it was different because this time I saw her face, crystal clear. That's when I recognized that the woman was Rachel."

"And that's when you went to her house to confront her, and then you killed her in a jealous fit of anger?"

"No. No, I didn't kill Rachel," protested Sarah. "I don't even remember going there."

"Why are your blood drenched fingerprints all over the cracked brick that was used to bash in Rachel Maxwell's skull, the brick that had been pulled from the drive that leads to her gate?"

"I don't know."

"Why are your fingerprints all over her car, your prints in her blood?"

"I don't know."

"And what about the bird? Why was a statue of a bird, a bird from inside her house, found broken to pieces just outside her car door? Did you break it? How did you get it? Why were you at the murder scene? What were you doing there if you didn't go there to kill Rachel Maxwell?"

"I don't know."

"Why were your clothes soaked in blood, your hands cut up—cuts made from gripping and striking with the brick? And how did you cut your forearms on the broken glass from Rachel Maxwell's car window?"

"I don't know."

"Sarah, is it because you murdered Rachel Maxwell?"

Sarah had lost all memory of that day. She looked at Michael with a blank stare.

"Sarah, you've got to do better than that if you want me to prove that you didn't kill Rachel Maxwell. All the evidence proves that you did. If you say that you did kill Rachel, I'll change your plea to guilty, and plea bargain. Or, I'll fight for you as temporarily insane."

Michael calmed down when he saw that Sarah was crying.

"I want you to go back to your cell and think long and hard about that night, Sarah. Try to remember something, anything, so I can have a nibble. If you didn't kill this woman, then someone did. I want to make sure that you're not just imagining that you didn't."

Sarah didn't respond.

Michael took a deep breath.

"Sarah, I'll come back tomorrow. Get some rest now."

Michael reached for Sarah's hand, but stopped. Her bandaged cuts were wrapped up to her elbows. He squeezed her shoulder instead.

"Sarah, if you are innocent of this murder, we'll prove it together. How—I don't know."

Now, Michael was sounding like Sarah. He walked over to the window and called for the guard. He turned to look at Sarah, faintly smiled, and left the room.

Sarah was returned to her cell. She struggled with Michael's questions, but failed to place herself at the scene of the crime.

Meanwhile, Michael called his investigator, Gil Riley, to see if he had turned up anything new on Sarah. They made an appointment to meet at the Broad Street Cafe within the hour.

Gil, a retired police sergeant, was well known throughout the San Diego area as the best in the business. He was fast and accurate, and had an uncanny ability of finding out information that others would spend months researching.

Gil plodded into the cafe with an overstuffed manila folder tightly clutched underneath his arm. Dog-eared pieces of paper were trying to escape.

"That Sarah Jenkins, I mean Boyington, whatever, is a real nut case," he said as he slumped his 300 pound, over-sized frame into the booth where Michael had been waiting for over ten minutes.

"What do you mean by that?"

"The police ransacked her apartment, not that there was anything to ransack. But they did find a pieces of glass, something broken, in her trash, and there were pieces of glass in the corner of her living room. Oh, and I talked to some old nursing broads who used to work with Sarah. It took some looking, cause some of them don't even live here anymore. Out of a list of seven, three of them are dead, already. One lives in Florida, another in Memphis. Only two of them still live here in San Diego."

"What did they tell you about Sarah?"

"Hold on there. Don't get too anxious. I got it all here," he said, as he rummaged through the crammed manila folder.

"Tess Levitt. Attended the same nursing school as Sarah. Started working at Valley Hospital at the same time, too. Tess said that Sarah was the most talented and professional nurse on the floor. Tess knew the guy that Sarah was engaged to, Dr. Philip Davenport. Here's his picture, and here's a young version of Sarah," said Gil, as he tossed the two photographs across the table.

"Sarah was some looker, looks nothing like that now," remarked Michael as he studied the eyes of the girl in the photo. Her smiling face looked happy and carefree.

"I wonder what makes a person go insane?" Gil asked as if he was talking to himself. "Sarah seemed to have had a lot going for her. This one man made her lose it, it seems. Oh, and another thing I found out. Sarah may be living like a pitiful, dried up old bag, but look at this?"

Gil slid a piece of paper across the table. It was a copy of a bank statement.

$20,370,301.68 was the balance. The name on the account—Sarah Boyington.

"Holy Mother of Christ," exclaimed Michael.

"And that's nothing. Take a gander at this," said Gil as he tossed another sheet of paper in front of Michael.

Michael sipped a mouthful of tea, but spat out when he read what Gil had given him.

"Are you sure this is right? This is way over my head, Gil. Are you sure this is real? Is this right? I can't believe this!"

"Well, you better believe it, cause it's true. Tess confirmed it, and so did I. It all checked out, and that's how I got that paper."

"Make sure that nobody else finds this out. I don't want a soul to hear of this until the trial."

"You got it, Mac," said Gil, who had called Michael by that name ever since they met.

Gil met Michael when he joined Markoo, Hayde & Markoo, a prestigious law firm that occupied the entire 27th floor of the World Bank. Gil was Markoo's most talented investigator and was hired by the firm after he retired from the San Diego Police Department.

Gil's imposing 6'7" frame was intimidating, and his deep, vibrating voice added to his tremendously immense presence.

Michael was astonished at the information that Gil had just shared.

"How did you get this?" he asked?

"Can't tell you that. But I will tell you that I had to move heaven and earth."

"How you got it may be important to the case."

"Mac, I've been doing this a long time, and believe me, when the time is right, I'll tell you. Don't worry, my sources are reliable, and you don't have to worry about the prosecution getting their hands on this information to use it against you. There's no way I'm letting it out of my hands."

"I'll have to show the prosecution this, you know that?"

"No, I don't know that. Until this information is confirmed by one more sources, it's just hearsay. Get it?"

Gil closed the folder, tucked it underneath his arm, and slid from the booth. When he stood, the folder fell from his arm, and all the papers spilled to the floor.

The waitress, who was walking past the table, stepped right onto the scattered papers.

"Damn, get off that," he shouted.

Michael looked down at the gigantic investigator who was squatting on the floor, gathering up mounds of paper.

"That's right Gil. You take good care that nothing happens to those papers."

"Go to hell," he responded, and then scooped up the pile of papers, crammed them back into the folder, and walked out.

Michael left the cafe soon afterwards. During the drive back to his office, he agonized over how he would use the information that Gil had presented to him.

"This makes Sarah look even guiltier," he thought to himself.

Michael fought back his fears that he had bitten off more than he could chew. He stopped at the next street and made a sharp U-turn.

"Sarah's gotta answer for this one," he adamantly told himself, then headed for the San Diego jail.

As he reached the jail, his cell phone rang. It was Gil.

"Where are you, Mac?"

"I'm in front of the jail. I'm gonna confront Sarah."

"Before you do that, stay put. I'll meet you there in about 20 minutes."

"What?"

"Just what I said. Don't go in to see Sarah yet. One of my buddies on the force has something he wants to give me and I think you'll want to show it to Sarah."

Michael spent the next twenty minutes on his cell phone talking to his secretary. Gil pulled up beside him.

"Sorry you had to wait," said Gil as he jumped into Michael's car. "I thought you'd want to have a look at this first."

"What is it?"

Gil handed Michael a photograph.

"This was taken at Sarah's apartment."

"Like I asked, what is it?

"It's the head of the little robin, or should I say 'a' little robin. It's just like the one that was found near Rachel Maxwell's dead body. It seems that glass that was found in the trash was part of this little bird."

"How did it get in Sarah's apartment?"

"It so happens that Sarah had one of her own. Let's take a guess where both these ladies got these little birds?"

"Dr. Philip Davenport?"

"Bingo! That doctor must have been getting a discount on these birds, cause it looks like he gave Sarah one, then after he met Rachel, probably gave her one, too."

"Thanks, Gil. I can't wait to hear what Sarah has to say about this?"

Gil got out of Michael's car and back into his and sped away.

Michael looked at the picture of the little decapitated robin's head and headed in to see Sarah. She was eager to see him. She even looked like she was finally getting a little rest, but was still very thin.

"Sarah, how are you? Have you been eating?"

"I can't eat."

Michael wasn't sure how to begin questioning her. He took the picture of the bird out of his briefcase and placed it on the table.

"My robin," Sarah immediately claimed. "That's my robin. What happened to it? Who broke my robin?"

"It was found in your apartment, in your trash can, along with the rest of it, all in pieces."

Suddenly Sarah remembered the night she had smashed the little bird on her kitchen floor.

"Oh Lord. I broke the robin, didn't I?"

"I don't know Sarah. Did you?"

"Yes, I remember now. I had just come back from Rachel's. When I realized that Rachel was the woman I had been dreaming about all this time, I just went crazy, and I crashed it on the floor."

"How did you and Rachel both come to have this bird? And how did one end up broken near Rachel's dead body?"

"I took Rachel's bird. I took it from her house that day, I mean, that Sunday evening. I remember now. I took it home with me. I didn't want anyone else to have one like it. When I saw Rachel had one on her fireplace mantel, something in me told me to just take it, so I did. I put it in my purse when no one was looking, and I brought it home."

"And if you broke Rachel's, how did the other one end up broken near Rachel's body?"

I took it to Rachel's that day. I remember I took it to give to Rachel since I'd broken hers."

Michael leaned forward and turned on his recorder. He listened closely as Sarah told him the story of how her bird ended up at the crime scene. She told him about the night before the murder and the following day, the day of Rachel's murder.

"The group, Nova's Arc, took a break. I wandered into Rachel's living room, just to look around. I didn't think anyone in the group would want to talk to me, and I was afraid to go up to any of them, so I just kept to myself. I walked over to her fireplace mantle and spotted the little robin statue. I couldn't believe that I was seeing the exact bird that Philip had given to me. My heart was pounding so fast I couldn't think, so I just grabbed it, opened my purse, and dropped it in. I almost fainted sitting in the room, that glass room, after the group was called back after the break."

"Go on, Sarah," said Michael while nodding.

"Well, the group got tired of talking about death, that was our subject that day, so Rachel decided to give a cocktail party, on the spot like that. I was glad we ended the meeting early. I had to get out of there and think. I told Curie I didn't feel well, and left. That's when I got home and got to thinking. I guess seeing that bird jarred some memories for me, and the sounds and sights I'd seen and heard at Rachel's opened the floodgates. I could see her face as clear as I'm seeing yours. She was the woman who looked out of the car window at me and drove off with Philip."

"Sarah, what can you tell me about the following day, that Monday—the day that Rachel was murdered."

"I can't tell you anything about that day. I honestly don't remember a single thing about it, except going over there to return the statue."

Michael clicked off his recorder."

"Thank you Sarah. I have some appointments," he said as he checked his watch. "I'll be back tomorrow. I've made arrangements for you to be examined by a psychiatrist."

"You think I'm crazy, don't you. I didn't kill Rachel, don't you believe me?" asked Sarah, searching Michael's face.

"I have to, Sarah. That's all I have to go on."

Michael departed the jail and went to see Tess Levitt, who lived in Ocean Beach.

Tess told Michael that she and Sarah were once best friends and about Sarah's breakup with Dr. Davenport. After interviewing Tess, he went to see the other nurse, Lorraine Smith, who worked with Sarah at Valley Hospital.

Lorraine wasn't much help to Michael. She had recently suffered a stroke and found it difficult to speak. He thanked her and returned to his office.

He met with his paralegal, and they called the nurses who no longer lived in San Diego, Gloria Harrington in Memphis and Barbara Dunbar in Orlando.

Both women had heard of Sarah's arrest. They spoke freely with Michael about how they came to know her and of their days at Valley Hospital.

After spending hours on the phone, Michael was exhausted. Everyone else at the firm had gone home for the day. He shut off all the lights and did the same.

Chapter Thirteen

"On Pins and Needles"

The two months waiting for Sarah's trail seemed to go by in slow motion. I felt like I was waiting for an earthquake to happen. I knew that no matter where I stepped, I was sure I'd get damaged.

Michael had interviewed, and subpoenaed members of Nova's Arc. I was nervous about testifying and what the prosecuting attorney would ask. I wanted to do anything I could to help Sarah, but I didn't want everyone to know about the group and everyone's private lives. After all, they had agreed to talk with me only if they could remain anonymous, but that was now out of the question.

Phyllis, Clarise, Judith and Jonathan were subpoenaed as witnesses for the prosecution, and the rest of us were subpoenaed by Michael to testify for the defense. It didn't make any difference to us, as we all were prepared to tell the truth, no matter who asked us.

Michael and two other attorneys were hard at work putting together a defense strategy for Sarah. Since Michael was the chief attorney on Sarah's case, he assumed a gallant leadership role, and began hiring experts, constructing exhibits, and interviewing anyone that he felt could give him some information that would help Sarah's defense.

Gil had spent over a month looking over old records, tracing Sarah's life from birth to the present. He even checked into the backgrounds of Rachel and Dr. Davenport. If Sarah didn't kill Rachel, Gil hoped that he could find a link to someone that was involved with both Rachel and Philip Davenport. His instincts told him that there was much more to the story that just a scorned woman seeking revenge.

In putting the pieces of Sarah's life together, Gil discovered a huge gap where she was not living in San Diego. At first, he figured that she must have been on an extended vacation, but decided to probe the lead anyway.

"Why would a woman go on a vacation alone when she's engaged to be married in less than a year?" He wondered why Dr. Davenport had not accompanied her. "Where is the good doctor all this time? And this is *before* Philip met and married Rachel."

Gil was determined to discover answers that he hoped would provide the lead he needed.

Michael and I met at least twice a week before the trial. Since I had invited Sarah to become a part of the group, he warned me that I might be ridiculed for involving her.

On one occasion, while we were meeting in Micael's office, he showed me several news stories about Nova's Arc, and what people from around the country were saying about us.

"Michael, I don't read the newspapers anymore, and I don't want you to read it to me. I know what people are saying. Reporters are jumping all over me, others are trying to get me to appear on talk shows, to say all kinds of crazy stuff, and some will even pay me to do it. They're trying to imply that Nova's Arc was a group of perverted people, and I won't hear of it. Some are even accusing us of being a cult. This stupidity doesn't deserve my attention."

"Curie, it might help clear up some misconceptions about your intentions. This thing has turned into a rich versus poor circus. You've gotta remember, Rachel Maxwell was very wealthy, well known all over the world, and loved by a lot of people. On the other hand, you have Sarah, who nobody knows—who walks into Rachel's home one day. Bam. A few weeks later, Rachel is dead. Can't you see why people are getting up in arms over this? The whole nation is interested in this case. Whenever you involve older people in a scandal, every group in the world comes out in either support for or against what's happening."

"OK, tell me what's in the article, don't read it to me. Paraphrase."

"In a nutshell, there's a major senior citizen's group called "Helping the Elderly Live Peacefully, or HELP, that has stirred up all kinds of raucous, and they plan to march outside the courthouse in support of Sarah. They'll camp out there until this the trial is over. They claim you used her for your own selfish purposes, and that you took advantage of the people in Nova's Arc."

"To hell with them. I didn't take advantage of anyone. The only good thing about what you said is that they support Sarah. Let them. God knows she needs someone to support her."

"Well, they might be supporting Sarah, but according to this article, they're mighty upset with you for dragging Sarah into your group in the first place."

"I don't care about that. And I didn't drag Sarah anywhere; I kindly asked her. Sarah didn't do anything, remember? I'm not going to be made to feel guilty by a group of people I don't even know."

The HELP group had recruited young and old, alike, to rally for Sarah. The press wasted no time in broadcasting statements from HELP, about Nova's Arc, you, and me, and it was they who turned the trial into a rich versus poor fiasco.

I stopped listening to the news altogether, and only received information, second hand, from Michael.

Chapter Fourteen

"The Trial of Sarah Jenkins"

The night before the trial, I was a nervous wreck. All I could think of was the guilt I felt over forming the group in the first place. It didn't make me feel none the better by reminding myself that it had been Rachel's idea to have group interviews.

I felt so bad about how everything had turned out. What had started as a book filled with the wise advice of older people, letting the world know that life could still be adventurous and wonderful after 55, had turned into a nightmare. What I had done was gotten a lot of people mixed up in a horrific tragedy. Although I could do nothing to bring Rachel back, I prayed that everyone else would survive unscathed.

I tossed and turned all night, dreaming about Rachel and the group, talking about their lives in the semi-circle that we called Nova's Arc.

Rachel walked into my dream, as if she were still alive. She raised a glass of sparkling water and led a toast.

"May we live every day with a song in our heart, our friends by our side, and a long life filled with cheer and good thoughts."

When the group clinked their glasses together, Jonathan shouted "salute!" and I woke up.

I moved in fast motion to get ready for day one of Sarah's trial. When I arrived at the courthouse, I had to bully my way through the press, and hundreds of zealous Sarah supporters. People of all ages paraded in front of the courthouse with signs reading "SARAH'S THE VICTIM" and 'SAVE SARAH."

"You were just using her," an angry woman shouted at me as I walked up the courthouse steps.

I ignored her ranting, and the crowd got louder, some screaming ugly words of condemnation, others wanting to know if I believed Sarah was guilty.

I wanted to cry, but I wouldn't give the press the luxury of capturing me that way. I wanted to keep a brave face for Sarah, and a respectful one for Rachel. I had no idea how I would react when asked questions by either attorney.

Although Michael reviewed my testimony over and over with me, I blocked it all out, and wanted to get on with answering my questions truthfully and without bias for either view.

I froze when I saw the other members of Nova's Arc scattered throughout the courtroom. Clarise smiled at me, and I was able to breathe again. It occurred to me that Clarise and I had talked very little since Rachel's murder. I felt bad that I couldn't bring myself to face Rachel's best friend, and was eased by her comforting smile. I hoped she had forgiven me for my cowardice.

I looked at the lineup of jurors. They were a mix of people from all walks of life, just like Nova's Arc. There was a tall, African American woman who wore glasses. She looked very serious.

Another juror was a Hispanic man, seemingly in his late fifties. He appeared anxious and ready to get started.

A young, white blonde woman held a notebook in her hand. She had a string of pearls around her neck and wore an expensive blazer. I had no way of knowing for sure, but I guessed that she was wealthy.

I scanned the faces of them all, wondering which ones would identify with Sarah and which would rally for Rachel. I imagined them all to be Nova's Arc, debating in the deliberation room just like we used to do in the glass room. Either way, I knew that this jury had been hand picked by both attorneys, and I prayed that Michael's case would be strong enough so that they didn't have to rally for either side.

I wanted Sarah to be innocent, and while I watched Michael's young face as he talked with Sarah—like a good son and his mother, I felt confident that Michael would do his best to save her.

The Bailiff called the Court to order. After the honorable Judge Richard Parker entered the courtroom, all was quiet.

Within a few minutes, it was time for opening statements.

Prosecutor Nicholas Robinson, who everyone called Nick, stood and walked to the jury box. He looked at Sarah, the mixture of reporters, and a mixture of others from all walks of life who jammed the courtroom, and then he turned and faced the jury. He made eye contact with each juror individually, then began his opening statement.

"You won't miss a thing, will you?" He cleverly paused, as if waiting for a response from the jury.

"After all," he continued, "you have a collective 24 eyes and 24 ears that will be seeing and listening carefully to everything going on in this courtroom during the trail of The State of California vs. Sarah Jenkins. What you'll see and hear will be so apparent to you, but I don't want you to waste your precious eyesight looking only at the obvious, or listening to what will be as clear as a bell to you. As you sit through these proceedings, I want you to dig deep to find any little thing that might help you to understand the defendant," he said dramatically as he pointed directly at Sarah.

Sarah flinched as the jury followed Nicholas Robinson's long index finger directly to where she sat. I sensed that she could almost feel the touch of his fingertip in the center of her forehead.

The courtroom savvy prosecutor paused to give the jury time to stare at Sarah, and then he continued.

"Is this woman guilty, ladies and gentlemen? Did Sarah Jenkins kill Rachel Maxwell on December 3, 2001?" he calmly asked, then paused again and took a deep breath.

"Will the defendant be held accountable for the crime that the State of California is prepared to prove, beyond a shadow of doubt, that she killed Rachel Maxwell? I'm asking you now, because you will need to know the answers later, beyond a reasonable doubt, and I will lead you right to these answers. After going over every detail of this horrendous crime with you, you will review the overwhelming, damning evidence against Sarah Jenkins, and you won't be able to see or hear anything else, because that's all there is. Yes, the State will prove to you, beyond a reasonable doubt, that Sarah Jenkins, in a fit of explosive anger, went to Rachel Maxwell's house and bludgeoned her to death on that fateful morning of December 3, 2001. You'll see and hear how this woman crossed the line of human decency and into a world of wicked intent soon after she realized that Rachel Maxwell was the woman who had married Dr. Philip Davenport—the same man that Miss Jenkins was engaged to marry more than 30 years ago. But that engagement fell apart, and so did she."

Nick began to pace before the jury.

"This is a very sad, yes, but an all too common, tragedy. Sarah Jenkins may be getting on in her years, but the emotions of passion, jealousy, and love knows no age. Feelings don't scan the body for age; feelings don't consult a gauge to determine the proper age for experiencing certain emotions. Feelings are what you experience in your mind and through your body in the now— instantaneously. And the feelings of betrayal and hatred overwhelmed Sarah Jenkins, and revenge is what drove her to this vile and ghastly act of murder. Yes—feelings are what overwhelmed Sarah Jenkins, and the agony that she had endured for most of her adult life came crashing down upon her like boulders from the side of a La Jolla, California mountain."

He looked up at the ceiling, like he was seeing a mountain, then back at the jury, and continued.

"My first thought after analyzing this crime was that for Sarah Jenkins to commit this act, she had to devoid of any feelings whatsoever. After all, Rachel Maxwell had welcomed Miss Jenkins into her home, fed her, talked with her, and laughed with her. But how did the accused repay Rachel Maxwell's kindness? We'll prove that she stole an item from her home, and then stole Rachel Maxwell's life from her, that's how she repaid her, ladies and gentlemen, that's how she repaid Rachel Maxwell's kindness. She did it by fusing cold, calculated, revengeful thoughts about Rachel with her scorching, boiling emotions, that's why she did it. That's how she got herself so impassioned that she got in her car and sped over to confront Rachel on that fateful day—to seek revenge and put an end to her own suffering. She used Rachel Maxwell in the ultimate selfish act. She went to Mrs. Maxwell's estate to bury her own anguish, and made sure that

Rachel would be buried right along with it. That's what your collective twenty-four eyes will clearly see—and your twenty-four listening ears will hear—you will see Rachel Maxwell rising from her grave to tell you that Sarah Jenkins tried to escape from feelings of self-hatred by murdering her. That's why I want you to look closely, and listen with your soul so that you can see the face and hear the voice of the late, once vitally alive, Mrs. Maxwell—may we convict her murderer so that Mrs. Maxwell may rest in peace. She was a loving woman who trusted just a little too much. She trusted Sarah Jenkins then, and she trusts you now. I trust you, too, to do the right thing. Thank you all.

Chills ran up and down my spine as the wordsmith, Prosecutor Robinson, delivered his Opening Statement.

It was now time for Michael to deliver his Statement. He rose from his seat to face the jury. He looked at Sarah, and gave her a nod of compassion and confidence.

"Fear, anger, emotion…those are subjective words,"

stated Michael, as he looked to the jury.

"Not one of you can feel the same way as Sarah does, so those words are meaningless here. I closed the Psych 101 book on elusive terms when I decided to represent Miss Sarah Jenkins. Miss Jenkins did not kill Rachel Maxwell and the proofs will fail to show otherwise."

He took a step away from the jury box, and quickly spun around to face them.

"I believe that!" he shouted out, "and you will, too." Everyone in the courtroom waited in silence as the young looking attorney stepped-up even closer to the jury box.

"Before this trial is over, the State of California will owe Miss Jenkins a serious apology. The state will apologize to Miss Jenkins for the pain that she has already suffered and will endure during this entire nightmare. The death of Rachel Maxwell is indeed a tragedy, but the state has assumed that Sarah Jenkins is guilty because she has feelings! Of course she has feelings, don't you? I do! I have a deep well of feelings, for a lot of things. I get angry, I sometimes get depressed because of my feelings, and I scream because of my feelings. But my feelings for my client are not what will clear her name. The facts of this case will—listen to me. There is a twisted tale to be told, and I am anxious to tell it, so that my client can be exonerated and walk out of this courtroom to mourn the death of someone that she has told me she cared so deeply for. Sarah Jenkins admired and respected Rachel Maxwell. She's not a murderer. This is a woman who has lived with her sad past for many, many years, and not one time did she act out against another because of it. Both she and Rachel are victims here. Mrs. Maxwell was extremely kind, and so is Miss Jenkins. The defense has a long road ahead, and I am prepared to walk down that road until my feet bleed. I will walk up that road, and down that road, and I'll stop on the side of that road, because I'm going to be all over the place. The prosecution will fail to prove that Sarah Jenkins killed Rachel Maxwell. My client's not crazy, demented, or insane. If I thought that, I'd have delivered an insanity plea. My plea is 'not guilty' and 'not insane.' The facts of this case will shock you, so prepare yourselves."

Michael paced up and down before the jury, and then stopped to face them again.

"You'll be one hundred percent convinced that my client, Sarah Jenkins, did not commit this crime."

Michael had worked up a sweat. He stood in front of the jury for a few second more, then ended his Statement.

"Thank you ladies and gentlemen."

When Michael returned to his seat, cold chills didn't run up and down my spine, but I was certainly curious. I was anxious to know why Michael said the jury would know one hundred percent that Sarah had not killed Rachel. And although his opening statement hadn't stated anything to the contrary, I felt better about the outcome. I felt already that Sarah was innocent.

Judge Parker looked out into the courtroom. He gave the jury their instructions.

"Mr. Robinson, you may call your first witness," he said, and leaned back in his chair.

"Thank you your honor," said Nick. "I'd like to call Clarise Jorgensen to the stand."

Clarise was sworn in and took a seat in the witness chair.

"Would you please state your full name for the court?"

"Yes. Clarise Jorgensen."

"Thank you, Miss Jorgensen. Would you please tell the court how you met the defendant, Miss Jenkins?"

"Yes. I met Sarah Jenkins at Rachel's house. She was a part of a group that Rachel and Curie Nova formed for the purpose of writing a book."

"For the record, your honor, I'd like to inform the court that Curie Nova is a writer."

My heart sank as I listened to the prosecutor call out my name.

"So noted. Continue counselor," said Judge Parker.

"Now, Miss Jorgensen," said Nick. "How is it that people were chosen to be a part of this so-called group?"

"Curie selected everyone, except me. Rachel told me all about a project that she and Curie were working on, and asked if I would like to participate."

"And what was your response?"

"I told her, sure. It sounded like a fascinating project to me, and I also wanted to do it because it pleased Rachel."

"You wanted to please Rachel. What was the nature of your and Rachel's relationship?"

"She was my closest friend."

"I see. Are you friends with Sarah, too?"

"Yes. I mean, I liked Sarah."

"But were you friends with her?"

"I wouldn't say that. Sarah kept mostly to herself. I didn't talk to her very much, and she seldom spoke."

"Did you ever hear her make any disparaging comments about Rachel, or anyone else in the group?"

"No. Like I said, Sarah was quite shy and reserved. I'd even say, withdrawn."

"Let's move forward in time, Miss Jorgensen. On the day before Mrs. Maxwell was murdered, did you see Miss Jenkins?"

"Yes. We were all at Rachel's, the group that is, and Rachel decided to have an impromptu cocktail party. Everyone stayed for the party, except for Sarah?"

"Why didn't Sarah stay?"

"Because she said she didn't feel well."

"What was wrong with her?"

"Nothing that I could tell—she looked fine to me."

"I object, your honor," shouted out Michael. "The witness is speculating about the physical state of my client that day. Neither is she a physician, your honor, nor did she actually talk to my client before she left Mrs. Maxwell's."

"Sustained," said the judge. "The jury will ignore the last statement made by the witness."

"What was this project you spoke about?" asked Nick, switching the subject.

"The project was to interview a group of people, over age fifty five. The responses were recorded for the purpose of Curie and Rachel writing a book about aging."

"Was this a question and answer type setting?"

"Yes. Curie would pose a question, and everyone would take turns answering. After the first meeting, she started giving us the topic in advance of the upcoming meeting."

"I see. What was the first question that Miss Nova asked the group?"

"I believe it was whether we were still actively having sex?"

Everyone in the courtroom started whispering. I felt self-conscious, and I just knew the reporters would make me sound like some sort of perverted creep.

"That's seems rather intrusive to me?" continued Nick.

"Objection," shouted Michael again.

"Withdrawn your honor," Nick calmly said.

"The jury is so instructed. Omit Counselor Robinson's last comment."

"What was Sarah Jenkins' answer to that first question?"

"Objection, that's irrelevant, your Honor. That has nothing to do with this case," challenged Michael.

"Your honor, I'm trying to establish the behavior of Miss Jenkins in relation to the group, and the mental state she was in," explained Nick.

"Would you be more precise in your explanation?" Judge Parker ordered.

"Your honor, at this time I'd like to enter into evidence selective tape recordings of Curie Nova. You will hear Miss Jenkins' response to that and other questions. It will be obvious that she is distraught over, even after more than thirty years, over the breakup of her relationship with the late Dr. Philip Davenport. You will hear that in her mind, it was as if the breakup happened only yesterday."

"Do you have any objections, Mr. Clark?" asked the Judge.

"No, your honor." Michael knew that all the other members of Nova's Arc had already been questioned and had corroborated the contents of the tapes.

I wanted to yell out, "object Michael, object!"

"Show that four cassette tapes are marked and entered into evidence as one, two, three, and four," the judge instructed the court clerk.

Tape number one was placed into a portable recorder and played for the jury. It was pre-set to begin where I asked the first question.

"Is there anyone in the room who is no longer sexually active?" my taped voice rang out through the silent courtroom.

Then the tape was forwarded to where Sarah responded.

"I used to love sex. I stopped having sex after I lost my fiancé. He was so handsome, so kind, and so in love with me. We never got married though. I never found anyone quite like him, and I knew that I never would, so I didn't try to find a replacement. I live a pretty sheltered life now, so I don't meet very many men. Besides, the ones in my neighborhood hardly speak to me. Most of them look pretty dangerous anyway. But there are some nice ones, I'm sure. I do fantasize. I fantasize about me and my fiancé—the man I am still in love with, although he's dead now."

Nick stopped the recorder. Whispers filled the courtroom. Sarah's response to Curie's question drove a long spike into her case, sealing her guilt in the minds of many.

The jury looked intense. Her taped monotone voice lingered in the air like smoke from a smoldering fire. Sarah was looking real guilty, real fast.

Michael gave Sarah's hand a gentle squeeze to reassure her.

"Miss Jorgensen, is this what you remember to be Sarah Jenkins' response during your first group meeting?" asked Nick.

"Yes. That's Sarah."

"Did you hear her mention her former lover at any other time during your meetings?"

"Yes. I believe on one other occasion when we were discussing our hopes and dreams. Sarah made the statement that she missed her fiancé, and some other things about teenagers, that sort of stuff."

"She used the words, 'I miss my fiancé?'"

"Yes, that's what I remember."

Nick asked Clarise several other questions regarding Sarah and the group.

"I have no more questions, your honor," he said and returned to his table.

Michael was anxious to cross-examine Clarise. He stood before Nick could get back to his seat.

"I'm ready to cross-examine the witness, your honor."

"Proceed," said Judge Parker.

He began in a very relaxed manner.

"Miss Jorgensen, you said that you were Rachel's best friend?"

"Yes. We were very close."

"How long were the two of you friends?"

"For more than fourteen years."

"Then, would you kindly tell the jury if Rachel ever mentioned Sarah's name to you before you met her as a member of the group?"

"No, she never mentioned her before."

"Don't you think that if your best friend had married someone that was engaged to another woman, and the other woman fell apart over it, don't you think your best friend would share that with you?"

"Objection, Your Honor! The question calls for a conclusion."

"Sustained. Please rephrase your question, counselor," advised the judge.

"OK. Did Rachel Maxwell ever tell you that Sarah was once engaged to the man she married, Dr. Philip Davenport?"

"No."

"If you didn't know that, then how well did you really know the deceased?"

"Clarise stammered, attempting to answer Michael's question. Before she could answer, Michael moved on.

"That's all, Miss Jorgensen. No further questions, your honor?"

Nick returned to re-examine Clarise.

"Miss Jorgensen, did Rachel ever use the name Davenport during any of your meetings?"

"No."

"That's all, Miss Jorgensen."

Judge Parker excused Clarise, but informed her that she was still under oath and may be called again to testify.

Nick called Gertie as his next witness. As she was being sworn in, she answered in Spanish, and Judge Parker asked if she understood English.

"I speak pretty good English, your honor. It's just that when I get nervous, I forget a lot of it."

143

"We'll try not to make you too nervous, Miss Ortiz."

"Thank you, your honor," she said and took a seat in the witness chair.

Gertie's evidence was very damaging to Michael's case. She told of how she had discovered Sarah encircling Rachel's car, and then kneeling over Rachel's dead body, with the brick that had struck the fatal blows, still in her hand.

Michael cross-examined her, but wasn't able to make any headway. To prevent further damage, he politely asked her a few more questions, and then she was dismissed from the stand.

Michael was distressed over Gertie's testimony, but he didn't show it. He knew that the jury would be looking at him and Sarah, and he didn't want to show any weaknesses.

Judge Parker called a lunch recess, and everyone was dismissed for an hour.

When Michael came out of the courtroom, he saw Gil walking down the hall, and ran to catch up with him.

"Let's talk," he hurriedly told Gil.

"What's up?"

"The housekeeper, Gertie Ortiz, has me worried. Her testimony landed a strong blow against Sarah. Have you been able to make any headway in finding out anything I can use to dampen the fire she's started?"

"Not yet. This housekeeper is clean. She's a devout Catholic, and I can't find a thing that we can use to contradict anything she said."

"How do you know what she said? Were you in court this morning?"

"Yea, I keep a low profile."

Gil and Michael finished their lunch. Michael headed back to court, while Gil went out in search of leads to help Michael.

When the trial resumed, Nick called some other witnesses.

Jonathan, Phyllis and Judith had shared pretty much the same information as Clarise, and Michael didn't show it, but he was devastated by their elaboration of how Sarah never joined in break-time discussions, and how she was a loner who went on and on about the love she'd lost. And Michael could do nothing to shake them.

The Coroner was called to establish the cause of Rachel's death. He confirmed that a fatal blow to the head had killed Rachel. She had been struck twice, and he demonstrated by encircling his own head where the first blow had landed, but hadn't killed her. It was the second blow to the temple that caused Rachel's death. He took out charts and x-rays to illustrate for the jury.

The first day of testimony swiftly made its way into the newspapers, and all over television, and I was none too happy. The reporters made my group sound like some kind of stupid old people's cult. I wanted to rebut their stories, but didn't want to bring any more attention to the group than we were already receiving.

Beatrice was the only one who exploited the situation by openly speaking with newspaper and television reporters.

After the trail adjourned for the day, I talked briefly with Phyllis. When she told me that Beatrice had already accepted offers to appear on several talk shows, I was shocked. According to Phyllis, Beatrice bragged to all her friends how she was going to appear on The Oprah Winfrey show to talk about aging, and become a star.

It was obvious that Beatrice didn't feel the same way as I did about Rachel, but I wished that she would keep a low profile and not discuss anything that went on inside the glass room. I had signed a confidentiality agreement with the group, but Beatrice hadn't. The members had only signed releases for me to publish our interviews. It didn't matter anyway now. The whole world knew who the members of Nova's Arc were, and there was nothing that I could do to prevent the rumors that grew more bizarre with each passing day.

The trial seemed to go on forever.

Michael and Nick had been back and forth with forensic scientists, psychologists, and a host of other experts.

Nick called Suzanne to the witness stand.

Suzanne shifted her weight in the witness chair. Artists hired by the press, and other freelancers, were drawing her picture faster than I could write her name, which I had scribbled on a sheet of paper in my notepad.

I was keeping notes of pertinent statements made by each witness, and I wanted to make sure that I captured everything interesting that came out of the mouth of a woman that I had barely spoken to since the day we met. And she never helped me sell my Willi Geiger art.

I hadn't written very much of her testimony under Nick's examination. She had said what I expected, that she didn't feel comfortable with her mother having strangers in her home, and that she had warned Rachel that something might one day happen if she didn't stop associating with Nova's Arc. I had already predicted that she would reiterate her objections to the group.

When Nick asked Suzanne how she felt about Sarah before the murder, Suzanne said that she didn't know her at all, and that she had never met her.

"My mother used to talk about her," she told the court, "and she used to say that one day she would like to get to know her better. My mother was very fond of everyone in the group, and she trusted them all," she said as she glared at Sarah. "I told her not to get too friendly, but she had a stubborn streak in her."

"Were you aware that Sarah Jenkins had been a patient at Serenity Hospital, a hospital for the mentally disturbed?"

Michael sprang from his seat like a bolt of lightning had struck him.

"Objection," your honor.

"Over-ruled," the judge smugly said. "You may answer the question, Miss Sullivan."

145

"No, I didn't," she responded.

Nick ended his questioning for the day.

Michael cross-examined Suzanne. I flipped to a fresh sheet of paper in my notebook.

Before Michael could begin his questioning, the judge ordered an hour's recess for lunch.

I couldn't eat. I avoided the press, and sat at my car drinking only a soda for lunch.

When court resumed, Michael seemed eager to cross-examine Suzanne.

"How are you doing, Miss Sullivan?" he asked and smiled.

"I'm doing OK," she responded.

Michael stopped smiling and began his cross-examination.

"Tell me Miss Sullivan, did you tell your mother that you were worried about her trusting the group because some members were dirt poor?"

"No. That's not the reason. I just didn't think it was a good idea to welcome perfect strangers into your home the way she did."

"You told the court earlier that you had never met Sarah Jenkins, is that correct?"

"Yes, that's correct. I had heard about her from my mother and Clarise, but I never went over to my mother's on Sunday's because I knew the group was there, and I didn't really want to interfere."

"How would going to your mother's house be interference?"

"Because she, Curie Nova, wanted to interview people over 55. I don't meet the qualifications."

"Miss Sullivan, were Rachel and Dr. Philip Davenport your biological parents?"

"No, but as far as I was concerned, they were my real parents?"

"That's good. Have you ever checked to find out who are your real parents?"

"Objection, your honor. What does who Suzanne's parent's are have to do with this case?" interrupted Nick.

"I'll tell you, your honor. May I approach the bench?"

Michael and Nick walked to face Judge Parker. He whispered something to them, and the Judge looked over at Nick.

They went back and forth, and Nick ranted objections, none that I could hear.

Nick looked surprised, and I heard him protesting that he had not had a chance to review whatever Michael had discovered.

Then I faintly heard Michael say, "I just got this confirmed, your honor."

"I'll allow it," was all I heard the judge say before both men were excused from the bench.

"Objection over-ruled. You may continue, but let me warn you, I'll be listening carefully to see where you're going with this. If I hear anything out of line, I'll stop you."

146

"Thank you, your honor," said Michael, and continued questioning Suzanne.

"Now, Miss Sullivan. Would you like me to repeat the question?"

"Yes, please."

"Have you ever checked to find out who are your real parents?"

"No. I never thought about it. I had two wonderful parents. I had everything I could ever ask for, and more."

"How old were you when your father passed away?"

"I was five, but I remember him and I loved him."

"Most parents who adopt tell the child eventually who their real parents are, if they know. Did your parents ever talk to you about your biological parents?"

"Yes. My mother said that my real mom was a 16-year old girl who was too young to raise me, so she gave me up for adoption and Rachel and my dad adopted me. That's all she really said, and I never asked further."

"That's all, Miss Sullivan."

"Have you any further questions for this witness," Judge Parker asked Nick.

"No your honor, not at this time," he answered.

"Then you may be excused, Miss Sullivan. Please keep in mind that you are still under oath and may be called at any time to testify again."

"Yes, your honor," said Suzanne as she stepped from the witness stand.

"You may call your next witness," said the judge.

"The prosecution rests its case, your honor."

"Then counselor Clark, you may call your first witness."

Michael proudly stood to call his first witness.

I was called to testify, trying to remain as neutral as I could. I hoped that somehow I would be able to paint Sarah in a positive light. Somewhere deep within me I felt that Sarah was innocent, but I had nothing concrete to support my feelings.

The trial had been going on for three weeks, and I still wasn't sure of Sarah's innocence.

Michael's was gentle, and he asked me questions that painted a harmless, sad, and endearing picture of Sarah, not one of a murderer. But Nick was not so tender with his cross-examination.

"Miss Nova, do you make a living by prying into the lives of vulnerable old people?"

"No," I said. I wanted to say more, but kept quiet.

"Did you know that Sarah Jenkins was formerly engaged to Philip Davenport, Rachel's second husband, when you asked her to join the group?"

"No, I didn't."

"Did you know that the defendant had been institutionalized years ago?"

"Yes."

"Didn't you think that maybe it was not a good idea to have her exposed to others, being that she had had some emotional problems in the past?"

"I didn't see what her past had to do with anything?"

"Just answer the question, Miss Nova."

"No."

"If you had to do it over, would you exclude the defendant from your group?"

"No, I wouldn't."

My answers sounded damning of Rachel, and supportive of Sarah. I wanted to sound like I was in support of both women, but Nick made sure that I sounded biased towards Sarah.

"Your honor, I'd like to call Tess Levitt to the stand," Michael said once I was dismissed.

Everyone turned around to look at the mysterious, pale-skinned woman. I had never heard of her, and was anxious to hear why Michael was calling her to testify.

Sarah seemed to recognize her, though. She looked like she had seen a ghost, and wrung her hands as Tess was sworn in.

"Would you tell the court your name please?"

"Yes. My name is Tess Levitt."

"Thank you Miss Levitt. Do you know the defendant?"

"Yes, I do. I haven't seen her in ages, but that's Sarah Boyington."

"Her name is recorded by the state as Sarah Jenkins. How do you know her as Sarah Boyington?"

"Sarah and I go way back. We not only worked together as nurses at Valley Hospital, critical care nurses, but we were best friends."

"You were Sarah's best friend?"

"Yes. We did everything together, we roomed together. We were like sisters."

"When was that?"

"We were in nursing school when we met. We graduated and started working at the same hospital. We became so close, most people thought we *were* sisters."

"What kind of person would you say Sarah was back then?"

"She was so full of life. Such a funny, happy girl. Volunteered all the time, helping others, delivering lunches to people who were shut in on her days off, headed a lot of charity events that the hospital sponsored, and most everybody at the hospital liked her."

"Did you ever witness Sarah lose her temper and get violent?"

"Never. I used to get mad all the time, and rant and rave about this and that, but not Sarah. She'd calm me down, and tell me to let it go."

"I'd like to ask you about Sarah's former fiancé. Did you know the late Dr. Philip Davenport?"

"Yes."

"How did you know Dr. Davenport?"

"He was a doctor. He delivered babies and treated his patients at Valley hospital. He and Sarah were engaged to be married for over a year."

"But they never got married, did they?"

"No."

"Miss Levitt, did Sarah ever tell you anything about her breakup with Dr. Davenport?"

"Objection, your honor. That's hearsay," screamed Nick.

"Overruled," decreed Judge Parker. "The witness may answer the question."

"No. After the breakup, she didn't talk with anyone about it that I know of.

Michael thought for a moment before continuing.

"Before Sarah's breakup with Dr. Davenport, when they were still engaged to be married, did she leave town for an extended period. October 1965 to March 1966, to be exact?"

"Objection again, your honor. These are irrelevant questions?" protested Nick.

"Counselor, establish relevancy, or I'll have to sustain the objection," admonished the judge.

"Your honor, I'm establishing a connection between Sarah Jenkins and Philip Davenport prior to his marriage to Rachel Maxwell. It is relevant because the prosecution's main argument is that Miss Jenkins' insane jealousy over her former lover's marriage to the deceased caused her to have a mental breakdown. I'm establishing that Miss Jenkins was not out for revenge against Rachel Maxwell, and, at the same time, clarifying the reason for her stay at Serenity Hospital. Your honor, you'll see the relevancy. I have documents that I'll be submitting for entry into evidence to support it."

The judge ordered Nick and Michael to approach the bench. After a few minutes of discussion, I could see veins rising on Nick's temple. The judge allowed Michael to continue.

"Miss Levitt, where did Sarah go during that period, and why?"

Tess hesitated. She looked over at Sarah as if she was about to betray her with her testimony.

"She went to Philadelphia."

"Why did Sarah go to Philadelphia, Miss Levitt?"

"She went to have a baby."

The words tumbled out of her mouth, and the entire courtroom was on the edge of their seat, waiting to hear details from the pale stranger, Tess Levitt.

"Do you know what happened to Sarah's baby?"

"She gave the baby up for adoption."

"Do you know who was the father of Sarah's baby?"

"Yes. Sarah said it was Dr. Philip Davenport's baby."

"Objection. That's ludicrous, your honor," screamed Nick.

Michael met his challenge.

"Your honor, it's not ludicrous. I'd like to enter these documents into evidence."

"What are they?"

"Two birth certificates, your Honor."

The judge and Nick reviewed Michael's evidence.

"Any objection, Mr. Robinson?"

"No, your Honor," answered Nick, angry that he had not seen the documents prior to that day. He felt that the judge was favoring Michael, and that to accept the documents without a delay of case was unreasonable.

"The documents are received as exhibits numbers 23 and 24, and are to be so marked.

Michael walked over to Tess and handed to her the birth certificates.

"Miss Levitt, I hand you these exhibits. What do they show?"

"This one shows that a baby girl was born to Rebecca Anderson and father unknown, on March 3, 1966, in Cedars Sinai Hospital in Philadelphia, Pennsylvania, and that the baby was named Suzanne Anderson."

"Let the records show that the witness is reading from Exhibit #23," said the Judge.

"And the other record, Miss Levitt. What does the other record say?"

"That a baby girl was born to Sarah Boyington and Philip Davenport on March 3, 1966 at Cedar Sinai Hospital in Philadelphia, Pennsylvania, and that the baby was named Robin Boyington."

"Let the records show that the witness is referring to Exhibit #24," said Judge Parker.

"Miss Levitt, did Sarah Boyington ever tell you what happened to Baby Robin?"

"She gave the baby up for adoption."

"Objection, your honor," angrily shouted Nick. This woman cannot possibly know exactly what happened if she wasn't there. This is all hearsay and speculation."

"Your honor, I've already established that these two women were like sisters, and shared everything long ago. These records, the ones I entered into evidence, Your Honor, can substantiate this witnesses testimony."

"You may proceed, counselor. Objection overruled."

"Thank you Your Honor. Now, Miss Levitt, what happened to Baby Robin?"

Tess looked at Sarah, and back at Michael. "Baby Robin is now..." Tess hesitated. "Baby Robin is now Suzanne Sullivan."

"What?" came several voices from all directions in the courtroom.

"And how do you know this?" asked Michael, his voice steady and firm.

"After Sarah's breakdown, I hired an investigator to find the baby. Sarah was like my sister, you see. It was so painful for me to just do nothing."

"Did Sarah know this, that Robin was presented to Mrs. Maxwell as the child of a poor 16-year old?"

"No. I visited Sarah at Serenity, and she was so far gone I knew the news would just kill her, on the spot. I'm sorry, Sarah!" Tess was sobbing loudly, and Judge Parker declared a recess.

Michael later revealed that Suzanne Sullivan's birth certificate, the one she had used all her life, was a fraud. Michael provided a legal, certified copy, showing that the baby girl named Robin was born to Sarah Boyington and Philip Davenport on March 3, 1966, in Philadelphia. The second record, that was proven to be fraudulent, was a copy of the certificate that Dr. Davenport secured, listing the baby girl as Suzanne Anderson, born to the 16 year old Rebecca Anderson.

The babies listed on both documents were one in the same, and the child adopted by Dr. Philip Davenport and Rachel Maxwell. Dr. Davenport had adopted his own baby girl, and had kept it a secret from Sarah, who at the time, was locked away in a mental institution.

Pandemonium broke out in the courtroom. Everyone was flabbergasted over Michael's bombshell—that Suzanne Sullivan was the daughter of Sarah Jenkins."

Suzanne gasped and fainted. The courtroom fell apart. Sarah wept loudly.

Reporters sprang from the courtroom to call their newsrooms. People talked loudly to one another, in shock over the startling revelation that the wealthy Suzanne Sullivan was the daughter of the woman who had been accused of murdering her adoptive mother.

The judge pounded his gavel, demanding order. When the crowd continued to rant, he ordered a recess, and cleared the courtroom.

The paramedics were dispatched for Suzanne, who had yet to be revived.

I was beyond shock. I was so confused. Although I had heard everything, it was still unbelievable to me that Sarah was Suzanne's mother. "Had Sarah known this before today?" I asked myself. She looked upset, but not surprised when Michael exploded the room with his revelation. I wondered why Sarah hadn't fainted, too.

Later, I learned that Michael had already told Sarah the astonishing news about the birth certificates, and about Suzanne being her baby, Robin. I also learned that when Michael first told her, she was admitted to the hospital, and refused to accept the news, saying that she wanted to die.

I couldn't wait to hear the rest of this amazing story.

The judge postponed the trial for two hours, and everyone outside the courtroom was in a state of panic. Many shouted words of ridicule at Michael for what they described as underhanded and cruel tactics.

"Why didn't he tell Suzanne before now?" I asked myself. Even I felt that it was cruel to spring such a shocking revelation on her that way. "What kind of man is Michael?" I began to wonder. "Would he stoop to any level just to win his case?"

When court resumed the courtroom was packed to capacity.

Judge Parker began by admonishing to crowd. "I will not tolerate any further outbursts in my courtroom. I will clear this room and have a closed trial if I have to, but everyone will respect these proceedings or be excused."

Tess was back in the witness chair. Michael stood ready with other documents in hand. We all waited on pins and needles, barely breathing, to see what other cards Michael was holding. The courtroom was deathly quiet.

"Miss Levitt, I'd like to ask you if you knew Miss Jenkins to be a poor woman, having little money."

"Sarah had plenty of money. Her father was quite wealthy."

Gasps and whispers were heard throughout the courtroom, but everyone bit their tongue so Judge Parker wouldn't have them tossed out of the courtroom.

"Did you know the defendant's father?"

"Yes. I spent a lot of time with Sarah and her family. Her father was like a father to me—very kind and very wealthy. He left all his money to Sarah when he died. Her mother had died several years earlier."

"I'd like to enter these documents into evidence. They will show that Sarah Jenkins is worth more than $20 million, and had no motive to be jealous of Mrs. Maxwell's wealth."

The crowd mumbled, but they did not yell out. Everyone's thoughts merged like one collective body—the thought that we had been had by a wealthy heiress pretending to be a pitiful pauper.

I wanted to yell the loudest, because Sarah was living like a vagabond, in that little dingy apartment in National City. All along she had more than $20 million. I didn't know what to think. I was more confused than ever about the woman I thought I knew and grew intensely angry just thinking about her pitiful act the day I met her.

Replays of that day swirled around in my head—her driving a broken down piece of junk for a car, when all along she had enough money to buy any car she wanted, a whole dealership, even.

Tess answered more of Michael's questions. Every time she spoke I expected a shocker, but I guess Michael had exposed all his bombshells for the day.

When I moved beyond my anger at Sarah, I realized how impressed I was at the way Michael was handling Sarah's trial, although I still didn't like the way he had traumatized Suzanne or the way I had been duped by the wealthy Lady Sarah.

The press was treating the trial like a soap opera. With all the excitement, the fact that my friend Rachel had been murdered was fading into the background, and Sarah's secret life had gained top billing. Even I was anxiously awaiting young Michael's next explosive blow. But I would have to wait. Court was adjourned for the day.

That evening, I couldn't wait to read the paper and watch the news. The mystery surrounding Sarah and Suzanne mystified me, and the press unraveled it even more.

According to the San Diego Times, Dr. Davenport had convinced Sarah to give up their baby up for adoption. She took a leave of absence from the hospital and went to Philadelphia to have the baby so as not to cause embarrassment for Dr. Davenport. It was reported that Sarah pleaded to keep the baby, and had even named the baby Robin, but Philip Davenport had her such power over her the she gave up her baby.

The media had a field's day. Award-winning journalists kept straight faces as they told the story of how Philip had fallen in love with Rachel, and before Robin's adoption was final, had gone back to the adoption agency and adopted his own child. All the while, Sarah was locked away at Serenity.

Despite the serious and impartial look on the face of a female news reporter, her voice blared through my television speakers with a distinct hint of "cold-blooded, insensitive bastard," in her voice for the late Dr. Davenport.

On another network, a male reporter told of how when Philip and Rachel met, Rachel was in the hospital having a hysterectomy and couldn't have any children. So Philip adopted Robin, after putting together, and paying for, a duplicate set of records, because Rachel wanted so to have a child of her own.

"Liar," I screamed at the television. I remembered Rachel telling me that she wasn't ready for a child when they adopted Suzanne, and that Philip had convinced her to adopt Suzanne.

"Philip gave his, and Sarah's baby, to Rachel Maxwell," blasted the voice of another reporter. I switched the channel, and there was another reporter giving his station's rendition of Sarah's trial.

"Sarah Jenkins, who is on trial for the murder of the wealthy socialite Rachel Maxwell, and the mother of Suzanne Sullivan, the victim's adopted daughter, didn't know anything of the adoption. According to statements made earlier today by one of the defense's key witnesses, Tess Levitt, Sarah Boyington had no idea of who adopted her child. Shortly after her breakup with the wealthy Dr. Davenport, she was admitted to Serenity Mental Hospital. It was revealed during questioning today that Dr. Philip Davenport had kept the actual adoption a secret from Miss Boyington, and obviously, he took that secret to his grave."

I switched off my television, but then turned it back on. I didn't want to hear the sensationalism, but needed to hear more of what the reporters were saying about Sarah.

"According to acquaintances of Suzanne Sullivan, neither Suzanne, nor her mother Rachel Maxwell, knew that Suzanne was Philip Davenport's biological daughter. In confirmed stories, we discovered that Philip Davenport told Rachel Maxwell that the little girl he called Suzanne was the daughter of a 16-year old who couldn't afford to raise the child."

I switched off the television again. But within seconds I had turned it back on. I couldn't resist hearing more about the shocking news of Sarah and Suzanne.

A network news reporter was discussing the trial with a notable psychologist.

The reported crossed his legs and leaned towards the psychologist. "When Sarah Jenkins left the hospital after having her baby, Dr. Davenport gave her a little porcelain robin, the robin that was found shattered at the scene of Rachel Maxwell's murder. He had also given an identical statue to Rachel, and it has been speculated that he gave her the porcelain robin so that he could always remember that Suzanne was really 'the little robin.' What do you make of that?"

The psychologist thought for a moment. "Well, obviously, Philip Davenport was a man suffering from immense guilt and shame."

"Shut up, you freaking hooligan," I screamed. "You don't know a damn thing about Philip Davenport." I switched the channel again. I listened to another psychologist on a talk show giving his opinion of Sarah's condition. I only listened to him because he reminded me of Andy.

"Sarah Boyington did not suffer a breakdown wholly because of her breakup with Dr. Davenport when he broke off their engagement to be with another woman. She was devastated, yes, but it was the fact that not only had she lost Philip, but also had given up her child because he asked her to. That is probably what sent her over the edge. Those two things combined caused Sarah to fall into a deep depression from which she found it almost impossible to deal with. She didn't care about her money; she didn't care about her life. She had spent the past 30 years living in a world of guilt and shame over allowing Philip to convince her to give up her baby. She never forgave herself for abandoning Robin."

I finally switched off my television for good.

I had no proof, but I presumed that Michael's firm had leaked most of the information about Sarah to the press.

Suzanne was devastated. She was receiving around-the-clock care after Michael had let the nation know that she was the daughter of a rich vagabond who was on trial for killing the only mother she had ever known.

The press was stationed outside Suzanne's house night and day, waiting for the moment that she would emerge. She had a nurse posted at her bedroom door, and wouldn't talk to anyone.

Michael felt bad about Suzanne's condition, but he needed the jolt that Suzanne's true identity had created. He was ready to continue with the trial, and the next day proved to be just as shocking as the previous one.

The next morning the judge called Michael and Nick into his chambers.

"Look counselor," he admonished Michael.

"I will not have cheap theatrics in my courtroom. I knew that you would be presenting the birth certificates as evidence, but I didn't know that you would incite a riot by overplaying your hand, and shocking even your own client with your startling news."

"Your honor, with all due respect, I had already told my client about the fraudulent birth certificate."

"Don't play stupid with me, Mr. Clark. You may have told your client about the two birth certificates, but I'm sure you didn't tell her you were going to send her newly discovered daughter into a state of emotional chaos. The next time you have information that sensitive, or should I say, explosive, have more humanity. Discuss it with the people involved, if at all possible, before you proceed. Do I make myself clear?"

"Yes, your honor. But I did tell you, and I did what I had to do. I'm sorry about the harm the news may have caused Suzanne Sullivan, but she's not fighting for her life, Sarah Jenkins is," argued Michael as he grabbed his brief case, anxious to start the day's proceedings.

Court convened. Judge Parker spoke with the jury about the scene that Michael had created the day before, and let them know that they could expect the proceedings to be less theatrical from now on.

"That's what you think," Michael thought to himself as the judge talked.

Michael called his first witness of the day. It appears that the day of Rachel's murder, a gardener named Hector Jiminez had noticed that Rachel was standing outside her gate, looking at her car.

Hector was sworn in, and spelled his name for the court reporter.

"Mr. Jiminez, would you please tell the court what you remember going back to December 3, 2001. Tell the court what you observed as you entered the neighborhood where Rachel Maxwell's estate is located?

"Yes. It's easy for me to remember because I was headed to Mr. Carlton's home. His is the house just before you get to Mrs. Maxwell's. Her house sits at the top of the hill. I was in my truck, and I was talking on my cell phone to Mr. Carlton. When I got near Mr. Carlton's, I noticed a beautiful Jaguar, the car that Mrs. Maxwell drove, parked just inside her gate. You can barely see up to her place, and I could barely see a little of the car through the thick brush. I really didn't think much of it. I reached Mr. Carlton's a few minutes before 10:00. I know this because I had to be at Mr. Carlton's at 10:00, and I'm always on time, or early. But at any rate, I walked out of my truck, and Mr. Carlton was there waiting at his gate for me. I remember teasing him that I wanted to meet that lovely, rich neighbor of his. He didn't say anything really. But I said, "I'd like to drive that jag."

"And what else did you see on your way to Mr. Carlton's?"

"Like I told the police, I saw this old Chevy, looked like an Impala, come down the road, real slow at first, then by the time I almost reached Mr. Carlton's, it sped up, and hauled ass. I'm sorry, I probably shouldn't say ass."

"What color was this car, and did you get a look at the driver, or see any other passengers?"

"It was a brown four-door Impala, and it had this funky primer door on the driver's side. I didn't get a good look at the driver because I was still in my truck, and I wasn't really paying attention to the driver. I was just looking at that funky door."

"Thank you Mr. Jiminez. That's all for now."

Hector looked around the courtroom, waiting for the prosecutor to approach the witness stand.

Nick walked up and began his cross-examination.

"Mr. Jiminez. Would you please explain to the court what you mean by primer, in case the jury is not familiar with that term?"

"Yes. Primer is when the metal is cleaned and a primer, or sealer, is applied to the metal to seal it just before the paint is applied."

"Thank you, Mr. Jiminez. Now, you said that you saw a portion of Mrs. Maxwell's silver Jaguar through the brush as you were in the area of her home on December 3rd. How did you know it was Mrs. Maxwell's car?"

"I have been Mr. Carlton's gardener for over two years. I see Mrs. Maxwell driving that beautiful silver Jaguar all the time. It was Mr. Carlton who told me who she was when I asked some time ago. She was a very friendly woman; she waived at me once when I was leaving Mr. Carlton's property. When I first started working for Mr. Carlton, she drove a Cadillac. Then she bought that Jaguar, I guess, because I didn't see the Caddy no more."

"That's all for now."

Hector waited before leaving the witness stand. He didn't know if he should just get up or wait for the judge to dismiss him.

"Counselor Clark, would you like to reexamine your witness?"

"Yes, your honor. I have one more question to ask Mr. Jiminez," responded Michael. "But first, I'd like to enter this telephone record into evidence."

"What is it counselor?"

"Your honor, this is the telephone record of Mr. Jiminez' cellular telephone. It will substantiate the precise time that he called, and ended his call, to Mr. Carlton."

Any objection, Mr. Robinson?" asked Judge Parker.

"No, your Honor."

"This document is received as exhibit #25."

Michael continued.

"You'll see that Mr. Jiminez placed a call to Steve Carlton's residence at exactly 9:51 a.m. on December 3, 2001 and that he terminated that call at 9:55 a.m. That substantiates what Mr. Jiminez said about the time that he saw Rachel Maxwell's car, and that he was at Steve Carlton's before 10:00 a.m."

Mr. Jiminez' telephone records were accepted and entered into evidence. Michael approached Hector with record in hand.

"Mr. Jiminez, is this your telephone record?"

Hector took the papers from Michael and looked them over briefly.

"Yes sir. That's my bill. It's expensive to have a cell phone."

"That's all. Thank you."

The judge dismissed Hector. Michael called Steve Carlton to the stand, and he substantiated everything that Hector had testified to.

Nick declined to question Mr. Carlton.

Chapter Fifteen

"Thou Shalt Not Kill"

Michael examined witnesses, Nick cross-examined those witnesses. The trial had been going on for over two months.

Time was closing in, and Michael felt that he would need a miracle if he were to save Sarah. Hector Jiminez' testimony didn't have the impact he had hoped for. He suspected that he had failed to tie the brown car in with the crime. Landscapers and other workers often traveled the private roads to and from the estates. The miracle he needed was to find the driver of the car. So far, Hector was the only witness who testified to actually having seen it.

Michael didn't want to rely on expert's testimony of tire tracks, and other forensic evidence. Nick had made the experts' testimony seem insubstantial, and had made the mysterious brown car seem inconsequential, and repeatedly reminded the jury of Sarah holding the bloody murder brick. Nick had wove a compelling argument, tying in Sarah's motive with the subtle thought that perhaps she did already knew that Suzanne was her daughter. Although his innuendos were over-ruled by the Judge, in the back of my mind even I suspected that Sarah may have completely lost it if she knew that Rachel not only had her man, but her child, too.

Nick said that no matter who was driving down that stretch of road, it was Sarah who was at the murder scene.

Michael wanted something more—another shocker. The idea of putting Sarah on the stand crossed his mind, but he immediately dismissed it.

After court was adjourned for the day, he headed home, exhausted after a long day and distressing day.

Michael couldn't get Sarah's face out of his mind. He knew that if he put her on the stand to testify, Nick Robinson would make mincemeat of her.

I saw Clarise as I stepped out of the courtroom. She waived at me, and I walked over to her.

"I read the cards. Sarah is innocent," whispered Clarise. "Michael knows it, too. That's why he said he'd prove one hundred percent that Sarah didn't kill Rachel."

"What are you talking about Clarise?" I whispered back.

"I'm talking about the fact that Sarah did not kill Rachel."

"I hope so, Clarise. But I think it's going to take a miracle. Nick seems to have convinced the press, and more than likely the jury, that Sarah is guilty."

"Miracles do happen," she said. "I have to go now, but I'll see you here tomorrow."

I watched Clarise as she walked away. It was four in the afternoon, and I decided to go home and get some rest so that I'd be mentally ready to hear the closing arguments.

I spotted Michael's car leaving the courthouse. He, too, looked tired, and frustrated. As he drove away, I wondered what he was going to say the next day that would inspire the jury to proclaim Sarah innocent.

His cell phone rang as he pulled off the interstate exit to his neighborhood. It was Gil.

"Meet me at the Cafe."

"Why?"

"Just do it."

Michael got on the freeway and headed downtown. When he got there, Gil was sitting in Michael's favorite booth.

"Sit down and take a look," Gil ordered as Michael approached him.

Gil pulled out a photograph of a group of Sarah supporters outside the courthouse.

"And?" Michael asked.

"Look at the woman over to the left of the one holding the 'Free Sarah' sign. Look at what she's got around her neck. Here's a blow up of that woman," he said, as he tossed another photograph at Michael.

"She's wearing a necklace."

"Bingo."

"And?"

"And this, counselor. A few weeks after Rachel Maxwell was murdered, Suzanne Sullivan called that housekeeper, Gertie, to meet her at Rachel's. She wanted to go through some of Rachel's things. When she got there, she asked Gertie about her mother's favorite necklace. It appears old Gertie forgot the fact that Rachel was wearing that necklace the day she was murdered. Suzanne called Detective Folson, who in turned called District Attorney Robinson. Suzanne had some pictures of her mother wearing the necklace sent downtown. Now, you know I have more contacts downtown than the mayor does, so I got copies of those picture, too. As soon as I got the pictures, I started combing the city, talking to everybody I thought could lead me to this necklace. I figured if Sarah didn't have it on her the day the police arrested her, then it had to be somewhere. I had to talk to a lot of people, and the last woman I talked to gave me the answers I needed."

"Who was this woman?"

"Her name is Beth Cunningham. She lives across the hall from Sarah's apartment. I showed her the pictures, and as unbelievable as it sounds, she recognized the necklace."

"Keep going. Where had she seen it?"

"Miss Cunningham has been following this trial like a woman possessed. She likes Sarah, even though Sarah hardly spoke a word to her. Said she felt sorry for her. She also said that she didn't believe for a second that Sarah killed Rachel. Told me she saw the necklace on CNN last night, on one of the Sarah's supporters outside the courthouse. And get this; she has seen the woman before. She said that's how she remembers seeing the necklace. When she spotted this woman on television, she thought that it looked odd for a woman Beth called a down and out drug addict to be wearing such an expensive looking necklace."

"How did Beth know this woman was a down and out drug addict?"

"She said she knows a little about the woman, remember?"

"How did you get these pictures of her?"

"I called up an old buddy of mine who works for CNN and had him comb the footage from last night until he found her."

"You didn't tell your buddy why, did you?"

"Hell no. I'm not stupid. I got these e-mailed to me. The cops don't even know about this…yet"

"This is the miracle I've been looking for. Now what do we do?"

"Well, Beth didn't know the woman's name, she just said she knew of her— saw her hanging around the complex with some scary looking characters, all drugged out. All I have to do is find this woman, and find out how she got her hands on Rachel's necklace. Then you'll find your killer."

Just then, Gil's cell phone rang. He clicked it off after listening to the caller for about thirty seconds.

"I've gotta go. Miss Cunningham has already spoken with the D.A. about this. They have the same pictures you're looking at. They're looking for the woman wearing the necklace. But ask me where I'm going?"

"Where you going, Gil?"

"I think we may have found your mystery woman. I'm going to check it out before the cops get to her."

Gil had pulled his large body from the booth and walked out of the door before Michael could ask another question. Michael immediately called Judge Parker.

I had gone home and fallen asleep on my sofa after leaving the courthouse. The seven-week trial had taken its toll on me, and I was drained physically and emotionally. I was awakened by the sound of my telephone. It was Michael.

"Curie, meet me at the Broad Street Cafe right now," he demanded.

"What?"

"Get in your car and meet me at the cafe. I'll explain when you get here."

"Michael is everything all right. Is it Sarah?"

"I have to tell you something, and I don't want to do it over the phone."

"OK, I said," and went to splash my face with water. I grabbed my purse and ran out of the house without locking the door. I sped all the way downtown, praying that I wouldn't be pulled over by the police for speeding.

When I walked into the cafe, Michael walked up and led me back to his booth.

"Sit down, Curie," he said, and then opened his briefcase. He pulled out a manila envelope and shoved a picture in front of me.

"What?" I asked.

"What do you see?"

"I see a picture of some people in front of the courthouse."

"I want you to take a look at this woman," he said while putting his index finger on the face of a woman in a white shirt.

"OK," I said, still confused as to what I was supposed to be looking for.

"Look at the necklace she's wearing."

"Oh my God, that's Rachel's necklace."

"That's exactly what I hoped you would say. You've seen that necklace before?"

"Yes. Several times. It was Rachel's favorite. Who is this woman? Where did you get this picture? Why is she wearing Rachel's necklace?"

"That's what we're gonna find out."

"Does this mean you'll have to postpone the closing arguments tomorrow?"

"I called Judge Parker. He said unless we can find this woman and the necklace, before 9:00 A.M. tomorrow, he's not interrupting the proceedings, and the closing arguments begin as scheduled."

"But you don't have enough time to find her before 9:00 tomorrow—do you?"

"Yes—plenty of time. I think Gil's already found her. I hope it's her, because unless Gil finds this woman, and Rachel's necklace, the judge won't budge."

"What do you want me to do?"

"You're going to the jail to see Sarah with me. After I talk to Sarah, I want you to go with me to my office."

"And do what?"

"Curie, you're going to help me re-write my closing argument?"

"What?" I looked at Michael as if he was losing his mind. "Why would you need me to help you? I'm no attorney. Shouldn't you ask the lawyers at your firm to help you?"

"No. I want you to do it. Look Curie," he said as he placed the photographs back into the envelope. "If Gil doesn't find this woman, Nick Robinson is going to hammer the evidence into the jury so hard that even I don't think that I can pull them back to thinking Sarah is innocent. The judge won't budge, because he says that even if we do find this mystery woman, we have no proof that she

161

didn't get the necklace from Sarah. He said that Gertie could have her dates mixed up. He's not going to put tomorrow's closings on hold and re-call witnesses. Sure Suzanne could verify her mother's necklace, so could you and Gertie. But he said that this crucial evidence is not crucial based on the ramblings of the housekeeper, who may have her dates mixed up."

"Michael I still don't understand why you want me to help you?"

"Curie, I need that jury to feel Sarah's innocence, not just hear about it. They're going to be listening to Nick, who by the way is the best prosecutor in all of California as far as I'm concerned, deliver a blow by blow string of damning words to the jury. The facts are stacked in his favor, and you know that. I can't overcome the state's evidence. Even after I revealed the truth about Suzanne, and the fact that Sarah's not some impoverished vagabond, I don't think I'm getting to them. In fact, I think it may have hurt her case. I need my statement to be prepared by a dramatic writer who knows and cares about Sarah, not some legalistic, mumbo jumbo. You see what I mean? I need the jury to listen to my evidence with their heart. What I'm planning to do, and what I want you to write, are my facts, and my evidence, placed into the center of a real heart, so that every word will sink deeply into the minds of the jury. You know as well as I do that Sarah did not kill Rachel Maxwell. But you also know that Nick's case is stronger than mine."

"OK Michael," I agreed from exhaustion. I didn't have any clue as to what Michael expected from me, but I knew he would not stop talking until I agreed.

"Let's go," he ordered, and grabbed his briefcase.

I was still sitting at the booth and hadn't noticed that Michael had left the café.

I grabbed my purse, tossed five dollars on the table, and ran after him. As I pushed open the door, I realized that I had paid the waitress five dollars although I hadn't ordered anything.

Michael was already pulling out of the parking lot. I jumped in my car and raced after him, following him to the jail.

Michael had entered the building by the time I parked my car. I sat out front, biting my fake nails, watching people walk back and forth in front of me, but not really seeing any of them.

In the meantime, Michael was sharing his revelation of the mysterious woman with Sarah, who had regained most of her memory of what happened the day of Rachel's murder.

"I didn't see any necklace the day I found Rachel," said Sarah after seeing the picture of the woman wearing the necklace.

She looked away, and then back at Michael. "Like I told you, when I got to Rachel's I got out of my car. I saw the door of Rachel's car open, and the window was already broken. That's how I got these cuts on my arms and hands. I panicked and just started running around in circles. Then, I ran up to Rachel and tripped right into the broken window. Rachel was covered in blood, bleeding real bad. I cried out her name. And, Mr. Clark, one thing I didn't tell anybody before." Sarah took a deep breath. "Rachel was still alive. She grabbed my hand. I didn't tell you before, because I couldn't. Before I busted it, Rachel told me to keep the robin."

"Sarah, what haven't you told me? Don't you know that closing arguments start tomorrow?" Michael asked, in disbelief that Sarah had waited until now to tell him something he considered the most crucial information of her case.

"It doesn't have anything to do with the case. Like I said, Rachel was still alive. She had blood all over her hands. I told Rachel not to talk, but she talked anyway. I told you that part. But you know how I told you that Rachel told me to keep the robin?"

"Yes. Go on?"

"Well, I leaned in real close to Rachel. Just before she died she told me..." Sarah hesitated. "She told me that before Philip died he told her 'ask Sarah to forgive me.' Rachel didn't know what that meant at the time, and there's no way she would have known that I was the Sarah that Philip had mentioned, until she was dying. I guess it just clicked as she was taking her last breaths. I went crazy after hearing that. I loved Rachel, and I had finally found some pieces that could help me put my life back together, and Rachel was dead. She died right there in my arms. That's when I went berserk, and broke the little robin. That's when I screamed, picked up the brick, and began pounding it on the ground, and on Rachel's car. I did not pound that brick into Rachel's skull. Someone else had already done that," she cried.

Michael sat speechless for a moment, and then he put the pictures back into his briefcase.

"Sarah, that was very important to your trial. Why did you say it has nothing to do with the case? It has everything to do with the case. Why didn't you think to tell me before now? Never mind," he said before she could speak. "What's important now is that Judge Parker won't let me use these pictures, and probably not your enormously crucial confession, unless we can prove that this is Rachel's necklace by delivering this woman, and the necklace, to him before 9:00 tomorrow. He said he won't allow suspension of the arguments unless...never mind, Sarah. I've got to go. I have to go and create some miracles."

Michael called for the guard to open the door. He found me sitting out front, with a handful of fake nails in my palm.

Michael and I went to his office to re-write his closing argument. I prayed all the way there for God to inspire me.

Michael and I worked long into the night to create what I felt was a plea inspired by angels to save Sarah.

I rose early the next morning. So far I had not received a call from Michael, which meant that the closing arguments would proceed as scheduled.

I arrived early at the courthouse. All of Nova's Arc was there. There we were, lined up on a bench, like birds on a wire, ready to hear the powerful closing words of the two attorneys—who both were ready to do battle. Nick looked confident and self-assured. Michael looked anxious.

Clarise leaned over and whispered in my ear.

"Miracles do happen," she said, then squeezed my arm.

Judge Parker entered the courtroom.

"All rise for the Honorable Judge Richard Parker," announced the bailiff.

The courtroom was deathly silent. The jury sat in waiting, looking alert for what they knew would be a long day. The mood of the courtroom was extremely tense.

Nick rose from his chair after Judge Parker reviewed the next phase of the trial with the jury—the closing arguments.

Nick walked over to face the jury.

"Ladies and gentlemen, I know this has been a long trial. Your families have suffered without you. And I thank you and them. We have traveled down a long and treacherous road together. We have listened to a parade of witnesses tell of how Rachel Maxwell was found at her La Jolla estate, after having been viciously murdered. It is Mrs. Maxwell's family who needs you now. They need you to bring justice and closure to this horrible event, the brutal murder of Rachel Maxwell. I could delay you getting back to your families by belaboring the obvious—reviewing the evidence over and over, but what you have seen and heard during this trial is more than enough to prove that Sarah Jenkins murdered Rachel Maxwell. Beyond a reasonable doubt."

Contrary to what Nick said to the jury about not going over and over the evidence, he went over every little shred of his case and wove a convincing summation of how Sarah had sought revenge and murdered Rachel. I had the feeling that even some of the members of Nova's Arc were convinced that Sarah was guilty. Even I thought so.

After Nick finished, Gil entered the courtroom and approached Michael's table and passed him a plain, white envelope. Michael read the contents, then squeezed Sarah's arm. He looked like he had just been handed the miracle he'd been looking for.

Michael rose from his chair. My heart raced. Michael and I were the only two people who knew that I had put together his closing argument. Michael may have been inexperienced in trial law, but he was extremely clever. For such a young man, he had an incredible knowledge of the workings of the human heart, and how to use that knowledge to reach the mind. I took a deep breath as Michael began.

"Your honor, I'd like to move to reopen the proofs on the basis of newly discovered evidence which was just presented to me by my investigator, Gil Rodriquez."

"What?" yelled out mostly everyone in the courtroom, including Judge Parker.

"Approach the Bench, counselors," ordered the judge.

"What on earth?" I asked myself. I was gnawing my new nails down to the nubs.

The two attorneys walked up to face Judge Parker.

Michael spoke to the judge.

"What?" I heard the judge say. Then he looked out over the courtroom with a look of irritation on his face.

"This court is in recess for half an hour," announced Judge Parker. He banged his gavel, hard, and walked out. "Counselors, into my chambers, now!"

"What are you doing?" shouted Nick, who looked like he would punch Michael.

"Your honor, I just found out this information just now. After Nick finished his closing argument, Gil, my investigator, handed me this envelope, your honor."

"Give me that!" snapped the Judge.

Michael passed the envelope to Judge Parker. In it contained a typewritten note from Gil's office, along with copies of checks written by Philip Davenport to Jonathan Severied back in 1966. Another paper was a signed confession of participation in an adoption scheme from a man named Abraham.

"Gil discovered Abraham while looking for the woman who was wearing Rachel Maxwell's necklace and the driver of the brown Impala. He found the woman, your honor," excitedly said Michael. "She told Gil that she had exchanged drugs for the necklace. The woman wearing the necklace didn't know anything about this being Rachel Maxwell's necklace. The woman who swapped drugs for the necklace did so with the girlfriend of the man who drove the brown Impala that Hector Jiminez saw that morning. We haven't been able to find him yet, your honor, but his girlfriend has been arrested. And Nick knows that."

The Judge gave Nick a look of confusion. "I'm holding you both in contempt right now unless you can explain to me what the hell is going on? Nick, if you knew about this why didn't you say something?"

"Because we were in the middle of closing arguments, your honor. This drugged out woman has no proof. For all I know she could have gotten this necklace from Sarah Jenkins."

"What more do you have, Clark?" asked Judge Parker, feeling certain that Michael had more surprises.

"This woman, the one who swapped the necklace is named Flora Jordan. She had no idea about the value of the necklace. She said that her boyfriend gave her the necklace. He didn't tell her where he got it, but she said that he had a lot of money, and told her that he had made a big drug sale. According to Miss Williams, he kept bragging about some score with who she referred to as, this big whig at the World Bank. Gil just put two and two together when he was reviewing Curie Nova's notes."

"You're not making sense yet, son," said the judge.

"Bear with me, your Honor. One of the members of Nova's Arc is the president of that bank, the World Bank. Jonathan Severied is the President of that bank. To follow the lead, your honor, my investigator had to make a connection with Jonathan Severied, the druggie, her boyfriend, and Rachel Maxwell. That led nowhere, really, not until Gil linked the druggie, Jonathan Severied, and Philip Davenport."

"Go on."

"Well, your honor, Gil was able to get ahold of a woman who used to work at this now defunct adoption agency. She told him the whole story of how a couple had signed adoption papers for Robin...some folks out of Illinois. But Philip Davenport was a very wealthy and influential man, and you gotta remember this was a long time ago. People didn't go to court as readily as they do now. But anyway, Jonathan started throwing money at the adoption agency, and they told that couple that a mistake had been made and that the adoption had fallen through. They took the baby from this couple because Davenport was there to adopt his own child. He made it look like an adoption so that Rachel would never find out it was his child. They couple from Illinois was never heard from again."

The adoption agency delivered the baby to Dr. Davenport. Jonathan made that happen. Abraham once worked at that adoption agency. He fell on hard times and tried to blackmail Jonathan. Jonathan's secretary, Alice, delivered Abraham to Gil on a silver platter. When Gil went to Jonathan's office, Jonathan wasn't there, so he questioned Alice. She volunteered that the day of the murder Rachel had been to see Jonathan, but she left because he spent so much time with Abraham."

"We already know that," chimed in Nick.

"Yes. But what you didn't know, until now, is that Abraham was blackmailing Jonathan. Gil tracked Abraham down right in this courthouse today, your honor."

"You still haven't proved a damn thing, son. You've proved blackmail, but not murder."

"Your honor, while Nick was giving his closing argument, Gil spotted Abraham just outside the courthouse. Gil has a special way of getting other people to talk your honor." Michael cleared his throat. "That's when he told Gil the whole story, and handed him that confession. He said he knows he'll be arrested, but he said he doesn't care. He said he just wants Jonathan to get what's coming to him, because he said he knew that Jonathan would never pay for his silence...and would probably just have him killed instead."

Michael passed the confession that Gil had given him to Judge Parker. The Judge furrowed his brow, then passed the paper to Nick.

As Nick read Abraham's confession, Michael continued to appeal to Judge Parker.

"Your honor, I knew that Gil was checking things out, but I didn't know about this until now, and that's because Gil just handed it to me. He had to check it out before disclosing it."

"Son, I don't appreciate anyone trying to shock the jury into a verdict, and I don't like your Perry Mason tactics worth a damn. But, I must admit that this is crucial information."

Nick interrupted after he read the contents of the envelope.

"With all due respect, this is ludicrous, your Honor. Surely you're not going to consider this!"

Nick's words irritated Judge Parker.

"Mr. Robinson, are you out of your mind. This changes this case entirely. Mr. Clark has a legitimate argument here. I'll give you my decision when court reconvenes. Now get out, both of you."

When Michael and Nick reentered the courtroom, everyone was in their seats anxiously awaiting the return of Judge Parker. Standing at the back of the courtroom was a short, balding man. He took a seat in one of the back rows.

The judge cleared his throat before speaking. Nick and Michael looked like they were about to explode from anxiety, waiting for the Judge's decision on his motion.

"Motion to reopen the proofs is granted," he announced.

Michael looked like he had just been touched by an angel, and Nick slumped in his seat like a deflated tire.

The members of Nova's Arc were whispering, and Jonathan, Frank and Phyllis got up and walked out.

I was curious as to why they left, and whispered to Clarise.

"Where are they going?"

"I don't know."

I wanted her to become the psychic she bragged to be and tell me where they went."

"This court is adjourned until 9:00 A.M. tomorrow," declared Judge Parker. He called the jurors into his chambers to explain more fully that the proofs stage of the trail was being reinstated.

I had never heard of the proofs stage being reintroduced, but I was sure Michael had. I was becoming very impressed with the young, brazen attorney. He was certainly making his name well known all over the country and I hoped that his trump card would work.

The next morning I arrived at the courthouse early. I could hardly wait to find out what was going to happen next.

At 9:00 A.M. we all stood, anyone hardly breathing, as Judge Parker entered the courtroom.

I saw Jonathan shifting his weight in his seat just as the judge announced that he was sealing the courtroom.

"I expect absolute silence in my court. I have given the bailiff specific instruction to remove anyone who makes a sound," the judge sternly spoke.

Michael was allowed to begin his questioning. "Your Honor, I'd like to call Gil Rodriguez to the stand."

Gil was sworn in and took a seat in the witness chair.

"Would you state your name for the court?" asked Michael.

"Gilbert Jesus Rodriquez."

"Thank you Mr. Rodriquez. Would you please inform the court what your profession is?"

"Yes, I'm a private investigator."

"Mr. Rodriquez, how have you been involved with this case?"

"I've been investigating leads for the law firm of Markoo, Hayde, and Markoo.

"During your investigation, what did you recently discover that you placed in an envelope and delivered to me in this courtroom yesterday?"

"I found three cancelled checks and a man named Mel Abraham. Mr. Abraham gave me a signed confession, admitting to the part that he played in the cover-up of Sarah Jenkins' adopted daughter, Robin."

"What?" I almost said out loud, as did a lot of other people in the courtroom. The Judge looked into the crowd, and everyone shut up immediately. Gil continued his testimony.

"There were also two documents from the Sunset Falls Adoption Agency with unquestionable verification that the little girl who was adopted by Philip Davenport was the biological daughter of Sarah Jenkins and Dr. Philip Davenport. Oh, and, there is also absolute verification that the records were changed to show a woman by the name of Rebecca Anderson, a non-existent person, as the mother of the little girl."

"Your Honor, I'd like to submit these six documents into evidence as exhibits."

"Let the record show the documents are accepted into evidence as Exhibits 87 through 92," said Judge Parker.

"Now," said Michael, who took a deep breath. "Mr. Rodriquez, would you tell us whose name is on the signature line of the cancelled checks and to whom they are made payable?"

"Jonathan Severied, and they're made payable to the Sunset Falls Adoption Agency."

A hush came over the courtroom and then pandemonium broke out. Everyone started looking around, trying to identify Jonathan. Everyone began to talk at once.

Judge Parker stood up, and banged his gavel repeatedly.

"Sit down, everyone, or I'll close this trial and throw you all out!"

Jonathan jumped from his seat and started running out of the courtroom. An officer in the rear of the room apprehended him. Everyone turned to look at Jonathan, as he yelled out.

"I didn't do anything. I didn't kill Rachel. Let me go, let go of me," he demanded.

He was removed from the courtroom and taken into custody for questioning.

"Clear this courtroom bailiff," shouted Judge Parker.

Everyone was ordered to leave. Judge Parker wanted to talk to both counselors. He dismissed the jury for the day and asked Nick and Michael to meet him in his chambers.

Michael looked satisfied that he had shaken up the courtroom. The jury was in just as frantic an uproar as the rest of us.

Extra security entered the courtroom.

I could hardly believe what I had heard. Jonathan had paid the Sunset Falls Adoption Agency to release the baby, Robin, to Philip Davenport—but who had paid Jonathan?"

Chapter Sixteen

"Honor Thy Mother and Thy Father"

Abraham's confession wasn't enough for the police to charge Jonathan with accessory to commit murder, but the girlfriend who had swapped the necklace for drugs was. Her name was Miranda Ferguson. She snitched on her boyfriend, Bo Williams, who was subsequently captured in Las Vegas, extradited back to California, and charged with the murder of Rachel Maxwell.

The girlfriend told her story to the district attorney for leniency. All charges were dropped against her in exchange for her testimony.

Judge Parker suspended Sarah's trial for two weeks to allow time to verify the new findings.

Abraham gave a complete confession. His statement included how Dr. Davenport had paid Jonathan to intervene and handle the fraudulent birth certificate of Robin, and who paid off the adoption agency officials to nullify the original adoption of baby Robin.

Bo Williams also confessed to the murder of Rachel Maxwell, implicating Jonathan as the man who hired him. According to his statement, Jonathan had not intended to have Rachel killed. Instead, Bo was to steal the envelope that Abraham had placed in Rachel's briefcase the day he purposely bumped into her on the steps of the bank. Abraham had already threatened to take this evidence to the police if Jonathan didn't pay him, and decided to give it to Rachel the day he stormed out of Jonathan's office.

Jonathan had watched Abraham's actions from his office window, and Bo was hired to take the incriminating envelope. Unfortunately, Williams had taken Rachel's life, too. In his panic, he bungled the robbery.

William's statement detailed how he parked his car down the road, and then tried to sneak through Rachel's gate on foot. His intentions were to break into her car and steal the briefcase, or demand it at gunpoint if necessary. But before he made it past the gate, he saw Rachel pulling out of her drive and hid in the brush. It was by sheer coincidence that Rachel had a flat tire and stopped after she opened the gate. If Rachel had not had the flat tire, she would have driven to the gallery. The worse that may have happened was a snatched briefcase. But after Rachel stepped from her car, Bo Williams panicked. When Rachel began to scream, to quiet her, Williams picked up a brick from her driveway, and struck her, twice. When she fell, he noticed the sparkling emerald necklace, which had come loose and fallen to the ground, and took it. Her briefcase was open, so the gloved attacker just snatched the envelope and ran, driving his brown Impala, which Gertie got a glimpse, and which Hector Jiminez saw, all the way down Sonoma Way, the Street where Rachel lived, then sped out of La Jolla.

As a result of the confessions, Sarah's case was dismissed and she was released.

When she walked out of jail, I was anxiously waiting for her. But I had not come alone—Suzanne had come with me to greet Sarah as her mother for the first time.

Suzanne didn't expect to welcome her mother without question. She didn't' know what to expect. Suzanne knew that she had lost the woman she had called "mother" all her life, and although she and Rachel were not close as adults, she loved and respected her.

I ran up and flung my arms around Sarah. She had lost a considerable amount of weight, but she looked relieved that her nightmare was over. I felt a twinge of guilt for believing less than a day ago that she had murdered Rachel.

"Sarah, before you go out there," I told her as we neared the front door, "Suzanne's here. She came to see you come out of this place. Sarah, it was her idea, not mine. I think that's a start. I know you don't know her at all, and I don't know how she'll respond after seeing you, but always know that just like that day your car broke down, I'll always be there for you, whenever, wherever. And I promise I won't ever bring up this trial, unless you do. You have time to get to know Suzanne," I said as tears streamed down my face.

"Take this chance, Sarah, if she gives it to you, and if you want it, one day at a time."

"Curie, I have no idea what to say to my little Robin. I thought I'd never see her again, and here I am, going to walk out that door and into my baby's life. I'm so scared, and nervous, and confused. Look at me, Curie. She's used to a beautiful, glamorous, exciting mother. I'm a sheltered, horrible wreck."

"Sarah, please don't. You're one of the kindest women I've met in a long time. And I know you loved Suzanne, I mean Robin, when she was born. You were very young, Sarah, and you did what you thought was the right thing to do. You have got to get someone professional to help you work through your feelings about all this, and about the best way to build a relationship with your daughter. Just be happy right now that you've been given a second chance. That's something that most people never get. And for God's sake, move out of that rattrap. Please don't get me wrong, but you are not a pauper. Stop punishing yourself. You've suffered enough. You're free. Live like it. Live, Sarah, live."

I tried my best to bring a smile to Sarah's face. I settled for the tears falling from her eyes. I hoped they were tears of joy.

We walked out of the door of the jail together. I slowed and let Sarah get ahead of me when Suzanne stepped towards her.

I wept openly, unashamed at the many snapshots that were being taken by the press.

Like weeds in a field, people sprang up everywhere. In addition to the press, Sarah supporters crowded the parking lot, some openly crying like me, others cheering her release.

All at once, the crowd quieted.

Suzanne and her mother stood face to face, neither one saying a word. Then, Suzanne did something that broke the damn, and a flood of tears streamed from my eyes in a seeming never ending flow. She kissed Sarah on the cheek, took her hand, and said, "I forgive you."

The press pushed microphone after microphone in their faces, but Michael had arranged security, and Sarah and Suzanne were escorted to a waiting limousine. I wondered where Suzanne was taking Sarah.

When the limo sped away, Michael pushed his way through the crowd, repeating "no comment" and grabbed my hand. He repeated strings of "no comment" and we jumped into his car and headed to, where else, the Broad Street Cafe.

"Michael, you're insane," I told him, feeling better than I had in a long time.

"What's the big idea of you not using my closing argument? Don't you know I put my whole heart into it?"

"Curie, I had every intention of using what you had prepared. But when Gil handed me the keys to Sarah's freedom, I had no choice but to unlock her cell with them."

"I don't know how we'll ever repay you."

"I do. Sarah has over $20 million. And Suzanne has over a gazillion. Somebody can afford to pay me now!"

We both broke out into ridiculous laughter. I wasn't laughing because Michael's comments were so funny; I was just happy inside.

"God, Michael, talk about timing, huh?"

Before Michael could answer, my cell phone rang. It was Suzanne calling from the limousine.

"Curie, its Suzanne. Sarah has made a request."

"What is it, Suzanne?"

"Sarah would like you to hold a meeting at my mother's…"

Suzanne stopped talking.

"Suzanne?" I asked.

"I'm sorry. It's just that it's going to take some time for me to get over Rachel's death. Sarah would like for you to hold a meeting of Nova's Arc, minus Jonathan, of course, at my mother's estate this Sunday."

"Oh Suzanne, nothing would please me more."

"Thank you Curie. I'd like to join you, if that's all right."

"Suzanne," I said, as the tears began to flow again, "I would consider it an honor."

Sarah's case had been thrown out of court on a Friday, and I was looking forward to a long, relaxing weekend. I didn't care that my weekend to just do nothing had been interrupted. The thought of having the group back together, one last time, sent chills up and down my spine.

Michael and I talked for hours that day at his favorite cafe, in his favorite booth. Later that evening, I called the members of Nova's Arc to tell them of the upcoming meeting.

"It will feel real strange without Rachel," said Phyllis. "I miss her."

"I miss her too. We'll have this meeting in her honor."

Everyone gladly accepted the invitation to meet at Rachel's on Sunday. After the last member had been called, my doorbell rang. It was Diana.

"Look what you've done? You and your group! I hate you, Curie, I hate you!" she yelled and screamed at me.

"Diana, I'm so sorry," I said. Until now, I had not thought about how all this would affect Diana. The guilt I had shed after Sarah's case had been replaced by the guilt I felt over Diana's predicament.

"Sorry? Is that all you've got to say to me? My father's been arrested and charged with accessory to commit murder, not to mention fraud, and a host of other charges."

"Diana, my group had nothing to do with your father's arrest. Think, Diana. It was just a coincidence that Sarah was in the same group as your father. But what your father did, he did long before I knew any of them. The man that tried to blackmail your father would have done that regardless of Nova's Arc. Don't you see?"

"I don't know what to see, or think, or feel right now."

"I know Diana. I'm so sorry about everything."

Diana slumped to the floor, and began to sob. I rushed over to comfort her.

"Diana, I love you. You're my best friend. Please talk to me. Please let me take care of you, the way you took care of me."

I held Diana all night. She left the next morning without saying a word to me. I hoped that over time she would come to accept that Nova's Arc had nothing to do with what her father had done, and forgive me.

It was only 6:00 A.M. when Diana left. I decided to pull out my notes from the first meeting I had had with Rachel, and listen to the tapes of us talking about her fantasies.

Her familiar "Oh, God" was special to me, and I sought comfort in her voice. I decided to listen to some of the other meetings.

Robert tiptoed out of the house so that he wouldn't disturb. I had fallen asleep listening to the tape where Carmen talked about life, and the fact that despite her age, she had a lot to look forward to. I had barely slept while keeping vigil over Diana all night, and when I awakened, I was surprised to see that it was 1:00 P.M. I had slept over half my day away, and I had so much to do to prepare for Sunday at Rachel's.

Although I knew our meeting would not be the same without Rachel, I felt the way I'm sure everyone else in the group did—that Rachel would be there with us.

I spent that Saturday afternoon preparing for Sunday. I looked in the back of my closet to a row of cocktail dresses. I wanted to look stunning and glamorous, like Rachel always did. I pulled out a shiny, long-sleeved royal blue dress and held it out for a look.

"Excellent," I said as I placed it on my bed.

I ran to the dresser and picked out my teardrop, diamond earrings. They were the only diamonds I owned, and I only wore them on special occasions. After I checked my shoes, purse, and other accessories, ensuring that they would be befitting for the last meeting of Nova's Arc, I sighed in satisfaction.

I knew that our final meeting was actually a memorial for Rachel—a woman who had shared her heart and her home with us all. I didn't want our salute to her to be dreary and downhearted, as Rachel had been such a brilliant spot in my life since the day I met her. Only my best outfit would do externally, and internally, I knew my love for her would shine through, as she had captured a spot in my heart forever.

Although I had slept through my beauty salon appointment, I called and insisted, no—begged my hairdresser to cut and style my hair. I explained that I absolutely had to look perfect for Sunday. She finally said yes, and I was out he door before she could say goodbye.

By the time I was finished at the salon, it was almost 4:00 P.M. I thought about calling Diana, but decided to give her some time. I missed my best friend. Diana and I often double-dated on Saturday nights.

Robert and I decided to stay in for the evening and go to bed early, so that I would wake refreshed and ready for Nova's Arc.

The next morning, I sprang from my bed feeling both happy and sad. I couldn't wait to the see the group together again, minus Jonathan. I wondered how he was doing for a brief moment.

I thought back to the days when we all gathered at Rachel's, and then of how horrid everything had turned out.

I picked up the Sunday paper, and Jonathan's face was and story was plastered all over the front page. I tossed the paper to the floor and shook the thoughts of him from my mind. I had a special meeting to attend.

It was 2:30 by the time I arrived at Rachel's. It was customary for me to get there before everyone else, and I didn't want to change things today. Gertie greeted me at the door dressed in her formal black and white uniform.

"Hello Miss Curie," she said, as she tried to manage a smile. I could feel that her heart was heavy.

"Gertie," I said, and hugged her. "It means so much to me to be here today. You look wonderful. Thank you for being here, too."

I didn't want to start talking about the good times I'd had with Rachel, or how strange it was being back at Rachel's estate. So I switched the subject to food.

"Gertie, you have really outdone yourself," I said as I walked into the sitting room where Nova's Arc always took their breaks.

"Yes. I prepared everything. I been here since 5:00 o'clock this morning, cleaning, and cooking, and getting everything all beautiful for you and your group."

"You're an angel Gertie. Thank you very much for everything."

"Yes, Miss Curie. You're nice too."

Gertie walked away, and I stood there alone, looking at the furniture, the pictures on the wall, everything. I walked back out to the living room, but this time I didn't look for things I'd never seen before. Instead, I looked at all the familiar things that I had discovered over time.

It was 3:00 o'clock. The doorbell rang. I had not yet entered the glass room, as I wanted us all to walk in together.

Everyone arrived at the same time, as if they had planned it. Beatrice entered first, dressed in a beautiful sea green dress with little pearls sewn around the collar. Frank was dressed in full military uniform. He looked so handsome and official.

Phyllis wore a fabulous navy blue suit with a satin white blouse.

Clarise looked enchanting wearing a white chiffon full-length dress.

Both Andy and Joe wore black tuxedos.

Judith looked like a different woman. She had colored her hair light brown, bought some new designer eyeglasses, and her face was made up. I noticed for the first time that she had beautiful, big, brown eyes. She wore a deep purple cocktail dress, which made her look regal.

Carmen, who looked divine wearing a silver, satin dress and elbow length silver gloves, gracefully and silently entered the room.

Next entered Sarah. What a transformation? Sarah didn't look like the same woman. Her hair had been professionally cut, colored, and styled. Her nails were manicured, and her makeup was flawless. Sarah wore an elegant French pink suit. She looked years younger.

Suzanne entered last. She no longer looked business-like and serious. Instead, she looked soft and refined in her light blue designer gown.

Everyone looked their best for Rachel. We all hugged one another over and over.

175

Gertie walked out and opened the door to the glass room. It was magnificently filled with exotic flowers and a sparkling ice sculpture of a dove with an olive branch in its mouth.

After we finished admiring the incredible sculpture, which was designed by Clarise, everyone took their usual seat in the Arc. Suzanne sat where Rachel normally sat, and the sight of her there consoled us.

I softly began. "Being here with you all makes me feel so very good. I wondered if we'd ever be together again. Today, there is no topic, so I think in honor of Rachel, we'll just say whatever we feel."

I looked into the faces of the beautiful group and smiled. Tears were coming to the surface, and I blinked. The tears rolled down my face, and I did not try to stop them.

Phyllis raised her hand and stood before the group.

"If Rachel were here, Curie, you'd be asking us about sex."

Everyone laughed. She continued. "I never thought in a million years that I'd be so privileged as to be a part of such beautiful lives, such as yours," Phyllis said, as she looked out at the group.

"My life has been so deeply enriched because I met all of you. And, the always elegant Rachel touched my life in ways that she'll never know."

Others nodded in agreement, and Phyllis continued.

"I think today is a very special day. It is a day when Nova's Arc has gathered to say 'I love you.' That is today's topic. Love."

The always-witty Phyllis was different today. She spoke softly, and seriously.

Phyllis looked at Beatrice.

"Beatrice, I love the way you giggle when you talk about your baby-sitting business, and I love the way your nose wrinkles and your eyes sparkle. Whenever I think about you I think about those things, but it's you I love. Thank you for giving me memories that makes me smile."

She switched her attention to Frank.

"Frank, I love the way you always say exactly what's on your mind, and the respect that you showed today by wearing your full military uniform in honor of Rachel, a woman that meant so much to all of us. You helped make today special, Frank. I love you."

She scanned the faces for Clarise.

"And Clarise, your spirit has touched us all, and our own spirit has soared because of being near you. Always kind, graceful, and encouraging, you helped me to see what being a friend is all about. Your friendship with Rachel was truly an example for all to follow. It was plain to see that you loved her unconditionally, faithfully, and genuinely—the way love is supposed to be. I love you for that, Clarise."

Joe fidgeted as she said his name.

"Joe, dear Joe. Although you could have given many reasons not to become a member of Nova's Arc, you faithfully came every week and shared yourself with us. We were selfish, Joe, because we never asked you what we could do to help your life be better. We saw you every Sunday, and you asked nothing of us but to be accepted. I was guilty of not accepting you unconditionally at first, Joe. But I do now. I love you for being here, with us, every Sunday since we met. The group wouldn't have been the same without you. And you look absolutely stunning and handsome in that tuxedo."

Sitting next to Joe was Judith.

"Judith," said Phyllis, "you look beautiful. I can see so much life in you since you started coming to Rachel's. It's plain to see that you're no longer hiding your soul. And, although you look so great on the outside, I can see so much beauty around you, radiating from out of your heart. You are truly a lesson to us all, a lesson not to just change the outside, but to dig deep, as Andy would say, and bring out the inner beauty, and let it shine. I love you Judith."

Then Phyllis smiled at Andy.

"Speaking of Andy, you, too, look great in your tux. You speak from the heart and soul, Andy, and I love you for your honesty. You never tried to be anyone other than Andy and you let us into your life from the day we met. You're smart, successful, and determined. But you're also kind, sincere, and an inspiration to us all to be honest with ourselves. I love you Andy, for being Andy. I'm glad that you came into my life."

Carmen smiled at Phyllis as their eyes met.

"Carmen, you touched our lives with your fire, your zest for living, and certainly your heaven-inspired music. You taught us how to enjoy ourselves, even at our age. You taught us that life doesn't stop just because the years continue. And the melodies you channeled directly from the angels filled my soul with joy. I love you Carmen, for being such a beautiful woman who's not afraid to share herself with the world. Your love is abundant, and replenishes itself because you give so much of it."

Sarah and Suzanne sat side by side. Phyllis' eyes lit up when she looked their way.

"And Sarah, I love you. Our prayers were answered, because we knew in our hearts that you were a reflection of so many people. When we prayed for you Sarah, we prayed for everyone out there who has a broken heart, for all those alone in their room, wondering where the joy of the soul has gone. You, Sarah, represent those who are diamonds buried in the sand, and I learned that I must look with my soul's eye, and recognize that all in heaven and on earth is precious. I learned that, like a flower garden, patience and care will yield beauty in abundance. You're beautiful Sarah. Welcome home."

She moved on to Suzanne.

"Suzanne, I love you, too. I watched you over these weeks endure a pain so great, and I see you now, reaching out to heal not only your shattered heart, but helping us all by allowing us into your life. By your reaching out to Sarah, we are all made stronger. I have never known someone such as you, with such a mighty heart. You are transcending beyond what earthly minds understand, and have reached a higher state of consciousness. I pray that you will soon come to heal from all that's gone before you."

Then she turned around and looked at me.

"And Curie" she said, as she swung around to face me, "I really love you, too. Without you, Curie, there would be no Nova's Arc. You have a special magic that brings love together. Wherever you go, and I know you'll go far, very far, continue to help others to dream. Help others, the way you've helped us, learn to share what's in our hearts. God chose you to bring us all together, and for that I will be forever grateful. And please, don't think that Rachel is gone, out there in some void. Remember what she told us about death and dying? She's lighting up the moon to cast a tender glow for many a tired and weary traveler."

Just then, Gertie walked in. She stopped when Phyllis called out her name.

"And you Gertie…Get in here Gertie," she playfully said. "I love you Gertie."

"Gracias, Miss Phyllis."

Everyone laughed and applauded, then Phyllis continued.

Phyllis concluded by addressing Rachel.

"And Rachel, as we sit here missing you, your smile, your bravado, your oh, so, charming ways, I know you already have read our hearts. You know that without you we would never had learned these valuable lessons and been touched by so special a group. We will love you always, and every time we hear the words, 'Oh, God," we will think of you."

Phyllis returned to her seat, and Clarise stood.

"And we love you, too, Phyllis. That was so beautiful. Without you there would have been moments when we were stuck for words, and hurting for a laugh. You reminded us not to take ourselves too seriously. Life is a never-ending journey. Thank you for coming along with us, and walking with us on ours."

At that point, Carmen stood and walked over to the Grand piano.

Slowly, she began to play and sing. "Like the ocean waves you never cease, sometimes rushing with a force. Other times you quietly came and washed our trodden shore. You let us in, and then we saw, the beauty of your love, touch us one more time, dear Rachel, gently, like feathers from a dove. Like a breeze that blows on fields of grass, so full of happy bees, we hear your laughter, as I sing to you, you dance across the keys."

Carmen continued singing her song for Rachel, and we all listened in silence.

As I heard the soft and moving song, I stared at the beautiful ice sculpture. I saw the dove as Rachel, reminding us that she was still watching over Nova's Arc, leading us on in our quest for a new vision, and to a peaceful and understanding heart.

Carmen finished her song, and we were all moved to tears.

I stopped crying when I looked again at the sculpture. The dove signaled that the flood of tears had ended, and that Nova's Arc had completed its long journey. We were now on solid ground.

Gertie, who walked in carrying a tray of sparkling water, interrupted my thoughts, and we all took a glass.

Suzanne raised her glass with outstretched arm.

"May we live every day with a song in our heart, our friends by our side, and a long life filled with cheer and good thoughts."

Frank stood tall in his military uniform and raised his glass… "Salute."

Chapter Seventeen

"Time to De-board The Arc"

We all left Rachel's with a new purpose in our lives. Beatrice went on the talk show circuit and talked of her relationship with Rachel and Nova's Arc. She was booked all over the country to give lectures on aging.

She no longer tended the two little children in her home because she was far too busy traveling from city to city. She was also being handsomely paid for her personal stories of the days of glory with "Lady Maxwell."

Phyllis retired from the real estate business. Suzanne asked her to assist her in running August House.

Clarise continued her business in production and film, and she and Phyllis became very close friends.

Judith moved away to live in West Palm Beach, Florida. She told her sister Moira that she wanted to contribute something to the world before she left it, and published an Internet web site for senior citizens. Her chat room was always full, with people of all ages sharing their lives.

Frank was, and always will be, Frank. He called Joe from time to time, and they even occasionally had dinner together.

Dan Cook kept his promise to Carmen. She signed a multi-million dollar contract and later performed at Madison Square Garden. She was an inspiration for her millions adoring fans of all age groups, and a year later, "Carmen the Virtuoso" went on to perform before audiences in countries all over the world. She said her greatest accomplishment was when her tribute song to Rachel was recorded and used as the theme song about an upcoming movie of Rachel's life.

Sarah purchased a mansion in Torrey Pines and hired Joe to help her. He supervised all the workers in her ten-bedroom estate.

Andy bought a percentage of a NFL team. He spent a lot of time in the skybox, shouting, and laughing, and enjoying football. He also helped Bradley become the facilities director at his old investment firm. Bradley now earned a handsome living, and bought flowers for Rhonda every weekend.

Jonathan never served time in jail. He suffered a massive heart attack just one week after he was sentenced to ten years in prison for conspiring to commit murder. He was pronounced dead on arrival at the hospital.

I never published my notes of Nova's Arc. Instead, I wrote another book on aging. I dedicated my book...*to Rachel...the oh, so fabulous woman. What about husband #3, Gary Maxwell? I guess I'll never know."*

Suzanne and Sarah went to therapy weekly together to try and work through all the pain and tragedy in their lives apart and together. Suzanne ran the gallery with perfection, and Andreas Vandiver's show was rescheduled as her first exhibition since her mother's death. The sign out front of August House read, "Open, in honor of Lady Maxwell."

THE END

Michael Anthony Clark's Closing Argument, authored by Curie Nova...

Dear Members of the Jury:

Until Sarah Jenkins became a member of Nova's Arc, she had no friends. You see, Sarah Jenkins lives alone in a tiny apartment, her emotions sheltered, just like her, because she endured years of agony at the hands of someone who professed to love her, and, who not only threw her away, but took her precious baby, too. Over time, her many layers of pain were stripped away by a young writer who recognized the kind of person Sarah Jenkins really is, beneath the insanity, the heartache, the loneliness. She saw a woman desperately in need of the light. Sarah embraced the light Nova's Arc brought into her life. Like a refuge through a storm, Nova's Arc brought Sarah Jenkins safely to a place of love among friends. Now, thanks to a system that has neglected to find out who actually killed the innocent, and beloved Rachel Maxwell, that bright light has been dimmed, and Sarah is in pain and being washed up in the rages of Armageddon—someone else's, the real killer's Judgment Day. The real killer should be sitting here, not Sarah Jenkins.

Sarah Jenkins loved Mrs. Maxwell. She did not go to Mrs. Maxwell's for revenge and murder, she went there to return a little statue of a baby robin, and to bring closure to the loss over her own real little baby, Robin, by asking for forgiveness from Mrs. Maxwell. That's it. It's not difficult to see that Sarah is a victim of circumstance...in the right place at the wrong time. Let me ask you— how would you feel if you suddenly discovered that your fiancé had duped you into giving away your child? How would you feel? You might feel enraged at the person who did it, but I doubt seriously that you'd comb the streets, striking out violently at the one group of people that cared about you. Mrs. Maxwell was part of that group. To harm her is to harm Nova's Arc. Don't you see? Out there somewhere is a killer, driving around in a brown car, laughing at you, laughing at me, laughing at Sarah, laughing at Nova's Arc, and laughing at the deceased. Yes, laughing. You know why? Because the killer is looking at this innocent woman, and thinking...it doesn't matter if she fries for a murder she didn't' commit. Who cares about her? She's just some poor, old white woman who has no friends and nobody will remember her once she's been electrocuted. Old people don't matter. But I suggest to the killer who drove that brown car, that you stop laughing right now and understand me when I say that we're gonna get you. We're gonna get you because you have not only committed a horrific crime against Mrs. Maxwell, but you are trying to kill yet another innocent victim. You wish her to burn for your sins. It's not going to happen. We're gonna get you because you have no idea who you're dealing with. You waste this good jury's time, you wreak havoc with the emotions of this courtroom audience, you tie up the TV and newspaper time with your cowardice, and you shall burn in earthly hell for that.

On the day of the murder Sarah Jenkins went out to see Rachel Maxwell to return the little statue she took from the mantle out of desperation. That's all. That's all. When she arrived, Rachel Maxwell was already down. Yes, listen to me carefully. I said, Rachel Maxwell was down, but it was Sarah Jenkins who lifted her up. Ladies and gentleman, Rachel Maxwell was not, I repeat, not dead at the time Sarah Jenkins arrived. But the only person who can prove that is my client. But my client doesn't have to prove it.

Follow along on this one with me. There was someone else at the murder scene, before Sarah Jenkins ever arrived. Does that give you reasonable doubt about my client? You bet it does! Never introduced by the prosecution. I had to bring it up. Don't you think that the prosecutor should have done everything in his power to convince you that the mysterious brown car is not linked to this crime? Yes, he should have, yes he should have, but he can't. He can't because he knows it is linked to this. It is not only linked to this, it is THIS! Trek with me here.

This is a funky, messed up twisted tale that involves a vulnerable woman, Sarah Jenkins, an innocent baby, Robin, a kind heiress, Rachel Maxell, a heartless fiancé, Philip Davenport, and a dirty, stinking murderer, who's walking around out there thinking he's off the hook. You're not off the hook, not by a long shot. You're gonna burn for this, I promise you, if it's the last thing I do, I'm gonna get your tail and send you screaming and gnashing your teeth right into the electric chair. Just you wait and see.

Forgive me ladies and gentlemen of the jury. I'm angry. I'm angry that my client has to endure this shameful accusation against a woman that she is grieving for. She is grieving the death of Rachel Maxwell. I am grieving for my client. There is evil here, all around us. Don't mistake trickery from the prosecution for concrete evidence. The only thing concrete you've heard is that Rachel Maxwell is dead. Don't kill my client, Sarah Jenkins. This is too much for even me to stand. Imagine what it's doing to the innocent, Sarah Jenkins. You must return a verdict of NOT GUILTY because the real killer will not, I repeat, not, have the last laugh. Deliberate as long as you need, think about the fact that the trial may be at an end, but my intentions are not. I intend to find out who really murdered Rachel Maxwell, and if that person or persons are out there, in here, over there, up yonder, no matter where, we will find you and bring you to justice.

Thank you, most kindly, ladies and gentlemen. May your heads decide what your hearts already know to be true. I rest my case.

###